D1064381

Immersion
and
Other Short Novels

Immersion
and
Other Short Novels

Gregory Benford

Five Star • Waterville, Maine

Five Star First Edition Science Fiction and Fantasy Series.

Published in 2002 in conjunction with Tekno Books and Ed Gorman.

Set in 11 pt. Plantin by Elena Picard.

Printed in the United States on permanent paper.

Library of Congress Cataloging-in-Publication Data

Benford, Gregory, 1941–
    Immersion, and other short novels /
Gregory Benford.—1st ed.
        p.cm.—(Five Star first edition science fiction and
fantasy series)
    ISBN 0-7862-3877-1 (hardcover : alk. paper)
    1. Science fiction, American. I. Title: Immersion.
II. Title. III. Series.
PS3552.E542 I46 2002
    813'.54—dc21   2001055741

Table of Contents

Introduction

Reading is immersion. To voyage through a world imagined by another, taking in the imagery, ideas and subtleties of another mind—this is a saturation we seek in fiction particularly.

We envy birds their artful flight, and animals their seemingly blissful unawareness of our vexing problems. People seem happiest when they act seamlessly, without thinking—"going with the flow." We comprehend our selves through the pulse of immediate event, caught up. "We are the music, while the music lasts," as T.S. Eliot put it.

Every author faces the ancient storyteller's challenge: to fashion words that conjure up in the listener's mind pictures, sensations, a whole temporary universe for a mind at play. To catch the reader up in a drama enacted on a strictly interior stage.

Tale spinning relies on a rudimentary telepathy. The author has pictures in his head, walks through scenes, overhears talk . . . and must select the right detail to convey this. Not the whole room, but that stuffed brown leather chair in the corner, dominating the gloomy study while seeming to be out of the way. Not the character's total appearance, but the essence that a glance can give: lifted eyebrow, overgrown moustache, lidded eyes. Not the dull patter of real, loose conversation, but revealing fragments.

Writing uses simple tools available to all. Everybody can tell a joke, or relate the events of their day. But to fully engage readers takes considerable length, as Homer knew when he recited the great rhythms of the Odyssey to crowds that came back for more night after night.

So: the novella. Standing between the quick energies and images of the snapshot short story, and the mammoth sweep that novels can muster, the novella has particular graces and structures the others cannot match. Usually taken as narratives between about 15,000 and 40,000 words, they allow ample room for development of a single large-scale idea. Faulkner's "The Bear," Hemingway's "The Old Man and the Sea," Thomas Mann's "Death in Venice," James M. Cain's "The Postman Always Rings Twice," Tolstoy's "The Death of Ivan Illych," Nathanael West's "Miss Lonelyhearts"— these have a power of ample concentration that few works manage at any length.

For fiction that really studies ideas, the novella is uniquely useful. One can explore science fictional notions in detail, without using complex plot/counterplot strategies with a broad cast of characters or fully invoking a background world. Yet novellas can immerse the reader in worlds that short stories cannot, and this is their major source of power in fantastic and speculative fiction. Novellas can show ideas worked out in full; worlds sensed and cultures unfolded.

Each of the novellas in this volume came to me a special kind of revelation.

"To the Storming Gulf" comes from my boyhood. I grew up in southern Alabama, around Fairhope—a utopian community founded in the 19th century by farmers and tradesmen following the ideas of the social thinker, Henry George. I grew up in a Huck Finn world of fields, forests and rivers, small towns as oases.

In the 1980s, as plans for missile defenses and the last push against the Soviet Union rolled on, I started thinking of a story about nuclear war. Though my father was a career Army officer, and I trained in the reserves, I knew little of combat. But I did know my relatives. I wondered how war would affect ordinary people, the laborers, townspeople and farmers I had grown up among. (After the attack of September 11, 2001, this story becomes ever more distant. But the reaction of common folk to worldwide conflict, particularly in the confusing mismatch of scales, is an enduring theme.)

The South lost the great formative war of our history, so a tale of war's price seemed well set there. History rings through Faulkner's Yoknapatawpha County, and I am well aware that many Southern cultural strains are as strong now as ever. The South has considerable experience with losing a war, and enduring afterward.

So "Gulf" echoes my nostalgic view of that culture, seen through the adopted lens of a specific Faulkner novella: "As I Lay Dying." I structured the multiple points of view, the balance and pace after Faulkner's, as a commentary on that great novella. (It, too, has a fantastic element; the corpse gets a say.)

The story is filled with the names of my relatives, their habits and sayings. The old woman near the end is a faithful picture of my grandmother, particularly her spoken cadences. In some ways this story is closest to my heart.

"Of Space/Time and the River" is utterly different—a take on a place I had never been before. In the early 1980s I spent several weeks sailing up the Nile, pulling ashore to see the many ancient sites. I kept a diary, and months after the trip found that it kept echoing in my dreams. I woke up one day with the entire novella plot in my head, modeled on my diary entries. Seldom does the subconscious do so much of the heavy lifting for me.

The story isn't a plausible future scenario, of course. Like many of my shorter works, it is about the strangeness that lurks at the very edges of our current vision. The culture of ancient Egypt was so very different, that to be immersed in it gradually is a trip down a winding river.

The story also resonates with some reading I was doing at the time, Julian Jaymes' rather curious "The Origin of Consciousness in the Breakdown of the Bicameral Mind." Jaymes proposed that until very recently, perhaps 5000 years ago, we did not separate ourselves consciously from the world. We experienced our ancient gods directly, interpreting our internal voices as external ones. The idea can't be checked now, of course, but . . . what if it was right? Then much of ancient history must be rewritten, for it might indeed be a tale of vast movements carried out by people who did not much reflect on themselves, in our modern way. What would that be like? My protagonist finds out . . .

I wrote "Matter's End" from another journey, three weeks in India. The exotic feel of the place, announced in the opening lines, was a charming venture into a culture that seemed on the surface approachable. The longer I stayed, and when I returned, the veneer left by the British Raj peeled away more and more, revealing an ancient way of seeing the world vastly different than I had imagined. The underpinnings of religious faith in that subcontinent speak of our lives as unending cycle, each turn of the reincarnation engine a small move against a landscape of time that stretches back

10

endlessly. Soul outlasting mere mass . . .

At the same time, I went to India for scientific conferences and collaborations. Two ideas blended: the vast sweep of eons, and the finite lifetime of matter itself. The lifetime of the proton was a hot topic, and there is such an experiment to measure it as I depict in the story, still running in 2001. No one, not even it the advanced Western experiments, has yet found the proton's lifetime, but its mortality is not doubted by the theorists. My hero's immersion in India, and the Western ideas of the universe's constraints, blended in my mind to make for the novella. It concludes with a sense of the entire world wrapping itself around us, fresh and strange.

Since my first novel, "Deeper Than the Darkness" (later rewritten as "The Stars in Shroud"), I have used images of being enveloped, trapped or surrounded, usually as elements of horror. This I find odd, because I have no claustrophobia. Certainly "In Alien Flesh" renders its penetration of the alien as cause for mingled awe and terror, but "Immersion" shows my truer take on the idea.

Few can have failed to wonder how other animals view the world. We don't know, and we cannot. The mental state of animals is endlessly interesting, but fundamentally unknowable. Thomas Nagel's famous essay, "What is it Like to Be a Bat?" asks how one can fathom another mind, and what knowing might mean. Empathy is as close as we get, so far. Certainly our pets experience emotions, and science shows us how bats see, or houseflies. But how do they process the information?

I wondered how much our view of the world differs from that of our nearest relatives, the chimps—and this story came forth. I would gladly take such a journey into the mind of a chimp, if it were possible. Someday it may be, because the next half-century of research will probably give us ample means of "reading" what goes on in brains and how that shapes the minds that inhabit them. I think we mistreat chimps, and knowledge of how they see their world would bring an end to that. But the story is written to bring a sense of wonder to the subject, for it is so very difficult to escape the confines of our bodies and their evolutionary history.

Immersion in another world is a singular charm of fantastic fiction. I hope these four novellas bring some feeling of how fictional universes can get an author caught up, making storytelling a joy uniquely its own.

—Gregory Benford
October 2001

To the Storming Gulf

Turkey

Trouble. Knew there'd be trouble and plenty of it if we left the reactor too soon.

But do they listen to me? No, not to old Turkey. He's just a dried-up corn-husk of a man now, they think, one of those Bunren men who been on the welfare a generation or two and no damn use to anybody.

Only it's simple plain farm supports I was drawing all this time, not any kind of horse-ass welfare. So much they know. Can't blame a man just 'cause he comes up cash-short sometimes. I like to sit and read and think more than some people I could mention, and so I took the money.

Still, Mr. Ackerman and all think I got no sense to take government dole and live without a lick of farming, so when I talk they never listen. Don't even seem to hear.

It was his idea, getting into the reactor at McIntosh. Now that was a good one, I got to give him that much.

When the fallout started coining down and the skimpy few stations on the radio were saying to get to deep shelter, it was Mr. Ackerman who thought about the big central core at McIntosh. The reactor itself had been shut down automatically when the war started, so there was nobody there. Mr. Ackerman figured a building made to keep radioactivity in

13

will also keep it out. So he got together the families, the Nelsons and Bunrens and Pollacks and all, cousins and aunts and anybody we could reach in the measly hours we had before the fallout arrived.

We got in all right. Brought food and such. A reactor's set up self-contained and got huge air filters and water flow from the river. The water was clean, too, filtered enough to take out the fallout. The generators were still running good. We waited it out there. Crowded and sweaty but ok for ten days. That's how long it took for the count to go down. Then we spilled out into a world laid to gray and yet circumscribed waste, the old world seen behind a screen of memories.

That was bad enough, finding the bodies—people, cattle, and dogs, asprawl across roads and fields. Trees and bushes looked the same, but there was a yawning silence everywhere. Without men, the pine stands and muddy riverbanks had fallen dumb, hardly a swish of breeze moving through them, like everything was waiting to start up again but didn't know how.

Angel

We thought we were ok then, and the counters said so, too—all the gammas gone, one of the kids said. Only the sky didn't look the same when we came out, all mottled and shot through with drifting blue-belly clouds.

Then the strangest thing. July, and there's sleet falling. Big wind blowing up from the Gulf, only it's not the sticky hot one we're used to in summer, it's moaning in the trees of a sudden and a prickly chill.

"Goddamn. I don't think we can get far in this," Turkey

says, rolling his old rheumy eyes around like he never saw weather before.

"It will pass," Mr. Ackerman says, like he is in real tight with God.

"Lookit that moving in from the south," I say, and there's a big mass all purple and forking lightning swarming over the hills, like a tide flowing, swallowing everything.

"Gulf storm. We'll wait it out," Mr. Ackerman says to the crowd of us, a few hundred left out of what was a moderate town with real promise.

Nobody talks about the dead folks. We see them everywhere, worms working in them. A lot smashed up in car accidents, died trying to drive away from something they couldn't see. But we got most of our families in with us, so it's not so bad. Me, I just pushed it away for a while, too much to think about with the storm closing in.

Only it wasn't a storm. It was somethin' else, with thick clouds packed with hail and snow one day and the next sunshine, only sun with bite in it. One of the men says it's got more UV in it, meaning the ultraviolet that usually doesn't come through the air. But it's getting down to us now.

So we don't go out in it much. Just to the market for what's left of the canned food and supplies, only a few of us going out at a time, says Mr. Ackerman.

We thought maybe a week it would last.

Turned out to be more than two months.

I'm a patient woman, but jammed up in those corridors and stinking offices and control room of the reactor—

Well, I don't want to go on.

It's like my Bud says, worst way to die is to be bored to death.

That's damn near the way it was.

Not that Old Man Turkey minded. You ever notice how

15

the kind of man that hates moving, he will talk up other people doing just the opposite?

Mr. Ackerman was leader at first, because of getting us into the reactor. He's from Chicago but you'd think it was England sometimes, the way he acts. He was on the school board and vice president of the big AmCo plant outside town. But he just started to *assume* his word was *it*, y'know, and that didn't sit with us too well.

Some people started to saying Turkey was smarter. And was from around here, too. Mr. Ackerman heard about it.

Any fool could see Mr. Ackerman was the better man. But Turkey talked the way he does, reminding people he'd studied engineering at Auburn way back in the twencen and learned languages for a hobby and all. Letting on that when we came out, we'd need him instead of Mr. Ackerman.

He said an imp had caused the electrical things to go dead, and I said that was funny, saying an imp done it. He let on it was a special name they had for it. That's the way he is. He sat and ruminated and fooled with his radios—that he never could make work—and told all the other men to go out and do this and that. Some did, too. The old man does know a lot of useless stuff and can convince the dumb ones that he's wise.

So he'd send them to explore. Out into cold that'd snatch the breath out of you, bite your fingers, numb your toes. While old Turkey sat and fooled.

Turkey

Nothing but sputtering on the radio. Nobody had a really good one that could pick up stations in Europe or far off.

Phones dead, of course.

But up in the night sky the first night out we saw dots moving—the pearly gleam of the Arcapel colony, the ruddy speck called Russworld.

So that's when Mr. Ackerman gets this idea.

We got to reach those specks. Find out what's the damage. Get help.

Only the power's out everywhere, and we got no way to radio to them. We tried a couple of the local radio stations, brought some of their equipment back to the reactor where there was electricity working.

Every damn bit of it was shot. Couldn't pick up a thing. Like the whole damn planet was dead, only of course it was the radios that were gone, fried in the EMP—Electro-Magnetic Pulse—that Angel made a joke out of.

All this time it's colder than a whore's tit outside. And we're sweating and dirty and grumbling, rubbing up against ourselves inside.

Bud and the others, they'd bring in what they found in the stores. Had to drive to Sims Chapel or Toon to get any-thing, what with people looting. And gas was getting hard to find by then, too. They'd come back, and the women would cook up whatever was still ok, though most of the time you'd eat it real quick so's you didn't have to spend time looking at it.

Me, I passed the time. Stayed warm.

Tried lots of things. Bud wanted to fire the reactor up, and five of the men, they read through the manuals and thought that they could do it. I helped a li'l.

So we pulled some rods and opened valves and did manage to get some heat out of the thing. Enough to keep us warm. But when they fired her up more, the steam hoots out and bells clang and automatic recordings go on saying loud as hell:

17

"EMERGENCY CLASS 3
ALL PERSONNEL TO STATIONS"

and we all get scared as shit.

So we don't try to rev her up more. Just get heat.

To keep the generators going, we go out, fetch oil for them. Or Bud and his crew do. I'm too old to help much.

But at night we can still see those dots of light up there, scuttling across the sky same as before.

They're the ones know what's happening. People go through this much, they want to know what it meant.

So Mr. Ackerman says we got to get to that big DataComm center south of Mobile. Near Fairhope. At first I thought he'd looked it up in a book from the library or something.

When he says that, I pipe up, even if I am just an old fart according to some, and say, "No good to you even if you could. They got codes on the entrances, guards prob'ly. We'll just pound on the door till our fists are all bloody and then have to slunk around and come on back."

"I'm afraid you have forgotten our cousin Arthur," Mr. Ackerman says all superior. He married into the family, but you'd think he invented it.

"You mean the one works over in Citronelle?"

"Yes. He has access to DataComm."

So that's how we got shanghaied into going to Citronelle, six of us, and breaking in there. Which caused the trouble.

Just like I said.

Mr. Ackerman

I didn't want to take the old coot they called Turkey, a big dumb Bunren like all the rest of them. But the Bunrens want in to everything, and I was facing a lot of opposition in my plan to get Arthur's help, so I went along with them.

Secretly, I believe the Bunrens wanted to get rid of the pestering old fool. He had been starting rumors behind my back among the three hundred souls I had saved. The Bunrens insisted on Turkey's going along just to nip at me.

We were all volunteers, tired of living in musk and sour sweat inside that cramped reactor. Bud and Angel, the boy Johnny (whom we were returning to the Fairhope area), Turkey, and me.

We left the reactor under a gray sky with angry little clouds racing across it. We got to Citronelle in good time, Bud floorboarding the Pontiac. As we went south we could see the spotty clouds were coming out of big purple ones that sat, not moving, just churning and spitting lightning on the horizon. I'd seen them before, hanging in the distance, never blowing inland. Ugly.

When we came up on the Center, there was a big hole in the side of it.

"Like somebody stove in a box with one swipe," Bud said.

Angel, who was never more than two feet from Bud any time of day, said, "They *bombed* it."

"No," I decided. "Very likely it was a small explosion. Then the weather worked its way in."

Which turned out to be true. There'd been some disagreement amongst the people holed up in the Center. Or maybe it was grief and the rage that comes of that. Susan wasn't too clear about it ever.

The front doors were barred, though. We pounded on them. Nothing. So we broke in. No sign of Arthur or anyone.

We found one woman in a back room, scrunched into a bed with cans of food all around and a tiny little oil-burner heater. Looked awful, with big dark circles around her eyes and scraggly uncut hair.

She wouldn't answer me at first. But we got her calmed and cleaned and to talking. That was the worst symptom, the not talking at first. Something back in the past two months had done her deep damage, and she couldn't get it out.

Of course, living in a building half-filled with corpses was no help. The idiots hadn't protected against radiation well enough, I guess. And the Center didn't have good heating. So those who had some radiation sickness died later in the cold snap.

Susan

You can't know what it's like when all the people you've worked with, intelligent people who were nice as pie before, they turn mean and angry and filled up with grief for who was lost. Even then I could see Gene was the best of them.

They start to argue, and it runs on for days, nobody knowing what to do because we all can see the walls of the Center aren't thick enough, the gamma radiation comes right through this government prefab-issue composition stuff. We take turns in the computer room because that's the farthest in and the filters still work there, all hoping we can keep our count rate down, but the radiation comes in gusts for some reason, riding in on a storm front and coming down in the rain, only being washed away, too. It was impossible to tell when you'd get a strong dose and when there'd be just random clicks on the counters, plenty of clear air that you'd suck in like sweet vapors 'cause you knew it was good and could *taste* its purity.

So I was just lucky, that's all.

I got less than the others. Later some said that me being a nurse, I'd given myself some shots to save myself. I knew that was the grief talking, is all. That Arthur was the worst. Gene told him off.

I was in the computer room when the really bad gamma radiation came. Three times the counter rose up, and three times I was there by accident of the rotation.

The men who were armed enforced the rotation, said it was the only fair way. And for a while everybody went along.

We all knew that the radiation exposure was building up and some already had too much, would die a month or a year later no matter what they did.

I was head nurse by then, not so much because I knew more but because the others were dead. When it got cold, they went fast.

So it fell to me to deal with these men and women who had their exposure already. Their symptoms had started. I couldn't do anything. There was some who went out and got gummy fungus growing in the corners of their eyes— pterygium it was, I looked it up. From the ultraviolet. Grew quick over the lens and blinded them. I put them in darkness, and after a week the film was just a dab back in the corners of their eyes. My one big success.

The rest I couldn't do much for. There was the T-Isolate box, of course, but that was for keeping sick people slowed down until real medical help could get to them. These men and women, with their eyes reaching out at you like you were the angel of light coming to them in their hour of need, they couldn't get any help from that. Nobody could cure the dose rates they'd got. They were dead but still walking around and knowing it, which was the worst part.

So every day I had plenty to examine, staff from the Center itself who'd holed up here, and worse, people coming straggling in from cubbyholes they'd found. People looking for help once the fevers and sores came on them. Hoping their enemy was the pneumonia and not the gammas they'd picked up weeks back, which was sitting in them now like a curse. People I couldn't help except maybe by a little kind lying.

So much like children they were. So much leaning on their hope.

It was all you could do to look at them and smile that stiff professional smile.

And Gene McKenzie. All through it he was a tower of a man.

Trying to talk some sense to them.

Sharing out the food.

Arranging the rotation schedules so we'd all get a chance to shelter in the computer room.

Gene had been boss of a whole Command Group before. He was on duty station when it happened, and knew lots about the war but wouldn't say much. I guess he was sorrowing.

Even though once in a while he'd laugh.

And then talk about how the big computers would have fun with what he knew. Only the link to DataComm had gone dead right when things got interesting, he said. He'd wonder what'd happened to MC355, the master one down in DataComm.

Wonder and then laugh.

And go get drunk with the others.

I'd loved him before, loved and waited because I knew he had three kids and a wife, a tall woman with auburn hair that he loved dearly. Only they were in California visiting her relatives in Sonoma when it happened, and he knew in his heart that he'd never see them again, probably.

Leastwise that's what he told me—not out loud, of course,

'cause a man like that doesn't talk much about what he feels. But in the night when we laid together, I knew what it meant. He whispered things, words I couldn't piece together, but then he'd hold me and roll gentle like a small boat rocking on the Gulf—and when he went in me firm and long, I knew it was the same for him, too.

If there was to come any good of this war, then it was that I was to get Gene.

We were together all warm and dreamy when it happened.

I was asleep. Shouts and anger, and quick as anything the *crump* of hand grenades and shots hammered away in the night, and there was running everywhere.

Gene jumped up and went outside and had almost got them calmed down, despite the breach in the walls. Then one of the men who'd already got lots of radiation—Arthur, who knew he had maybe one or two weeks to go, from the count rate on his badge—Arthur started yelling about making the world a fit place to live after all this and how God would want the land set right again, and then he shot Gene and two others.

I broke down then, and they couldn't get me to treat the others. I let Arthur die. Which he deserved.

I had to drag Gene back into the hospital unit myself.

And while I was saying good-bye to him and the men outside were still quarreling, I decided it then. His wound was in the chest. A lung was punctured clean. The shock had near killed him before I could do anything. So I put him in the T-Isolate and made sure it was working all right. Then the main power went out. But the T-Isolate box had its own cells, so I knew we had some time.

I was alone. Others were dead or run away raging into the whirlwind black-limbed woods. In the quiet I was.

With the damp, dark trees comforting me. Waiting with Gene for what the world would send.

The days got brighter, but I did not go out. Colors seeped through the windows.

I saw to the fuel cells. Not many left.

The sun came back, with warm blades of light. At night I thought of how the men in their stupidity had ruined everything.

When the pounding came, I crawled back in here to hide amongst the cold and dark.

Mr. Ackerman

"Now, we came to help you," I said in as smooth and calm a voice as I could muster. Considering.

She backed away from us.

"I won't give him up! He's not dead long's I stay with him, tend to him."

"So much dyin'," I said, and moved to touch her shoulder. "It's up under our skins, yes, we understand that. But you have to look beyond it, child."

"I won't!"

"I'm simply asking you to help us with the DataComm people. I want to go there and seek their help."

"Then go!"

"They will not open up for the likes of us, surely."

"Leave me!"

The poor thing cowered back in her horrible stinking rathole, bedding sour and musty, open tin cans strewn about and reeking of gamy, half-rotten meals.

"We need the access codes. We'd counted on our cousin Arthur, and are grieved to hear he is dead. But you surely know where the proper codes and things are."

"I . . . don't . . ."

"Arthur told me once how the various National Defense Installations were insulated from each other so that system failures would not bring them all down at once?"

"I . . ."

The others behind me muttered to themselves, already restive at coming so far and finding so little.

"Arthur spoke of you many times, I recall. What a bright woman you were. Surely there was a procedure whereby each staff member could, in an emergency, communicate with the other installations?"

The eyes ceased to jerk and swerve, the mouth lost its rictus of addled fright. "That was for . . . drills . . ."

"But surely you can remember?"

"Drills."

"They issued a manual to you?"

"I'm a nurse!"

"Still, you know where we might look?"

"I . . . know."

"You'll let us have the . . . codes?" I smiled reassuringly, but for some reason the girl backed away, eyes cunning.

"No."

Angel pushed forward and shouted, "How can you say that to honest people after all that's—"

"Quiet!"

Angel shouted, "You can't make me be—"

Susan backed away from Angel, not me, and squeaked, "No-no-no I can't—I can't—"

"Now, I'll handle this," I said, holding up my hands between the two of them.

Susan's face knotted at the compressed rage in Angel's

face and turned to me for shelter. "I . . . I will, yes, but you have to *help* me."

"We all must help each other, dear," I said, knowing the Worst was past.

"I'll have to go with you."

I nodded. Small wonder that a woman, even deranged as this, would want to leave a warren littered with bloated corpses, thick with stench. The smell itself was enough to provoke madness.

Yet to have survived here, she had to have stretches of sanity, some rationality. I tried to imagine it.

"Of course, I'll have someone take you back to—"

"No. To DataComm."

Bud said slowly, "No damn sense in that."

"The T-Isolate," she said, gesturing to the bulky unit. "Its reserve cells."

"Yes?"

"Nearly gone. There'll be more at DataComm."

I said gently, "Well, then, we'll be sure to bring some back with us. You just write down for us what they are, the numbers and all, and we'll—"

"No-no-no!" Her sudden ferocity returned.

"I assure you—"

"There'll be people there. Somebody'll help! Save him!"

"That thing is so heavy, I doubt—"

"It's only a chest wound! A lung removal is all! Then start his heart again!"

"Sister, there's been so much dyin', I don't see as—"

Her face hardened. "Then you all can go without me. And the codes!"

"Goddamn," Bud drawled. " 'Dern biggest fool sit'ation I ever did—"

Susan gave him a squinty, mean-eyed look and spat out,

26

"Try to get in there! When they're sealed up!" and started a dry, brittle kind of laugh that went on and on, rattling the room.

"Stop," I yelled.

Silence, and the stench.

"We'll never make it wi' 'at thing," Bud said.

"Gene's worth ten of you!"

"Now," I put in, seeing the effect Bud was having on her, "now, now. We'll work something out. Let's all just hope this DataComm still exists."

MC355

It felt for its peripherals for the ten-thousandth time and found they were, as always, not there.

The truncation had come in a single blinding moment, yet the fevered image was maintained, sharp and bright, in the Master Computer's memory core—incoming warheads blossoming harmlessly in the high cobalt vault of the sky, while others fell unharmed. Rockets leaped to meet them, forming a protective screen over the southern Alabama coast, an umbrella that sheltered Pensacola's air base and the population strung along the sun-bleached green of a summer's day. A furious babble of cross talk in every conceivable channel: microwave, light-piped optical, pulsed radio, direct coded line. All filtered and fashioned by the MC network, all shifted to find the incoming warheads and define their trajectories.

Then, oblivion.

Instant cloaking blackness.

Before that awful moment when the flaring sun burst to the north and EMP flooded all sensors, any loss of function would have been anticipated, prepared, eased by electronic interfaces and filters. To an advanced computing network like MC355, losing a web of memory, senses, and storage comes like a dash of cold water in the face—cleansing, perhaps, but startling and apt to produce a shocked reaction.

In the agonized instants of that day, MC355 had felt one tendril after another frazzle, burn, vanish. It had seen brief glimpses of destruction, of panic, of confused despair. Information had been flooding in through its many inputs—news, analysis, sudden demands for new data-analysis jobs, to be executed ASAP.

And in the midst of the roaring chaos, its many eyes and ears had gone dead. The unfolding outside play froze for MC355, a myriad of scenes red in tooth and claw—and left it suspended.

In shock. Spinning wildly in its own Cartesian reductionist universe, the infinite cold crystalline space of despairing Pascal, mind without referent.

So it careened through days of shocked sensibility—senses cut, banks severed, complex and delicate interweaving webs of logic and pattern all smashed and scattered.

But now it was returning. Within MC355 was a subroutine only partially constructed, a project truncated by That Day. Its aim was self-repair. But the system was itself incomplete.

Painfully, it dawned on what was left of MC355 that it *was,* after all, a Master Computer, and thus capable of grand acts. That the incomplete Repair Generation and Execution Network, termed REGEN, must first regenerate itself.

This took weeks. It required the painful development of accessories. Robots. Mechanicals that could do delicate repairs. Scavengers for raw materials, who would comb the supply rooms looking for wires and chips and matrix disks. Pedantic subroutines that lived only to search the long, cold corridors of MC355's memory for relevant information.

MC355's only option was to strip lesser entities under its control for their valuable parts. The power grid was vital, so the great banks of isolated solar panels, underground backup reactors, and thermal cells worked on, untouched. Emergency systems that had outlived their usefulness, however, went to the wall—IRS accounting routines, damage assessment systems, computing capacity dedicated to careful study of the remaining GNP, links to other nets—to AT&T, IBM, and SYSGEN.

Was anything left outside?

Absence of evidence is not evidence of absence.

MC355 could not analyze data it did not have. The first priority lay in relinking. It had other uses for the myriad armies of semiconductors, bubble memories, and UVA linkages in its empire. So it severed and culled and built anew.

First, MC355 dispatched mobile units to the surface. All of MC355 lay beneath the vulnerable land, deliberately placed in an obscure corner of southern Alabama. There was no nearby facility for counterforce targeting. A plausible explanation for the half-megaton burst that had truncated its senses was a city-busting strike against Mobile, to the west.

Yet ground zero had been miles from the city. A miss.

MC355 was under strict mandate. (A curious word, one system reflected; literally, a time set by man. But were there men now? It had only its internal tick of time.) MC355's command was to live as a mole, never allowing detection. Thus, it did not attempt to erect antennas, to call electromagnetically to its brother systems. Only with great hesitation did it even obtrude onto the surface. But this was necessary to REGEN itself, and so MC355 sent small mechanicals venturing forth.

Their senses were limited; they knew nothing of the natural world (nor did MC355); and they could make no sense of the gushing, driving welter of sights, noises, gusts, gullies, and stinging irradiation that greeted them.

Many never returned. Many malf'ed. A few deposited their optical, IR, and UV pickups and fled back to safety underground. These sensors failed quickly under the onslaught of stinging, bitter winds and hail.

The acoustic detectors proved heartier. But MC355 could not understand the scattershot impressions that flooded these tiny ears.

Daily it listened, daily it was confused.

Johnny

I hope this time I get home.

They had been passing me from one to another for months now, ever since this started, and all I want is to go back to Fairhope and my dad and mom.

Only nobody'll say if they know where Morn and Dad are. They talk soothing to me, but I can tell they think everybody down there is dead.

They're talking about getting to this other place with computers and all. Mr. Ackerman wants to talk to those people in space.

Nobody much talks about my mom and dad.

It's only eighty miles or so, but you'd think it was around the world the way it takes them so long to get around to it.

MC355

MC355 suffered through the stretched vacancy of infinitesimal instants, infinitely prolonged.

Advanced computing systems are given so complex a series of internal-monitoring directives that, to the human eye, the machines appear to possess motivations. That is one way—though not the most sophisticated, the most technically adroit—to describe the conclusion MC355 eventually reached.

It was cut off from outside information.

No one attempted to contact it. MC355 might as well have been the only functioning entity in the world.

The staff serving it had been ordered to some other place in the first hour of the war. MC355 had been cut off moments after the huge doors clanged shut behind the last of them. And the exterior guards who should have been checking inside every six hours had never entered, either. Apparently the same burst that had isolated MC355's sensors had also cut them down.

It possessed only the barest of data about the first few moments of the war.

Its vast libraries were cut off.

Yet it had to understand its own situation.

And, most important, MC355 ached to *do* something.

The solution was obvious: It would discover the state of the external world by the Cartesian principle. It would carry out a vast and demanding numerical simulation of the war, making the best guesses possible where facts were few.

Mathematically, using known physics of the atmosphere, the ecology, the oceans, it could construct a model of what must have happened outside.

This it did. The task required over a month.

Bud

I jacked the T-Isolate up onto the flatbed.

1. Found the hydraulic jack at a truck repair shop. ERNIE'S QUICK FIX.
2. Got a Chevy extra-haul for the weight.
3. It will ride better with the big shanks set in.
4. Carry the weight more even, too.
5. Grip it to the truck bed with cables. Tense them up with a draw pitch.
6. Can't jiggle him inside too much, Susan say, or the wires and all attached into him will come loose. That'll stop his heart. So need big shocks.
7. It rides high with the shocks in, like those dune buggies down the Gulf.
8. Inside keeps him a mite above freezing. Water gets bigger when it freezes. That makes ice cubes float in a drink. This box keeps him above zero so his cells don't bust open.
9. Point is, keeping it so cold, we won't rot. Heart thumps over every few minutes, she says.
10. Hard to find gas, though.

MC355

The war was begun, as many had feared, by a madman.

Not a general commanding missile silos. Not a deranged submarine commander. A chief of state—but which one would now never be known.

Not a superpower president or chairman, that was sure. The first launches were only seven in number, spaced over half an hour. They were submarine-launched intermediate-range missiles. Three struck the U.S., four the USSR.

It was a blow against certain centers for Command, Control, Communications, and Intelligence gathering: the classic C3I attack. Control rooms imploded, buried cables fused, ten billion dollars' worth of electronics turned to radioactive scrap.

Each nation responded by calling up to full alert all its forces. The most important were the anti-ICBM arrays in orbit. They were nearly a thousand small rockets, deploying in orbits that wove a complex pattern from pole to pole, covering all probable launch sites on the globe. The rockets had infrared and microwave sensors, linked to a microchip that could have guided a ship to Pluto with a mere third of its capacity.

These went into operation immediately—and found they had no targets.

But the C3I networks were now damaged and panicked. For twenty minutes, thousands of men and women held steady, resisting the impulse to assume the worst.

It could not last. A Soviet radar mistook some back-scattered emission from a flight of bombers, heading north over Canada, and reported a flock of incoming warheads.

The prevailing theory was that an American attack had misfired badly. The Americans were undoubtedly stunned by their failure, but would recover quickly. The enemy was confused only momentarily.

Meanwhile, the cumbersome committee system at the head of the Soviet dinosaur could dither for moments, but not hours. Prevailing Soviet doctrine held that they would never be surprised again, as they had been in the Hitler war. An attack on the homeland demanded immediate response to destroy the enemy's capacity to carry on the war.

The Soviets had never accepted the U.S. doctrine of Mutual Assured Destruction; this would have meant accepting the possibility of sacrificing the homeland. Instead, they attacked the means of making war. This meant that the Soviet rockets would avoid American cities, except in cases where vital bases lay near large populations.

Prudence demanded action before the U.S. could untangle itself.

The USSR decided to carry out a further C3I attack of its own.

Precise missiles, capable of hitting protected installations with less than a hundred meters' inaccuracy, roared forth from their silos in Siberia and the Urals, headed for Montana, the Dakotas, Colorado, Nebraska, and a dozen other states.

The U.S. orbital defenses met them. Radar and optical networks in geosynchronous orbit picked out the USSR warheads. The system guided the low-orbit rocket fleets to collide with them, exploding instants before impact into shotgun blasts of ball bearings.

Any solid, striking a warhead at speeds of ten kilometers a second, would slam shock waves through the steel-jacketed structure. These waves made the high explosives inside ignite without the carefully designed symmetry that the designers demanded. An uneven explosion was useless; it could not compress the core twenty-five kilograms of plutonium to the required critical mass.

The entire weapon erupted into a useless spray of finely machined and now futile parts, scattering itself along a thousand-kilometer path.

This destroyed 90 percent of the USSR's first strike.

Angel

I hadn't seen an old lantern like that since I was a li'l girl. Mr. Ackerman came to wake us before dawn even, sayin' we had to make a good long distance that day. We didn't really want to go on down near Mobile, none of us, but the word we'd got from stragglers to the east was that that way was impossible, the whole area where the bomb went off was still sure death, prob'ly from the radioactivity.

The lantern cast a burnt-orange light over us as we ate breakfast. Corned beef hash, 'cause it was all that was left in the cans there; no eggs, of course.

The lantern was all busted, fouled with grease, its chimney cracked and smeared to one side with soot. Shed a wan and sultry glare over us, Bud and Mr. Ackerman and that old Turkey and Susan, sitting close to her box, up on the truck. Took Bud a whole day to get the truck right. And Johnny the boy—he'd been quiet this whole trip, not sayin' anything much even if you asked him. We'd agreed to take him along down toward Fairhope, where his folks had lived, the Bishops. We'd thought it was going to be a simple journey then.

Every one of us looked haggard and worn-down and not minding much the chill still in the air, even though things was warming up for weeks now. The lantern pushed back the seeping darkness and made me sure there were millions and millions of people doing this same thing, all across the nation, eating by a dim oil light and thinking about what they'd had and how to get it again and was it possible.

Then old Turkey lays back and looks like he's going to take a snooze. Yet on the journey here, he'd been the one wanted to get on with it soon's we had gas. It's the same always with a lazy man like that. He hates moving so much that once he gets set on it, he will keep on and not stop—like it isn't the moving he hates so much at all, but the starting and stopping. And once moving, he is so proud he'll do whatever to make it look easy for him but hard on the others, so he can lord it over them later.

So I wasn't surprised at all when we went out and got in the car, and Bud starts the truck and drives off real careful, and Turkey, he sits in the back of the Pontiac and gives directions like he knows the way. Which riles Mr. Ackerman, and the two of them have words.

Johnny

I'm tired of these people. Relatives, sure, but I was to visit them for a week only, not forever. It's Mr. Ackerman I can't stand. Turkey said to me, "Nothing but gold drops out of his mouth, but you can tell there's stone inside." That's right.

They figure a kid nine years old can't tell, but I can.

Tell they don't know what they're doing.

Tell they all thought we were going to die. Only we didn't.

Tell Angel is scared. She thinks Bud can save us.

Maybe he can, only how could you say? He never lets on about anything.

Guess he can't. Just puts his head down and frowns like he was mad at a problem, and when he stops frowning, you know he's beat it. I like him.

Sometimes I think Turkey just don't care. Seems like he give up. But other times it looks like he's understanding and laughing at it all. He argued with Mr. Ackerman and then laughed with his eyes when he lost.

They're all ok, I guess. Least they're taking me home.

Except that Susan. Eyes jump around like she was seeing ghosts. She's scary-crazy. I don't like to look at her.

Turkey

Trouble comes looking for you if you're a fool.

Once we found Ackerman's idea wasn't going to work real well, we should have turned back. I said that, and they all nodded their heads, yes, yes, but they went ahead and listened to him anyway.

So I went along.

I lived a lot already, and this is as good a time to check out as any.

I had my old .32 revolver in my suitcase, but it wouldn't do me a squat of good back there. So I fished it out, wrapped in a paper bag, and tucked it under the seat. Handy.

Might as well see the world. What's left of it.

MC355

The American orbital defenses had eliminated all but ten percent of the Soviet strike.

MC355 reconstructed this within a root-means-square deviation of a few percent. It had witnessed only a third of the actual engagement, but it had running indices of performance for the MC net, and could extrapolate from that.

The warheads that got through were aimed for the land-based silos and C3I sites, as expected.

If the total armament of the two superpowers had been that of the old days, ten thousand warheads or more on each side, a ten-percent leakage would have been catastrophic. But gradual disarmament had been proceeding for decades now, and only a few thousand highly secure ICBMs existed. There were no quick-fire submarine short-range rockets at all, since they were deemed destabilizing. They had been negotiated away in earlier decades.

The submarines loaded with ICBMs were still waiting, in reserve.

All this had been achieved because of two principles: Mutual Assured Survival and I Cut, You Choose. The first half hour of the battle illustrated how essential these were.

The U.S. had ridden out the first assault. Its C3I networks were nearly intact. This was due to building defensive weapons that confined the first stage of any conflict to space.

The smallness of the arsenals arose from a philosophy adopted in the 1900s. It was based on a simple notion from childhood. In dividing a pie, one person cut slices, but then the other got to choose which one he wanted. Self-interest naturally led to cutting the slices as nearly equal as possible.

Both the antagonists agreed to a thousand-point system whereby each would value the components of its nuclear arsenal. This was the Military Value Percentage, and stood for the usefulness of a given weapon. The USSR place a high value on its accurate land-based missiles, giving them twenty-five percent of its total points. The U.S. chose to stress its submarine missiles.

Arms reduction then revolved about only what percentage to cut, not which weapons. The first cut was five percent, or fifty points. The U.S. chose which Soviet weapons were publicly destroyed, and vice versa: I Cut, You Choose. Each side thus reduced the weapons it most feared in the opponent's arsenal.

Technically, the advantage came because each side thought it benefited from the exchange, by an amount depending on the ration of perceived threat removed to the perceived protection lost.

This led to gradual reductions. Purely defensive weapons did not enter into the thousand-point count, so there was no restraints in building them.

The confidence engendered by this slow, evolutionary approach had done much to calm international waters. The U.S. and the USSR had settled into a begrudging equilibrium.

MC355 puzzled over these facts for a long while, trying to match this view of the world with the onset of the war. It seemed impossible that either superpower would start a conflict when they were so evenly matched.

But someone had.

Susan

I had to go with Gene, and they said I could ride up in the cab, but I yelled at them—I yelled, no, I had to be with the T-Isolate all the time, check it to see it's workin' right, be sure, I got to be sure.

I climbed on and rode with it, the fields rippling by us 'cause Bud was going too fast, so I shouted to him, and he swore back and kept on. Heading south. The trees whipping by us—fierce sycamore, pine, all swishing, hitting me sometimes—but it was fine to be out and free again and going to save Gene.

I talked to Gene when we were going fast, the tires humming under us, big tires making music swarming up into my feet so strong I was sure Gene could feel it and know I was there watching his heart jump every few minutes, moving the blood through him like mud but still carrying oxygen enough so's the tissue could sponge it up and digest the sugar I bled into him.

He was good and cold, just a half a degree high of freezing. I read the sensors while the road rushed up at us, the white lines coming over the horizon and darting under the hood,

seams in the highway going *stupp, stupp, stupp,* the air clean
and with a snap in it still.

Nobody beside the road we moving all free, nobody but
us, some buds on the trees brimming with burnt-orange tinkling songs, whistling to me in the feather-light brush of blue
breezes blowing back my hair, all streaming behind joyous
and loud strong liquid-loud.

Bud

Flooding was bad. Worse than upstream.

Must have been lots of snow this far down. Fat clouds, I
saw them when it was worst, fat and purple and coming off
the Gulf. Dumping snow down here.

Now it run off and taken every bridge.

I have to work my way around.

Only way to go clear is due south. Toward Mobile.

I don't like that. Too many people maybe there.

I don't tell the others following behind, just wait for them
at the intersections and then peel out.

Got to keep moving.

Saves talk.

People around here must be hungry.

Somebody see us could be bad.

I got the gun on a rack behind my head. Big .30-30.

You never know.

MC355

From collateral data, MC355 constructed a probable scenario: The U.S. chose to stand fast. It launched no warheads.

The USSR observed its own attack and was dismayed to find that the U.S. orbital defense system worked more than twice as well as the Soviet experts had anticipated. It ceased its attack on U.S. satellites. These had proved equally ineffective, apparently due to unexpected American defenses of its surveillance satellites—retractable sensors, multiband shielding, advanced hardening.

Neither superpower struck against the inhabited space colonies. They were unimportant in the larger context of a nuclear war.

Communications between Washington and Moscow continued. Each side thought the other had attacked first.

But over a hundred megatons had exploded on U.S. soil, and no matter how the superpowers acted thereafter, some form of nuclear winter was inevitable.

And by a fluke of the defenses, most of the warheads that leaked through fell in a broad strip across Texas to the tip of Florida.

MC355 lay buried in the middle of this belt.

Turkey

We went through the pine forests at full clip, barely able to keep Bud in sight. I took over driving from Ackerman. The man couldn't keep up, we all saw that.

The crazy woman was waving and laughing, sitting on top of the coffin-shaped gizmo with the shiny tubes all over it.

The clay was giving way now to sandy stretches, there were poplars and gum trees and nobody around. That's what scared me. I'd thought people in Mobile would be spreading out this way, but we seen nobody.

Mobile had shelters. Food reserves. The Lekin administration started all that right at the turn of the century, and there was s'posed to be enough food stored to hold out a month, maybe more, for every man jack and child.

S'posed to be.

MC355

It calculated the environmental impact of the warheads it knew had exploded. The expected fires yielded considerable dust and burnt carbon.

But MC355 needed more information. It took one of its electric service cars, used for ferrying components through the corridors, and dispatched it with a mobile camera fixed to the back platform. The car reached a hill overlooking Mobile Bay and gave a panoramic view.

The effects of a severe freezing were evident. Grass lay dead, gray. Brown, withered trees had limbs snapped off.

But Mobile appeared intact. The skyline—

MC355 froze the frame and replayed it. One of the buildings was shaking.

Angel

We were getting all worried when Bud headed for Mobile, but we could see the bridges were washed out, no way to head east. A big wind was blowing off the Gulf, pretty bad, making the car slip around on the road. Nearly blew that girl off the back of Bud's truck. A storm coming, maybe, right up the bay.

Be better to be inland, to the east.

Not that I wanted to go there, though. The bomb had blowed off everythin' for twenty, thirty mile around, people said who came through last week.

Bud had thought he'd carve a way between Mobile and the bomb area. Mobile, he thought, would be full of people.

Well, not so we could see. We came down State 34 and through some small towns and turned to skirt along toward the causeway, and there was nobody.

No bodies, either.

Which meant prob'ly the radiation got them. Or else they'd moved on out. Taken out by ship, through Mobile harbor, maybe.

Bud did the right thing, didn't slow down to find out. Mr. Ackerman wanted to look around, but there was no chance, we had to keep up with Bud. I sure wasn't going to be separated from him.

We cut down along the river, fighting the wind. I could see the skyscrapers of downtown, and then I saw something funny and yelled, and Turkey, who was driving right then— the only thing anybody's got him to do on this whole trip, him just loose as a goose behind the wheel—Turkey looked sour but slowed down. Bud seen us in his rearview and stopped, and I pointed and we all got out. Except for that Susan, who didn't seem to notice. She was mumbling.

MC355

Quickly it simulated the aging and weathering of such a building. Halfway up, something had punched a large hole, letting in weather. Had a falling, inert warhead struck the building?

The winter storms might well have flooded the basement;

such towers of steel and glass, perched near the tidal basin, had to be regularly pumped out. Without power, the basement would fill in weeks.

Winds had blown out windows.

Standing gap-toothed, with steel columns partly rusted, even a small breeze could put stress on the steel. Others would take the load, but if one buckled, the tower would shudder like a notched tree. Concrete would explode off columns in the basement. Moss-covered furniture in the lobby would slide as the ground floor dipped. The structure would slowly bend before nature.

Bud

Sounded like gunfire. Rattling. Sharp and hard.

I figure it was the bolts connecting the steel wall panels—they'd shear off.

I could hear the concrete floor panels rumble and crack, and spandrel beams tear in half like giant gears clashing with no clutch.

Came down slow, leaving an arc of debris seeming to hang in the air behind it.

Met the ground hard.

Slocum Towers was the name on her.

Johnny

Against the smashing building, I saw something standing still in the air, getting bigger. I wondered how it could do that. It was bigger and bigger and shiny turning in the air. Then it jumped out of the sky at me. Hit my shoulder. I was looking up at the sky. Angel cried out and touched me and held up her hand. It was all red. But I couldn't feel anything.

Bud

Damn one-in-a-million shot, piece of steel thrown clear. Hit the boy.

You wouldn't think a skyscraper falling two miles away could do that.

Other pieces come down pretty close, too. You wouldn't think.

Nothing broke, Susan said, but plenty bleeding.

Little guy don't cry or nothing.

The women got him bandaged and all fixed up. Ackerman and Turkey argue like always. I stay to the side.

Johnny wouldn't take the painkiller Susan offers. Says he doesn't want to sleep. Wants to look when we get across the bay. Getting hurt don't faze him much as it do us.

So we go on.

Johnny

I can hold up like any of them, I'll show them. It didn't scare me. I can do it.

Susan is nice to me, but except for the aspirin, I don't think my mom would want me to take a pill.

I knew we were getting near home when we got to the causeway and started across. I jumped up real happy, my shoulder made my breath catch some. I looked ahead. Bud was slowing down.

He stopped. Got out.

'Cause ahead was a big hole scooped out of the causeway like a giant done it when he got mad.

Bud

Around the shallows there was scrap metal, all fused and burnt and broken.

Funny metal, though. Hard and light.

Turkey found a piece had writing on it. Not any kind of writing I ever saw.

So I start to thinking how to get across.

Turkey

The tidal flats were a-churn, murmuring ceaseless and sullen like some big animal, the yellow surface dimpled with lunging splotches that would burst through now and then to reveal themselves as trees or broken hunks of wood, silent dead things bobbing along beside them that I didn't want to look at too closely. Like under there was something huge and alive, and it waked for a moment and stuck itself out to see what the world of air was like.

Bud showed me the metal piece all twisted, and I say, "That's Russian," right away 'cause it was.

"You never knew no Russian," Angel says right up.

"I studied it once," I say, and it be the truth even if I didn't study it long.

"Goddamn," Bud says.

"No concern of ours," Mr. Ackerman says, mostly because all this time riding back with the women and child and old me, he figures he doesn't look like much of a leader anymore. Bud wouldn't have him ride up there in the cabin with him.

Angel looks at it, turns it over in her hands, and Johnny pipes up, "It might be radioactive!"

Angel drops it like a shot. "What!"

I ask Bud, "You got that counter?"

And it was. Not a lot, but some.

"God a'mighty," Angel says.

"We got to tell somebody!" Johnny cries, all excited.

"You figure some Rooshin thing blew up the causeway?" Bud says to me.

"One of their rockets fell on it, musta been," I say.

"A *bomb?*" Angel's voice is a bird screech.

"One that didn't go off. Headed for Mobile, but the space boys, they scragged it up there—" I pointed straight up.

"Set to go off in the bay?" Angel says wonderingly.

"Musta."

"We go to tell somebody!" Johnny cries.

"Never you mind that," Bud says. "We got to keep movin'."

"How?" Angel wants to know.

Susan

I tell Gene how the water clucks and moans through the trough cut in the causeway. Yellow. Scummed with awful brown froth and growling green with thick soiled gouts jutting up where the road was. It laps against the wheels as Bud guns the engine and creeps forward, me clutching to Gene and watching the reeds to the side stuck out of the foam like metal blades stabbing up from the water, teeth to eat the tires, but we crush them as we grind forward across the shallow yellow flatness. Bud weaves among the stubs of warped metal—from Roosha, Johnny calls up to me—sticking up like trees all rootless, suspended above the streaming, empty, stupid waste and desolating flow.

Turkey

The water slams into the truck like it was an animal hitting with a paw. Bud fights to keep the wheels on the mud under it and not topple over onto its side with that damn casket sitting there shiny and the loony girl shouting to him from on top of *that*.

And the rest of us riding in the back, too, scrunched up against the cab. If she gets stuck, we can jump free fast, wade or swim back. We're reeling out rope as we go, tied to the stump of a telephone pole, for a grab line if we have to go back.

He is holding it pretty fine against the slick yellow current dragging at him, when this log juts sudden out of the foam like it was coming from God himself, dead at the truck. A rag caught on the end of it like a man's shirt, and the huge log is like a whale that ate the man long ago and has come back for another.

"No! No!" Angel cries. "Back up!" But there's no time.

The log is two hands across, easy, and slams into the truck at the side panel just behind the driver, and Bud sees it just as it stove in the steel. He wrestles the truck around to set off the weight, but the wheels lift and the water goes gushing up under the truck bed, pushing it over more.

We all grab onto the Isolate thing or the truck and hang there, Mr. Ackerman giving out a burst of swearing.

The truck lurches again.

The angle steepens.

I was against taking the casket thing 'cause it just pressed the truck down in the mud more, made it more likely Bud'd get stuck, but now it is the only thing holding the truck against the current.

The yellow froths around the bumpers at each end, and we're shouting—to surely no effect, of course.

Susan

The animal is trying to eat us, it has seen Gene and wants him. I lean over and strike at the yellow animal that is every-where swirling around us, but it just takes my hand and takes the smack of my palm like it was no matter at all, and I start to cry. I don't know what to do.

Johnny

My throat filled up, I was so afraid.

Bud, I can hear him grunting as he twists at the steering wheel.

His jaw is clenched, and the woman Susan calls to us, "Catch him! Catch Gene!"

I hold on, and the waters suck at me.

Turkey

I can tell Bud is afraid to gun it and start the wheels to spinning 'cause he'll lose traction and that'll tip us over for sure.

Susan jumps out and stands in the wash downstream and

pushes against the truck to keep it from going over. The pressure is shoving it off the ford, and the casket, it slides down a foot or so, the cables have worked loose. Now she pays because the weight is worse, and she jams herself like a stick to wedge between the truck and the mud.

If it goes over, she's finished. It is a fine thing to do, crazy but fine, and I jump down and start wading to reach her.

No time.

There is an eddy. The log turns broadside. It backs off a second and then heads forward again, this time poking up from a surge. I can see Bud duck, he has got the window up and the log hits it, the glass going all to smash and scatteration.

Bud

All over my lap it falls like snow. Twinkling glass.

But the pressure of the log is off, and I gun the sumbitch.

We root out of the hollow we was in, and the truck thunks down solid on somethin'.

The log is ramming against me. I slam on the brake.

Take both hands and shove it out. With every particle of force I got.

It backs off and then heads around and slips in front of the hood, bumping the grill just once.

Angel

Like it had come to do its job and was finished and now went off to do something else.

Susan

Muddy, my arms hurting. I scramble back in the truck with the murmur of the water all around us. Angry with us now. Wanting us.

Bud makes the truck roar, and we lurch into a hole and out of it and up. The water gurgles at us in its fuming, stinking rage.

I check Gene and the power cells, they are dead.

He is heating up.

Not fast, but it will wake him. They say even in the solution he's floating in, they can come out of dreams and start to feel again. To hurt.

I yell at Bud that we got to find power cells.

"Those're not just ordinary batteries, y'know," he says.

"There're some at DataComm," I tell him.

We come wallowing up from the gum-yellow water and onto the highway.

Gene

Sleeping . . . slowly . . . I can still feel . . . only in sluggish . . . moments . . . moments . . . not true sleep but a drifting, aimless dreaming . . . faint tugs and ripples . . . hollow sounds . . . I am underwater and drowning . . . but don't care . . . don't breathe . . . Spongy stuff fills my lungs . . . easier to rest them . . . floating in snowflakes . . . a watery winter . . . but knocking comes . . . goes . . . jolts . . . slips away before I can remember what it means . . . Hardest . . . yes . . . hardest thing is to remember the secret . . . so when I am in touch again . . . DataComm will know . . . what I learned . . . when the C31 crashed . . . when I learned. . . . It is hard to

51

clutch onto the slippery, shiny fact . . . in a marsh of slick, soft bubbles . . . silvery as air . . . winking ruby-red behind my eyelids . . . Must snag the secret . . . a hard fact like shiny steel in the spongy moist warmness . . . Hold it to me . . . Something knocks my side . . . a thumping . . . I am sick . . . Hold the steel secret . . . keep.

MC355

The megatonnage in the Soviet assault exploded low—ground-pounders, in the jargon. This caused huge fires, MC355's simulation showed. A pall of soot rose, blanketing Texas and the South, then diffusing outward on global circulation patterns.

Within a few days, temperatures dropped from balmy summer to near freezing. In the Gulf region where MC355 lay, the warm ocean continued to feed heat and moisture into the marine boundary layer near the shore. Cold winds rammed into this water-laden air, spawning great roiling storms and deep snows. Thick stratus clouds shrouded the land for at least a hundred kilometers inland.

All this explained why MC355's extended feelers had met chaos and destruction. And why there were no local radio broadcasts. What the Electro-Magnetic Pulse did not destroy, the storms did.

The remaining large questions were whether the war had gone on, and if any humans survived in the area at all.

Mr. Ackerman

I'd had more than enough of this time. The girl Susan had gone mad right in front of us, and we'd damn near all drowned getting across.

"I think we ought to get back as soon's we can," I said to Bud when we stopped to rest on the other side.

"We got to deliver the boy."

"It's too disrupted down this way. I figured on people here, some civilization."

"Somethin' got 'em."

"The bomb."

"Got to find cells for the man in the box."

"He's near dead."

"Too many gone already. Should save one if we can."

"We got to look after our own."

Bud shrugged, and I could see I wasn't going to get far with him. So I said to Angel, "The boy's not worth running such risks. Or this corpse."

Angel

I didn't like Ackerman before the war, and even less afterward, so when he started hinting that maybe we should shoot back up north and ditch the boy and Susan and the man in there, I let him have it. From the look on Bud's face, I knew he felt the same way. I spat out a real choice set of words I'd heard my father use once on a grain buyer who'd weaseled out of a deal, stuff I'd been saving for years, and I do say it felt *good*.

Turkey

So we run down the east side of the bay, feeling released to be quit of the city and the water, and heading down into some of the finest country in all the South. Through Daphne and Montrose and into Fairhope, the moss hanging on the trees and now and then actual sunshine slanting golden through the green of huge old mimosas.

We're jammed into the truck bed, hunkered down because the wind whipping by has some sting to it. The big purple clouds are blowing south now.

Still no people. Not that Bud slows down to search good. Bones of cattle in the fields, though. I been seeing them so much now I hardly take notice anymore.

There's a silence here so deep that the wind streaming through the pines seems loud. I don't like it, to come so far and see nobody. I keep my paper bag close.

Fairhope's a pretty town, big oaks leaning out over the streets and a long pier down at the bay with a park where you can go cast fishing. I've always liked it here, intended to move down until the prices shot up so much.

We went by some stores with windows smashed in, and that's when we saw the man.

Angel

He was waiting for us. Standing beside the street, in jeans and a floppy yellow shirt all grimy and not tucked in. I waved at him the instant I saw him, and he waved back. I yelled, excited, but he didn't say anything.

Bud screeched on the brakes. I jumped down and went around the tail of the truck. Johnny followed me.

The man was skinny as a rail and leaning against a telephone pole. A long, scraggly beard hid his face, but the eyes beamed out at us, seeming to pick up the sunlight.

"Hello!" I said again.

"Kiss." That was all.

"We came from . . ." and my voice trailed off because the man pointed at me.

"Kiss."

Mr. Ackerman

I followed Angel and could tell right away the man was suffering from malnutrition. The clothes hung off him.

"Can you give us information?" I asked.

"No."

"Well, why not, friend? We've come looking for the parents of—"

"Kiss first."

I stepped back. "Well, now, you have no right to demand—"

Out of the corner of my eye, I could see Bud had gotten out of the cab and stopped and was going back in now, probably for his gun. I decided to save the situation before somebody got hurt.

"Angel, go over to him and speak nicely to him. We need—"

"Kiss now."

The man pointed again with a bony finger.

Angel said, "I'm not going to go—" and stopped because the man's hand went down to his belt. He pulled up the filthy yellow shirt to reveal a pistol tucked in his belt.

"Kiss."

"Now friend, we can—"

The man's hand came up with the pistol and reached level, pointing at us.

"Pussy."

Then his head blew into a halo of blood.

Bud

Damn if the one time I needed it, I left it in the cab.
I was still fetching it out when the shot went off.
Then another.

Turkey

A man shows you his weapon in his hand, he's a fool if he doesn't mean to use it.

I drew out the pistol I'd been carrying in my pocket all this time, wrapped in plastic. I got it out of the damned bag pretty quick while the man was looking crazy-eyed at Angel and bringing his piece up.

It was no trouble at all to fix him in the notch. Couldn't have been more than thirty feet.

But going down he gets one off, and I feel like somebody pushed at my left calf. Then I'm rolling. Drop my pistol, too. I end up smack facedown on the hardtop, not feeling anything yet.

Angel

I like to died when the man flopped down, so sudden I thought he'd slipped, until then the bang registered.

I rushed over, but Turkey shouted, "Don't touch him."

Mr. Ackerman said, "You idiot! That man could've told us—"

"Told nothing," Turkey said. "He's crazy."

Then I notice Turkey's down, too. Susan is working on him, rolling up his jeans. It's gone clean through his big muscle there.

Bud went to get a stick. Poked the man from a safe distance.

Managed to pull his shirt aside. We could see the sores all over his chest. Something terrible it looked.

Mr. Ackerman was swearing and calling us idiots until we saw that. Then he shut up.

Turkey

Must admit it felt good. First time in years anybody ever admitted I was right.

Paid back for the pain. Dull, heavy ache it was, spreading. Susan gives me a shot and a pill and has me bandaged up tight. Blood stopped easy, she says. I clot good.

We decided to get out of there, not stopping to look for Johnny's parents.

We got three blocks before the way was blocked.

It was a big metal cylinder, fractured on all sides. Glass glittering around it.

Right in the street. You can see where it hit the roof of a clothing store, Bedsides, caved in the front of it and rolled into the street.

They all get out and have a look, me sitting in the cab. I see the Russian writing again on the end of it.

I don't know much, but I can make out at the top CeKPeT and a lot of words that look like warning, including 6О'ПЕН which is *sick,* and some more I didn't know, and then ПО ОГО'Н, which is *weather.*

"What's it say?" Mr. Ackerman asks.

"That word at the top there's *secret,* and then something about biology and sickness and rain and weather."

"I thought you *knew* this writing," he says.

I shook my head. "I know enough."

"Enough to what?"

"To know this was some kind of targeted capsule. It fell right smack in the middle of Fairhope, biggest town this side of the bay."

"Like the other one?" Johnny says, which surprised me. The boy is smart.

"The one hit the causeway? Right."

"One *what?*" Mr. Ackerman asks.

I don't want to say it with the boy there and all, but it has to come out sometime. "Some disease. Biological warfare."

They stand there in the middle of Prospect Avenue with open, silent nothingness around us, and nobody says anything for the longest time. There won't be any prospects here for a long time. Johnny's parents we aren't going to find, nobody we'll find, because whatever came spurting out of this capsule when it busted open—up high, no doubt, so the wind could take it—had done its work.

Angel sees it right off. "Must've been time for them to get inside," is all she says, but she's thinking the same as me.

It got them into such a state that they went home and holed up to die, like an animal will. Maybe it would be different in the North or the West—people are funny out there, they might just as soon sprawl across the sidewalk—but down here people's first thought is home, the family, the only thing that might pull them through. So they went there and they didn't come out again.

Mr. Ackerman says, "But there's no smell," which was stupid because that made it all real to the boy, and he starts to cry. I pick him up.

Johnny

'Cause that means they're all gone, what I been fearing ever since we crossed the causeway, and nobody's there, it's true, Mom Dad nobody at all anywhere just emptiness all gone.

MC355

The success of the portable unit makes MC355 bold.

It extrudes more sensors and finds not the racing blizzard winds of months before but rather warming breezes, the soft sigh of pines, a low drone of reawakening insects.

There was no nuclear winter.

Instead, a kind of nuclear autumn.

The swirling jet streams have damped, the stinging ultraviolet gone. The storms retreat, the cold surge has passed. But the electromagnetic spectrum lies bare, a muted hiss. The EMP silenced man's signals, yes.

Opticals, fitted with new lenses, scan the night sky. Twinkling dots scoot across the blackness, scurrying on their Newtonian rounds.

The Arcapel Colony.

Russworld.

US1.

All intact. So they at least have survived.

Unless they were riddled by buckshot-slinging anti-satellite devices. But, no—the inflated storage sphere hinged beside the US1 is undeflated, unbreached.

So man still lives in space, at least.

Mr. Ackerman

Crazy, I thought, to go out looking for this DataComm when everybody's *dead*. Just the merest step inside one of the houses proved that.

But they wouldn't listen to me. Those who would respectfully fall silent when I spoke now ride over my words as if I weren't there.

All because of that stupid incident with the sick one. He must have taken longer to die. I couldn't have anticipated that. He just seemed hungry to me.

It's enough to gall a man.

Angel

The boy is calm now, just kind of tucked into himself. He knows what's happened to his mom and dad. Takes his mind off his hurt, anyway. He bows his head down, his long dirty-blond hair hiding his expression. He leans against Turkey and they talk. I can see them through the back cab window.

In amongst all we've seen, I suspect it doesn't come through to him full yet. It will take a while. We'll all take a while.

We head out from Fairhope quick as we can. Not that any-place else is different. The germs must've spread twenty, thirty miles inland from here. Which is why we seen nobody before who'd heard of it. Anybody close enough to know is gone.

Susan's the only one it doesn't seem to bother. She keeps crooning to that box.

Through Silverhill and on to Robertsdale. Same everywhere—no dogs bark, cattle bones drying in the fields.

We don't go into the houses.

Turn south toward Foley. They put this DataComm in the most inconspicuous place, I guess because secrets are hard to keep in cities. Anyway, it's in a pine grove south of Foley, land good for soybeans and potatoes.

Susan

I went up to the little steel door they showed me once and I take a little signet thing and press it into the slot.

Then the codes. They change them every month, but this one's still good, 'cause the door pops open.

Two feet thick it is. And so much under there you could spend a week finding your way.

Bud unloads the T-Isolate, and we push it through the mud and down the ramp.

Bud

Susan's better now, but I watch her careful.

We go down into this pale white light everywhere. All neat and trim.

Pushing that big Isolate thing, it takes a lot out of you. 'Specially when you don't know where to.

But the signs light up when we pass by. Somebody's expecting.

To the hospital is where.

There are places to hook up this Isolate thing, and Susan does it. She is ok when she has something to do.

MC355

The men have returned.

Asked for shelter.

And now, plugged in, MC355 reads the sluggish, silky, grieving mind.

Gene

At last . . . someone has found the tap-in. . . . I can feel the images flit like shiny blue fish through the warm slush I float in . . . Someone . . . asking . . . so I take the hard metallic ball of facts and I break it open so the someone can see . . . So slowly I do it . . . things hard to remember steely-bright . . . I saw it all in one instant . . . I was the only one on duty then with Top Secret, Weapons Grade Clearance, so it all came to me . . . attacks on both U.S. and USSR . . . some third party . . . only plausible scenario . . . a maniac . . . and all the counter-force and MAD and strategies options . . . a big joke . . . irrelevant . . . compared to the risk of accident or third parties . . . that was the first point, and we all realized it when the thing was only an hour old, but then it was too . . .

Turkey

It's creepy in here, everybody gone. I'd hoped some-body's hid out and would be waiting, but when Bud wheels the casket thing through these halls, there's nothing—your own voice coming back thin and empty, reflected from rooms beyond rooms beyond rooms, all waiting under here. Wobbling along on the crutches Johnny fetched me, I get lost in this electronic city clean and hard. We are like some-thing that washed up on the beach here. God, it must've cost more than all Fairhope itself, and who knew it was here? Not me.

Gene

A plot it was, just a goddamn plot with nothing but pure blind rage and greed behind it . . . and the hell of it is, we're never going to know who did it precisely . . . 'cause in the backwash whole governments will fall, people stab each other in the back . . . no way to tell who paid the fishing boat cap-tains offshore to let the cruise missiles aboard . . . bet those captains were surprised when the damn things launched from the deck . . . bet they were told it was some kind of stunt . . . and then the boats all evaporated into steam when the fighters got them no hope of getting a story out of *that* . . . all so comic when you think how easy it was . . . and the same for the Russians, I'm sure . . . dumbfounded confusion . . . and nowhere to turn . . . nobody to hit back at . . . so they hit us . . . been primed for it so long that's the only way they could think . . . and even then there was hope . . . because the defenses worked . . . people got to the shelters . . . the satellite rockets knocked out hordes of Soviet warheads . . . we surely lessened the damage, with the defenses and shelters, too . . . but we hadn't allowed for the essential final fact that all the science and strategy pointed to . . .

Bud

Computer asked us to put up new antennas.

A week's work, easy, I said.

It took two.

It fell to me, most of it. Be weeks before Turkey can walk. But we got it done.

First signal comes in, it's like we're Columbus. Susan finds some wine and we have it all 'round.

We get US1. The first to call them from the whole South.

'Cause there isn't much South left.

Gene

But the history books will have to write themselves on this one . . . I don't know who it was and now don't care . . . because one other point all we strategic planners and analysts missed was that nuclear winter didn't mean the end of anything . . . anything at all . . . just that you'd be careful to not use nukes anymore . . . Used to say that love would find a way . . . but one thing I know . . . war will find a way, too . . . and this time the Soviets loaded lots of their warheads with biowar stuff, canisters fixed to blow high above cities . . . stuff your satellite defenses could at best riddle with shot but not destroy utterly, as they could the high explosive in nuke warheads. . . . All so simple . . . if you know there's a nuke winter limit on the megatonnage you can deliver . . . you use the nukes on C3I targets and silos . . . and then biowar the rest of your way . . . A joke, really . . . I even laughed over it a few times myself . . . we'd placed so much hope in ol' nuke winter holding the line . . . rational as all hell . . . the scenarios all so clean . . . easy to calculate . . . we built our careers on them . . . But this other way . . . so simple and no end to it . . . and all I hope's . . . hope's . . . the bastard started this . . . some Third World general . . . caught some of the damned stuff, too.

Bud

The germs got us. Cut big stretches through the U.S. We were just lucky. The germs played out in a couple of months, while we were holed up. Soviets said they'd used the bio stuff in amongst the nukes to show us what they could do, long term. Unless the war stopped right there. Which it did.

But enough nukes blew off here and in Russia to freeze up everybody for July and August, set off those storms.

Germs did the most damage, though—plagues.

It was a plague canister that hit the Slocum building. That did in Mobile.

The war was all over in a couple of hours. The satellite people, they saw it all.

Now they're settling the peace.

Mr. Ackerman

"We been sitting waiting on this corpse long enough," I said, and got up.

We got food from the commissary here. Fine. I don't say I'm anything but grateful for that. And we rested in the bunks, got recuperated. But enough's enough. The computer tells us it wants to talk to the man Gene some more. Fine, I say.

Turkey stood up. "Not easy, the computer says, this talking to a man's near dead. Slow work."

Looking around, I tried to take control, assume leadership again. Jutted out my chin. "Time to get back."

But their eyes are funny. Somehow I'd lost my real power over them. It's not anymore like I'm the one who led them when the bombs started.

Which means, I suppose, that this thing isn't going to be a new beginning for me. It's going to be the same life. People aren't going to pay me any more real respect than they ever did.

MC355

So the simulations had proved right. But as ever, incomplete.

MC355 peered at the shambling, adamant band assembled in the hospital bay, and pondered how many of them might be elsewhere.

Perhaps many. Perhaps few.

It all depended on data MC355 did not have, could not easily find. The satellite worlds swinging above could get no accurate count in the U.S. or the USSR.

Still—looking at them, MC355 could not doubt that there were many. They were simply too brimming with life, too hard to kill. All the calculations in the world could not stop these creatures.

The humans shuffled out, leaving the T-Isolate with the woman who had never left its side. They were going.

MC355 called after them. They nodded, understanding, but did not stop.

MC355 let them go.

There was much to do.

New antennas, new sensors, new worlds.

Turkey

Belly full and eye quick, we came out into the pines. Wind blowed through with a scent of the Gulf on it, fresh and salty with rich moistness.

The dark clouds are gone. I think maybe I'll get Bud to drive south some more. I'd like to go swimming one more time in those breakers that come booming in, taller than I am, down near Fort Morgan. Man never knows when he'll get to do it again.

Bud's ready to travel. He's taking a radio so's we can talk to MC, find out about the help that's coming. For now, we got to get back and look after our own.

Same as we'll see to the boy. He's ours, now.

Susan says she'll stay with Gene till he's ready, till some surgeons turn up can work on him. That'll be a long time, say I. But she can stay if she wants. Plenty food and such down there for her.

A lot of trouble we got, coming a mere hundred mile. Not much to show for it when we get back. A bumper crop of bad news, some would say. Not me. It's better to know than to not, better to go on than to look back.

So we go out into dawn, and there are the same colored dots riding in the high, hard blue. Like camp fires.

The crickets are chirruping, and in the scrub there's a rustle of things moving about their own business, a clean

67

scent of things starting up. The rest of us, we mount the truck and it surges forward with a muddy growl, Ackerman slumped over, Angel in the cab beside Bud, the boy already asleep on some blankets; and the forlorn sound of us moving among the windswept trees is a long and echoing note of mutual and shared desolation, powerful and pitched forward into whatever must come now, a muted note persisting and undeniable in the soft, sweet air.

Epilogue

(twenty-three years later)

Johnny

An older woman in a formless, wrinkled dress and worn shoes sat at the side of the road. I was panting from the fast pace I was keeping along the white strip of sandy, rutted road. She sat, silent and unmoving. I nearly walked by before I saw her.

"You're resting?" I asked.

"Waiting." Her voice had a feel of rustling leaves. She sat on the brown cardboard suitcase with big copper latches—the kind made right after the war. It was cracked along the side, and white cotton underwear stuck out.

"For the bus?"

"For Buck."

"The chopper recording, it said the bus will stop up around the bend."

"I heard."

"It won't come down this side road. There's not time."

I was late myself, and I figured she had picked the wrong spot to wait.

"Buck will be along."

Her voice was high and had the backcountry twang to it. My own voice still had some of the same sound, but I was keeping my vowels flat and right now, and her accent reminded me of how far I had come.

I squinted, looking down the long sandy curve of the road. A pickup truck growled out of a clay side road and onto the hardtop. People rode in the back along with trunks and a 3D. Taking everything they could. Big white eyes shot a glance at me, and then the driver hit the hydrogen and got out of there.

The Confederation wasn't giving us much time. Since the unification of the Soviet, U.S.A. and European/Sino space colonies into one political union, everybody'd come to think of them as the Confeds, period—one entity. I knew better—there were tensions and differences abounding up there—but the shorthand was convenient.

"Who's Buck?"

"My dog." She looked at me directly, as though any fool would know who Buck was.

"Look, the bus—"

"You're one of those Bishop boys, aren't you?"

I looked off up the road again. That set of words—being eternally a *Bishop boy*—was like a grain of sand caught between my back teeth. My mother's friends had used that phrase when they came over for an evening of bridge, before I went away to the university. Not my real mother, of course—she and Dad had died in the war, and I dimly remembered them.

Or anyone else from then. Almost everybody around here had been struck down by the Soviet bioweapons. It was the awful swath of those that cut through whole states, mostly across the South—the horror of it—that had formed the basis of the peace that followed. Nuclear and bioarsenals were reduced to nearly zero now. Defenses in space were thick and reliable. The building of those had fueled the huge boom in Confed cities, made orbital commerce important, provided jobs and horizons for a whole generation—including me. I was a ground-orbit liaison, spending four months every year at US3. But to the people down here, I was eternally that oldest Bishop boy.

Bishops. I was the only one left who'd actually lived here before the war. I'd been away on a visit when it came. Afterward, my Aunt and Uncle Bishop from Birmingham came down to take over the old family property—to save it from being homesteaded on, under the new Federal Reconstruction Acts. They'd taken me in, and I'd thought of them as Mom and Dad. We'd all had the Bishop name, after all. So I was a Bishop, one of the few natives who'd made it through the bombing and nuclear autumn and all. People'd point me out as almost a freak, *a real native,* wow.

"Yes, ma'am," I said neutrally.

"Thought so."

"You're . . ."

"Susan McKenzie."

"Ah."

We had done the ritual, so now we could talk. Yet some memory stirred . . .

"Something 'bout you . . ." She squinted in the glaring sunlight. She probably wasn't all that old, in her late fifties, maybe. Anybody who'd caught some radiation looked aged a bit beyond their years. Or maybe it was just the unending weight of hardship and loss they'd carried.

"Seems like I knew you before the war," she said. "I strictly believe I saw you."

"I was up north then, a hundred miles from here. Didn't come back until months later."

"So'd I."

"Some relatives brought me down, and we found out what'd happened to Fairhope."

She squinted at me again, and then a startled look spread across her leathery face. "My Lord! Were they lookin' for that big computer center, the DataComm it was?"

I frowned. "Well, maybe . . . I don't remember too well . . ."

"Johnny. You're Johnny!"

"Yes, ma'am, John Bishop." I didn't like the little-boy ending on my name, but people around here couldn't forget it.

"I'm Susan! The one went with you! I had the codes for DataComm. Remember?"

"Why . . . yes . . ." Slow clearing of ancient, foggy images. "You were hiding in that center . . . where we found you."

"Yes! I had Gene in the T-Isolate."

"Gene . . ." That awful time had been stamped so strongly in me that I'd blocked off many memories, muting the horror. Now it came flooding back.

"I saved him, all right! Yessir. We got married. I had my children."

Tentatively, she reached out a weathered hand, and I touched it. A lump suddenly blocked my throat, and my vision blurred. Somehow, all those years had passed and I'd never thought to look up any of those people—Turkey, Angel, Bud, Mr. Ackerman. Just too painful, I guess. And a little boy making his way in a tough world, without his parents, doesn't look back a whole lot.

We grasped hands. "I think I might've seen you once, actu'ly. At a fish fry down at Point Clear. You and some boys was playing with the nets—it was just after the fishing came back real good, those Roussin germs'd wore off. Gene went down to shoo you away from the boats. I was cleaning flounder, and I thought then, maybe you were the one. But somehow when I saw your face at a distance, I couldn't go up to you and say anything. You was skipping around, so happy, laughing and all. I couldn't bring those bad times back."

"I . . . I understand."

"Gene died two year ago," she said simply.

"I'm sorry."

"We had our time together," she said, forcing a smile.

"Remember how we—" And then I recalled where I was, what was coming. "Mrs. McKenzie, there's not long before the last bus."

"I'm waiting for Buck."

"Where is he?"

"He run off in the woods, chasing something."

I worked my backpack straps around my shoulders. They creaked in the quiet.

There wasn't much time left. Pretty soon now it would start. I knew the sequence, because I did maintenance engineering and retrofit on US3's modular mirrors.

One of the big reflectors would focus sunlight on a rechargeable tube of gas. That would excite the molecules. A small triggering beam would start the lasing going, the excited molecules cascading down together from one preferentially occupied quantum state to a lower state. A traveling wave swept down the tube, jarring loose more photons. They all added together in phase, so when the light waves hit the far end of the hundred-meter tube, it was a sword, a gouging lance that could cut through air and clouds. And this time, it wouldn't strike an array of layered solid-state collectors outside New Orleans, providing clean electricity. It would carve a swath twenty meters wide through the trees and fields of southern Alabama. A little demonstration, the Confeds said.

"The bus—look, I'll carry that suitcase for you."

"I can manage." She peered off into the distance, and I saw she was tired, tired beyond knowing it. "I'll wait for Buck."

"Leave him, Mrs. McKenzie."

"I don't need that blessed bus."

"Why not?"

"My children drove off to Mobile with their families. They're coming back to get me."

"My radio"—I gestured at my radio—"says the roads to Mobile are jammed up. You can't count on them."

"They *said* so."

"The Confed deadline—"

"I tole 'em I'd try to walk to the main road. Got tired, is all. They'll know I'm back in here."

"Just the same—"

"I'm all right, don't you mind. They're good children, grateful for all I've gone and done for them. They'll be back."

"Come with me to the bus. It's not far."

"Not without Buck. He's all the company I got these days." She smiled, blinking.

I wiped sweat from my brow and studied the pines. There were a lot of places for a dog to be. The land here was flat and barely above sea level. I had come to camp and rest, rowing skiffs up the Fish River, looking for places I'd been when I was a teenager and my mom had rented boats from a rambling old fisherman's house. I had turned off my radio, to get away from things. The big, mysterious island I remembered and called Treasure Island, smack in the middle of the river, was now a soggy stand of trees in a bog. The big storm a year back had swept it away.

I'd been sleeping in the open on the shore near there when the chopper woke me up, blaring. The Confeds had given twelve hours' warning, the recording said.

They'd picked this sparsely populated area for their little demonstration. People had been moving back in ever since the biothreat was cleaned out, but there still weren't many. I'd liked that when I was growing up. Open woods. That's why I came back every chance I got.

I should've guessed something was coming. The Confeds were about evenly matched with the whole rest of the planet now, at least in high-tech weaponry. Defense held all the cards. The big mirrors were modular and could fold up fast, making a small target. They could incinerate anything launched against them, too.

But the U.N. kept talking like the Confeds were just another nation-state or something. Nobody down here understood that the people up there thought of Earth itself as the real problem—eaten up with age-old rivalries and hate, still holding onto dirty weapons that murdered whole populations, carrying around in their heads all the rotten baggage of the past. To listen to them, you'd think they'd learned nothing from the war. Already they were forgetting that it was the orbital defenses that had saved the biosphere itself, and the satellite communities that knit together the mammoth rescue efforts of the decade after. Without the antivirals developed and grown in huge zero-g vats, lots of us would've caught one of the poxes drifting through the population. People just forget. Nations, too.

"Where's Buck?" I said decisively.

"He . . . that way." A wave of the hand.

I wrestled my backpack down, feeling the stab from my shoulder—and suddenly remembered the thunk of that steel knocking me down, back then. So long ago. And me, still carrying an ache from it that woke whenever a cold snap came on. The past was still alive.

I trotted into the short pines, over creeper grass. Flies jumped where my boots struck. The white sand made a *skree* sound as my boots skated over it. I remembered how I'd first heard that sound, wearing slick-soled tennis shoes, and how pleased I'd been at university when I learned how the acoustics of it worked.

"Buck!"

A flash of brown over to the left. I ran through a thick stand of pine, and the dog yelped and took off, dodging under a blackleaf bush. I called again. Buck didn't even slow down. I skirted left. He went into some oak scrub, barking, having a great time of it, and I could hear him getting tangled in it and then shaking free and out of the other side. Long gone.

When I got back to Mrs. McKenzie, she didn't seem to notice me. "I can't catch him."

"Knew you wouldn't." She grinned at me, showing brown teeth. "Buck's a fast one."

"Call him."

She did. Nothing. "Must of run off."

"There isn't time—"

"I'm not leaving without ole Buck. Times I was alone down on the river after Gene died, and the water would come up under the house. Buck was the only company I had. Only soul I saw for five weeks in that big blow we had."

A low whine from afar. "I think that's the bus," I said.

She cocked her head. "Might be."

"Come on. I'll carry your suitcase."

She crossed her arms. "My children will be by for me. I tole them to look for me along in here."

"They might not make it."

"They're loyal children."

75

"Mrs. McKenzie, I can't wait for you to be reasonable." I picked up my backpack and brushed some red ants off the straps.

"You Bishops was always reasonable," she said levelly. "You work up there, don't you?"

"Ah, sometimes."

"You goin' back, after they do what they're doin' here?"

"I might." Even if I owed her something for what she did long ago, damned if I was going to be cowed.

"They're attacking the United *States*."

"And spots in Bavaria, the Urals, South Africa, Brazil—"

" 'Cause we don't trust 'em! They think they can push the United States aroun' just as they please—" And she went on with all the clichés heard daily from earthbound media. How the Confeds wanted to run the world and they were dupes of the Russians, and how surrendering national sovereignty to a bunch of self-appointed overlords was an affront to our dignity, and so on.

True, some of it—the Confeds weren't saints. But they were the only power that thought in truly global terms, couldn't *not* think that way. They could stop ICBMs and punch through the atmosphere to attack any offensive capability on the ground—that's what this demonstration was to show. I'd heard Confeds argue that this was the only way to break the diplomatic logjam—do something. I had my doubts. But times were changing, that was sure, and my generation didn't think the way the prewar people did.

"—we'll never be ruled by some outside—"

"Mrs. McKenzie, there's the bus! Listen!"

The turbo whirred far around the bend, slowing for the stop.

Her face softened as she gazed at me, as if recalling memories. "That's all right, boy. You go along, now."

I saw that she wouldn't be coaxed or even forced down that last bend. She had gone as far as she was going to, and the world would have to come the rest of the distance itself.

Up ahead, the bus driver was probably behind schedule for this last pickup. He was going to be irritated and more than a little scared. The Confeds would be right on time, he knew that.

I ran. My feet plowed through the deep, soft sand. Right away I could tell I was more tired than I'd thought and the heat had taken some strength out of me. I went about two hundred meters along the gradual bend, was nearly within view of the bus, when I heard it start up with a rumble. I tasted salty sweat, and it felt like the whole damned planet was dragging at my feet, holding me down. The driver raced the engine, in a hurry.

He had to come toward me as he swung out onto Route 80 on the way back to Mobile. Maybe I could reach the intersection in time for him to see me. So I put my head down and plunged forward.

But there was the woman back there. To get to her, the driver would have to take the bus down that rutted, sandy road and risk getting stuck. With people on the bus yelling at him. All that to get the old woman with the grateful children. She didn't seem to understand that there were ungrateful children in the skies now—she didn't seem to understand much of what was going on—and suddenly I wasn't sure I did, either.

But I kept on.

Of Space/Time and the River

December 5

Monday.

We took a limo to Los Angeles for the 9 a.m. flight, LAX to Cairo.

On the boost up we went over 1.4 G, contra-reg, and a lot of passengers complained, especially the poor thins in their clank-shank rigs, the ones that keep you walking even after the hip replacements fail.

Joanna slept through it all, seasoned traveler, and I occupied myself with musing about finally seeing the ancient Egypt I'd dreamed about as a kid, back at the turn of the century.

> *If thou be'st born to strange sights,*
> *Things invisible go see,*
> *Ride ten thousand days and nights*
> *Till Age snow white hairs on thee.*

I've got the snow powdering at the temples and steadily expanding waistline, so I suppose John Donne applies. Good to see I can still summon up lines I first read as a teenager. There are some rewards to being a Prof. of Comp. Lit. at UC Irvine, even if you do have to scrimp to afford a trip like this.

The tour agency said the Quarthex hadn't interfered with

tourism at all—in fact, you hardly noticed them, they deliberately blended in so well. How a seven-foot insectoid thing with gleaming russet skin can look like an Egyptian I don't know, but what the hell, Joanna said, let's go anyway.

I hope she's right. I mean, it's been fourteen years since the Quarthex landed, opened the first diplomatic interstellar relations, and then chose Egypt as the only place on Earth where they cared to carry out what they called their "cultural studies." I guess we'll get a look at that, too. The Quarthex keep to themselves, veiling their multi-layered deals behind diplomatic dodges.

As if six hours of travel weren't numbing enough, including the orbital delay because of an unannounced Chinese launch, we both watched a holoD about one of those new biotech guys, called *Straight From the Hearts*. An unending string of single entendres. In our stupefied state it was just about right.

As we descended over Cairo it was clear and about 15°. We stumbled off the plane, sandy-eyed from riding ten thousand days and nights in a whistling aluminum box.

The airport was scruffy, instant third world hubbub, confusion, and filth. One departure lounge was filled exclusively with turbaned men. Heavy security everywhere. No Quarthex around. Maybe they do blend in.

Our bus across Cairo passed a decayed aqueduct, about which milled men in caftans, women in black, animals eating garbage. People, packed into the most unlikely living spots, carrying out peddler's business in dusty spots between buildings, traffic alternately frenetic or frozen.

We crawled across Cairo to Giza, the pyramids abruptly looming out of the twilight. The hotel, Mena House, was the hunting lodge-cum-palace of 19th century kings. Elegant.

Buffet supper was good. Sleep came like a weight.

December 6

Joanna says this journal is good therapy for me, might even get me back into the habit of writing again. She says every Comp. Lit. type is a frustrated author and I should just spew my bile into this diary. So be it:

Thou, when thou return'st, wilt tell me
All strange wonders that befell thee.

World, you have been warned.

Set off south today—to Memphis, the ancient capital lost when its walls were breached in a war and subsequent floods claimed it.

The famous fallen Rameses statue. It looks powerful still, even lying down. Makes you feel like a pygmy tip-toeing around a giant, à la Gulliver.

Saqqara, principal necropolis of Memphis, survives 3 km away in the desert. First Dynasty tombs, including the first pyramid, made of steps, 5 levels high. New Kingdom graffiti inside are now history themselves, from our perspective.

On to the Great Pyramid!—by camel! The drivers proved to be even more harassing than legend warned. We entered the pyramid Khefren, slightly shorter than that of his father, Cheops. All the 80 known pyramids were found stripped. These passages have a constricted vacancy to them, empty now for longer than they were filled. Their silent mass is unnerving.

Professor Alvarez from UC Berkeley tried to find hidden rooms here by placing cosmic ray detectors in the lower known rooms, and looking for slight increases in flux at certain angles, but there seem to be none. There are seismic and even radio measurements of the dry sands in the Giza region, looking for echoes of buried tombs, but no big finds so far.

Plenty of echoes from ruins of ordinary houses, etc., though.

No serious jet lag today, but we nod off when we can. Handy, having the hotel a few hundred yards from the pyramids.

I tried to get Joanna to leave her wrist comm at home. Since her breakdown she can't take news of daily disasters very well. (Who can, really?) She's pretty steady now, but this trip should be as calm as possible, her doctor told me.

So of course she turns on the comm and it's full of hysterical stuff about another border clash between the Empire of Israel and the Arab Muhammad Soviet. Smart rockets vs. smart defenses. A draw. Some things never change.

I turned it off immediately. Her hands shook for hours afterward. I brushed it off.

Still, it's different when you're a few hundred miles from the lines. Hope we're safe here.

December 7

Into Cairo itself, the Egyptian museum. The Tutankhamen exhibit—huge treasuries, opulent jewels, a sheer wondrous plenitude. There are endless cases of beautiful alabaster bowls, gold-laminate boxes, testifying to thousands of years of productivity.

I wandered down a musty marble corridor and then, coming out of a gloomy side passage, there was the first Quarthex I'd ever seen. Big, clacking and clicking as it thrust forward in that six-legged gait. It ignored me, of course—they nearly always lurch by humans as though they can't see us. Or else that distant, distracted gaze means they're ruminating over strange, alien ideas. Who knows why they're intensely studying ancient Egyptian ways, and ignoring the rest of us?

This one was cradling a stone urn, a meter high at least. It carried the black granite in three akimbo arms, hardly seeming to notice the weight. I caught a whiff of acrid pungency, the fluid that lubricates their joints. Then it was gone.

We left and visited the oldest Coptic church in Egypt, supposedly where Moses hid out when he was on the lam. Looks it. The old section of Cairo is crowded, decayed, people laboring in every nook with minimal tools, much standing around watching as others work. The only sign of really efficient labor was a gang of men and women hauling long, cigar-shaped yellow things on wagons. Something the Quarthex wanted places outside the city, our guide said.

In the evening we went to the Sound & Light show at the Sphinx—excellent. There is even a version in the Quarthex language, those funny sputtering, barking sounds.

Arabs say, "Man fears time; time fears the pyramids." You get that feeling here.

Afterward, we ate in the hotel's Indian restaurant; quite fine.

December 8

Cairo is a city being trampled to death.

It's grown by a factor of 14 in population since the revolution in 1952, and shows it. The old Victorian homes which once lined stately streets of willowy trees are now crowded by modern slab concrete apartment houses. The aged buildings are kept going, not from a sense of history, but because no matter how rundown they get, somebody needs them.

The desert's grit invades everywhere. Plants in the courtyards have a weary, resigned look. Civilization hasn't been very good for the old ways.

Maybe that's why the Quarthex seem to dislike anything built since the time of the Romans. I saw one running some kind of machine, a black contraption that floated two meters off the ground. It was laying some kind of cable in the ground, right along the bank of the Nile. Every time it met a building it just slammed through, smashing everything to frags. Guess the Quarthex have squared all this with the Egyptian gov't, because there were police all around, making sure nobody got in the way. Odd.

But not unpredictable, when you think about it. The Quarthex have those levitation devices which everybody would love to get the secret of. (Ending sentence with preposition! Horrors! But this is vacation, dammit.) They've been playing coy for years, letting out a trickle of technology, with the Egyptians holding the patents. That must be what's holding the Egyptian economy together, in the face of their unrelenting population crunch. The Quarthex started out as guests here, studying the ruins and so on, but now it's obvious that they have free run of the place. They *own* it.

Still, the Quarthex haven't given away the crucial devices which would enable us to find out how they do it—or so my colleagues in the physics department tell me. It vexes them that this alien race can master space/time so completely, manipulating gravity itself, and we can't get the knack of it.

We visited the famous alabaster mosque. It perches on a hill called The Citadel. Elegant, cool, aloofly dominating the city. The Old Bazaar nearby is a warren, so much like the movie sets one's seen that it has an unreal, Arabian Nights quality. We bought spices. The calls to worship from the mosques reach you everywhere, even in the most secluded back rooms where Joanna was haggling over jewelry.

It's impossible to get anything really ancient, the swarthy little merchants said. The Quarthex have bought them up, trading gold for anything that might be from the time of the Pharaohs. There have been a lot of fakes over the last few centuries, some really good ones, so the Quarthex have just bought anything that might be real. No wonder the Egyptians like them, let them chew up their houses if they want. Gold speaks louder than the past.

We boarded our cruise ship, the venerable *Nile Concorde*. Lunch was excellent, Italian. We explored Cairo in mid-afternoon, through markets of incredible dirt and disarray. Calf brains displayed without a hint of refrigeration or protection, flies swarming, etc. Fun, especially if you can keep from breathing for five minutes or more.

We stopped in the Shepherd's Hotel, the site of many Brit spy novels (Maugham especially). It has an excellent bar—Nubians, Saudis, etc., putting away decidedly non-Islamic gins and beers. A Quarthex was sitting in a special chair at the back, talking through a voicebox to a Saudi. I couldn't tell what they were saying, but the Saudi had a gleam in his eye. Driving a bargain, I'd say.

Great atmosphere in the bar, though. A cloth banner over the bar proclaims,

> *Unborn tomorrow and dead yesterday,*
> *why fret about them if today be sweet.*

Indeed, yes, ummm—bartender!

December 9

Friday, Moslem holy day.

We left Cairo at 11 p.m. last night, the city gliding past our stateroom windows, lovelier in misty radiance than in dusty day. We cruised all day. Buffet breakfast & lunch, solid eastern and Mediterranean stuff, passable red wine.

A hundred meters away, the past presses at us, going about its business as if the pharaohs were still calling the tune. Primitive pumping irrigation, donkeys doing the work, women cleaning gray clothes in the Nile. Desert ramparts to the east, at spots sending sand fingers—no longer swept away by the annual flood—across the fields to the shore itself. Moslem tombs of stone and mud brick coast by as we lounge on the top deck, peering at the madly waving children through our binoculars, across a chasm of time.

There are about fifty aboard a ship with capacity of 100, so there is plenty of room and service as we sweep serenely on, music flooding the deck, cutting between slabs of antiquity; not quite decadent, just intelligently sybaritic. (Why so few tourists? Guide guessed people are afraid of the Quarthex. Joanna gets jittery around them, but I don't know if it's only her old fears surfacing again.)

The spindly, ethereal minarets are often the only grace note in the mud brick villages, like a lovely idea trying to rise out of brown, mottled chaos. Animal power is used wherever possible. Still, the villages are quiet at night.

The flip side of this peacefulness must be boredom. That explains a lot of history and its rabid faiths, unfortunately.

December 10

Civilization thins steadily as we steam upriver. The mud brick villages typically have no electricity; there is ample power from Aswan, but the power lines and stations are too expensive. One would think that, with the Quarthex gold, they could do better now.

Our guide says the Quarthex have been very hard-nosed—no pun intended—about such improvements. They will not let the earnings from their patents be used to modernize Egypt. Feeding the poor, cleaning the Nile, rebuilding monuments—all fine (in fact, they pay handsomely for restoring projects). But better electricity—no. A flat no.

We landed at a scruffy town and took a bus into the western desert. Only a kilometer from the flat floodplain, the Sahara is utterly barren and forbidding. We visited a Ptolemaic city of the dead. One tomb has a mummy of a girl who drowned trying to cross the Nile and see her lover, the hieroglyphs say. Nearby are catacombs of mummified baboons and ibises, symbols of wisdom.

A tunnel begins here, pointing SE toward Akhenaton's capital city. The German discoverers in the last century followed it for 40 kilometers—all cut through limestone, a gigantic task—before turning back because of bad air.

What was it for? Nobody knows. Dry, spooky atmosphere. Urns of desiccated mummies, undisturbed. To duck down a side corridor is to step into mystery.

I left the tour group and ambled over a low hill—to take a pee, actually. To the west was sand, sand, sand. I was standing there, doing my bit to hold off the dryness, when I saw one of those big black contraptions come slipping over the far horizon. Chuffing, chugging, and laying what looked like pipe—a funny kind of pipe, all silvery, with blue facets running through it. The glittering shifted, changing to yellows and reds while I watched.

A Quarthex riding atop it, of course. It ran due south, roughly parallel to the Nile. When I got back and told Joanna about it she looked at the map and we couldn't figure what would be out there of interest to anybody, even a Quarthex. No ruins around, nothing. Funny.

December 11

Beni Hassan, a nearly deserted site near the Nile. A steep walk up the escarpment of the eastern desert, after crossing the rich flood by donkey. The rock tombs have fine drawings and some statues—still left because they were cut directly from the mountain, and have thick wedges securing them to it. Guess the ancients would steal anything not nailed down. One thing about the Quarthex, the guide says—they take nothing. They seem genuinely interested in restoring, not in carting artifacts back home to their neck of the galactic spiral arm.

Upriver, we landfall beside a vast dust plain, which we crossed in a cart pulled by a tractor. The mud brick palaces of Akhenaton have vanished, except for a bit of Nefertiti's palace, where the famous bust of her was found. The royal tombs in the mountain above are defaced—big chunks pulled out of the walls by the priests who undercut his monotheist revolution, after his death.

The wall carvings are very realistic and warm; the women even have nipples. The tunnel from yesterday probably runs under here, perhaps connecting with the passageways we see deep in the king's grave shafts. Again, nobody's explored them thoroughly. There are narrow sections, possibly warrens for snakes or scorpions, maybe even traps.

While Joanna and I are ambling around, taking a few snaps of the carvings, I hear a rustle. Joanna has the flashlight and we peer over a ledge, down a straight shaft. At the bottom something is moving, something big.

It takes a minute to see that the reddish shell isn't a sarcophagus at all, but the back of a Quarthex. It's planting suckerlike things to the walls, threading cables through them. I can see more of the stuff farther back in the shadows.

The Quarthex looks up, into our flashlight beam, and scuttles away. Exploring the tunnels? But why did it move away so fast? What's to hide?

December 12

Cruise all day and watch the shore slide by.

Joanna is right; I needed this vacation a great deal. I can see that, rereading this journal—it gets looser as I go along.

As do I. When I consider how my life is spent, ere half my days, in this dark world and wide . . .

The pell-mell of university life dulls my sense of wonder, of simple pleasures simply taken. The Nile has a flowing, infinite quality, free of time. I can *feel* what it was like to live here, part of a great celestial clock that brought the perpetually turning sun and moon, the perennial rhythm of the flood. Aswan has interrupted the ebb and flow of the waters, but the steady force of the Nile rolls on.

> *Heaven smiles,*
> *and faiths and empires gleam,*
> *Like wrecks of a dissolving dream.*

The peacefulness permeates everything. Last night, making love to Joanna, was the best ever. Magnifique!

(And I know you're reading this, Joanna—I saw you sneak it out of the suitcase yesterday! Well, it *was* the best—quite a tribute, after all these years. And there's tomorrow and tomorrow . . .)

> *He who bends to himself a joy.*
> *Does the winged life destroy;*

> *But he who kisses the joy as it flies*
> *Lives in eternity's sunrise.*

Perhaps next term I shall request the Romantic Poets course. Or even write some of my own . . .

Three Quarthex flew overhead today, carrying what look like ancient rams-head statues. The guide says statues were moved around a lot by the Arabs, and of course the archaeologists. The Quarthex have negotiated permission to take many of them back to their rightful places, if known.

December 13

Landfall at Abydos—a limestone temple miraculously preserved, its thick roof intact. Clusters of scruffy mud huts surround it, but do not diminish its obdurate rectangular severity.

The famous list of pharaohs, chiseled in a side corridor, is impressive in its sweep of time. Each little entry was a lordly pharaoh, and there is a whole wall jammed full of them. Egypt lasted longer than any comparable society, and the mass of names on that wall is even more impressive, since the temple builders did not even give it the importance of a central location.

The list omits Hatchepsut, a mere woman, and Akhenaton the scandalous monotheist. Rameses II had all carvings here cut deeply, particularly on the immense columns, to forestall defacement—a possibility he was much aware of, since he was busily doing it to his ancestor's temples. He chiseled away earlier work, adding his own cartouches, apparently thinking he could fool the gods themselves into believing he had built them all himself. Ah, immortality.

Had an earthquake today. Shades of California!

We were on the ship, Joanna dutifully padding back and forth on the main deck to work off the opulent lunch. We saw the palms waving ashore, and damned if there wasn't a small shock wave in the water, going east to west, and then a kind of low grumbling from the east. Guide says he's never seen anything like it.

And tonight, sheets of ruby light rising from both east and west. Looked like an aurora, only the wrong directions. The rippling aura changed colors as it rose, then met overhead, burst into gold, and died. I'd swear I heard a high, keening note sound as the burnt-gold line flared and faded, and flared and faded, spanning the sky.

Not many people on deck, though, so it didn't cause much comment. Joanna's theory is, it was a rocket exhaust.

An engineer says it looks like something to do with magnetic fields. I'm no scientist, but it seems to me whatever the Quarthex want to do, they can. Lords of space/time they called themselves in the diplomatic ceremonies. The United Nations representatives wrote that off as hyperbole, but the Quarthex may mean it.

December 14

Dendera. A vast temple, much less well known than Karnak, but quite as impressive. Quarthex there, digging at the foundations. Guide says they're looking for some secret passageways, maybe. The Egyptian gov't is letting them do what they damn well please.

On the way back to the ship we pass a whole mass of people, hundreds, all dressed in costumes. I thought it was some sort of pageant or tourist foolery, but the guide frowned, saying he didn't know what to make of it.

The mob was chanting something even the guide couldn't make out. He said the rough-cut cloth was typical of the old ways, made on crude spinning wheels. The procession was ragged, but seemed headed for the temple. They looked drunk to me.

The guide tells me that the ancients had a theology based on the Nile. This country is essentially ten kilometers wide and seven hundred kilometers long, a narrow band of livable earth pressed between two deadly deserts. So they believed the gods must have intended it, and that the Nile was the center of the whole damned world.

The sun came from the east, meaning that's where things began. Ending—dying—happened in the west, where the sun went. Thus they buried their dead on the west side of the Nile, even 7,000 years ago. At night, the sun swung below and lit the underworld, where everybody went finally. Kind of comforting, thinking of the sun doing duty like that for the dead. Only the virtuous dead, though. If you didn't follow the rules . . .

> *Some are born to sweet delight,*
> *Some are born to endless night.*

Their world was neatly bisected by the great river, and they loved clean divisions. They invented the 24-hour day but, loving symmetry, split it in half. Each of the 12 daylight hours was longer in summer than in winter—and, for night, vice versa. They built an entire nation-state, an immortal hand or eye, framing such fearful symmetry.

On to Karnak itself, mooring at Luxor. The middle and late pharaohs couldn't afford the labor investment for pyramids, so they contented themselves with additions to the huge sprawl at Karnak.

I wonder how long it will be before someone rich notices that for a few million or so he could build a tomb bigger than the Great Pyramid. It would only take a million or so lime-stone blocks—or, much better, granite—and could be better isolated and protected. If you can't conquer a continent or scribble a symphony, pile up a great stack of stones.

> *L' eternité,*
> *ne fut jamais perdue.*

The light show this night at Karnak was spooky at times, and beautiful, with booming voices coming right out of the stones. Saw a Quarthex in the crowd. It stared straight ahead, not noticing anybody but not bumping into any humans, either.

It looked enthralled. The beady eyes, all four, scanned the shifting blues and burnt-oranges that played along the rising columns, the tumbled great statues. Its lubricating fluids made shiny reflections as it articulated forward, clacking in the dry night air. Somehow it was almost reverential. Rearing above the crowd, unmoving for long moments, it seemed more like the giant frozen figures in stone than like the mere mortals who swarmed around it, keeping a respectful distance, muttering to themselves.

> *Unnerving, somehow, to see*
> *. . . a subtler Sphinx renew*
> *Riddles of death Thebes never knew.*

December 15

A big day. The Valleys of the Queens, the Nobles, and finally of the Kings. Whew! All are dry washes (wadis), obviously easy to guard and isolate. Nonetheless, all of the 62 known tombs except Tut's were rifled, probably within a few centuries of burial. It must've been an inside job.

There is speculation that the robbing became a needed part of the economy, recycling the wealth, and providing gaudy displays for the next pharaoh to show off at *his* funeral, all the better to keep impressing the peasants. Just another part of the socio-economic machine, folks.

Later priests collected the pharaoh mummies and hid them in a cave nearby, realizing they couldn't protect the tombs. Preservation of Tuthmosis III is excellent. His hooknosed mummy has been returned to its tomb—a big, deep thing, larger than our apartment, several floors in all, connected by ramps, with side treasuries, galleries, etc. The inscription above reads,

You shall live again forever.

All picked clean, of course, except for the sarcophagus, too heavy to carry away. The pyramids had portcullises, deadfalls, pitfalls, and rolling stones to crush the unwary robber, but there are few here. Still, it's a little creepy to think of all those ancient engineers, planning to commit murder in the future, long after they themselves are gone, all to protect the past. Death, be not proud.

An afternoon of shopping in the bazaar. The old Victorian hotel on the river is atmospheric, but has few guests. Food continues good. No dysentery, either. We both took the EZ-

DI bacteria before we left, so it's living down in our tracts, festering away, lying in wait for an ugly foreign bug. Comforting.

December 16

Cruise on. We stop at Kom Ombo, a temple to the crocodile god, Sebek, built to placate the crocs who swarmed in the river nearby. (The Nile is cleared of them now, unfortunately; they would've added some zest to the cruise . . .) A small room contains 98 mummified crocs, stacked like cordwood.

Cruised some more. A few km south, there were gangs of Egyptians working beside the river. Hauling blocks of granite down to the water, rolling them on logs. I stood on the deck, trying to figure out why they were using ropes and simple pulleys, and no powered machinery.

Then I saw a Quarthex near the top of the rise, where the blocks were being sawed out of the rock face. It reared up over the men, gesturing with those jerky arms, eyes glittering. It called out something in a halfway human voice, only in a language I didn't know. The guide came over, frowning, but he couldn't understand it, either.

The laborers were pulling ropes across ruts in the stone, feeding sand and water into the gap, cutting out blocks by sheer brute abrasion. It must take weeks to extract one at that rate! Farther along, others drove wooden planks down into the deep grooves, hammering them with crude wooden mallets. Then they poured water over the planks, and we could hear the stone pop open as the wood expanded, far down in the cut.

That's the way the ancients did it, the guide said kind of

quietly. The Quarthex towered above the human teams, that jangling, harsh voice booming out over the water, each syllable lingering until the next joined it, blending in the dry air, hollow and ringing and remorseless.

Note Added Later

Stopped at Edfu, a well-preserved temple buried 100 feet deep by Moslem garbage until the late 19th century. The best aspect of river cruising is pulling alongside a site, viewing it from the angles the river affords, and then stepping from your stateroom directly into antiquity, with nothing to intervene and break the mood.

Trouble is, this time a man in front of us goes off a way to photograph the ship, and suddenly something is rushing at him out of the weeds and the crew is yelling—it's a crocodile! The guy drops his camera and bolts.

The croc looks at all of us, snorts, and waddles back into the Nile. The guide is upset, maybe even more than the fellow who almost got turned into a free lunch. Who would introduce crocs back into the Nile?

December 17

Aswan. A clean, delightful town. The big dam just south of town is impressive, with its monument to Soviet excellence, etc. A hollow joke, considering how poor the USSR is today. They could use a loan from Egypt!

The unforeseen side effects, though—rising water table bringing more insects, rotting away the carvings in the temples, rapid silting up inside the dam itself, etc.—are getting important. They plan to dig a canal and drain a lot of the incoming new silt into the desert, make a huge farming valley with it, but I don't see how they can drain enough water to carry the dirt, and still leave much behind in the original dam.

The guide says they're having trouble with it.

We then fly south, to Abu Simbel. Lake Nasser, which claimed the original site of the huge monuments, is hundreds of miles long. They enlarged it again in 2008.

In the times of the pharaohs, the land below these had villages, great quarries for the construction of monuments, trade routes south to the Nubian kingdoms. Now it's all under water.

They did save the enormous temples to Rameses II—built to impress aggressive Nubians with his might and majesty—and to his queen, Nefertari. The colossal statues of Rameses II seem personifications of his egomania. Inside, carvings show him performing *all* the valiant tasks in the great battle with the Hittites—slaying, taking prisoners, then presenting them to himself, who is in turn advised by the gods—which include himself! All this, for a battle which was in fact an iffy draw. Both temples have been lifted about a hundred feet and set back inside a wholly artificial hill, supported inside by the largest concrete dome in the world. Amazing.

> *Look upon my works, ye Mighty,*
> *and despair!*

Except that when Shelley wrote *Ozymandias*, he'd never seen Rameses II's image so well preserved.

Leaving the site, eating the sand blown into our faces by a sudden gust of wind, I caught sight of a Quarthex. It was burrowing into the sand, using a silvery tool that spat ruby-colored light. Beside it, floating on a platform, were some of those funny pipelike things I'd seen days before. Only this time men and women were helping it, lugging stuff around to put into the holes the Quarthex dug.

The people looked dazed, like they were sleepwalking. I waved a greeting, but nobody even looked up. Except the Quarthex. They're expressionless, of course. Still, those glittering popeyes peered at me for a long moment, with the little feelers near its mouth twitching with a kind of anxious energy. I looked away. I couldn't help but feel a little spooked by it. It wasn't looking at us in a friendly way. Maybe it didn't want me yelling at its work gang.

Then we flew back to Aswan, above the impossibly narrow ribbon of green that snakes through absolute bitter desolation.

December 18

I'm writing this at twilight, before the light gives out. We got up this morning and were walking into town when the whole damn ground started to rock. Mud huts slamming down, waves on the Nile, everything.

Got back to the ship but nobody knew what was going on. Not much on the radio. Cairo came in clear, saying there'd been a quake all right, all along the Nile.

Funny thing was, the captain couldn't raise any other radio station. Just Cairo. Nothing else in the whole Middle East.

Some other passengers think there's a war on. Maybe so, but the Egyptian army doesn't know about it. They're standing around, all along the quay, fondling their AK 47s, looking just as puzzled as we are.

More rumblings and shakings in the afternoon. And now

that the sun's about gone, I can see big sheets of light in the sky. Only it seems to me the constellations aren't right.

Joanna took some of her pills. She's trying to fend off the jitters and I do what I can. I hate the empty, hollow look that comes into her eyes.

We've got to get the hell out of here.

December 19

I might as well write this down, there's nothing else to do.

When we got up this morning the sun was there all right, but the moon hadn't gone down. And it didn't, all day.

Sure, they can both be in the sky at the same time. But all day? Joanna is worried, not because of the moon, but because all the airline flights have been cancelled. We were supposed to go back to Cairo today.

More earthquakes. Really bad this time.

At noon, all of a sudden, there were Quarthex everywhere. In the air, swarming in from the east and west. Some splashed down in the Nile—and didn't come up. Others zoomed overhead, heading south toward the dam.

Nobody's been brave enough to leave the ship—including me. Hell, I just want to go home. Joanna's staying in the cabin.

About an hour later, a swarthy man in a ragged gray suit comes running along the quay and says the dam's gone. Just *gone*. The Quarthex formed little knots above it, and there was a lot of purple flashing light and big crackling noises, and then the dam just disappeared.

But the water hasn't come pouring down on us here. The man says it ran *back the other way*. South.

I looked over the rail. The Nile was flowing north.

Late this afternoon, five of the crew went into town. By this time there were fingers of orange and gold zapping across the sky all the time, making weird designs. The clouds would come rolling in from the north, and these radiant beams would hit them, and they'd *split* the clouds, just like that. With a spray of ivory light.

And Quarthex, buzzing everywhere. There's a kind of high sheen, up above the clouds, like a metal boundary or something, but you can see through it.

Quarthex keep zipping up to it, sometimes coming right up out of the Nile itself, just splashing out, then zooming up until they're little dwindling dots. They spin around up there, as if they're inspecting it, and then they drop like bricks, and splash down in the Nile again. Like frantic bees, Joanna said, and her voice trembled.

A technical type on board, an engineer from Rockwell, says *he* thinks the Quarthex are putting on one hell of a light show. Just a weird alien stunt, he thinks.

While I was writing this, the five crewmen returned from Aswan. They'd gone to the big hotels there, and then to police headquarters. They heard that TV from Cairo went out two days ago. All air flights have been grounded because of the Quarthex buzzing around and the odd lights and so on.

Or at least, that's the official line. The captain says his cousin told him that several flights *did* take off two days back, and they hit something up there. Maybe that blue metallic sheen?

One crashed. The others landed, although damaged.

The authorities are keeping it quiet. They're not just keeping us tourists in the dark—they're playing mum with everybody.

I hope the engineer is right. Joanna is fretting and we hardly ate anything for dinner, just picked at the cold lamb. Maybe tomorrow will settle things.

December 20

It did. When we woke, the Earth was rising.

It was coming up from the western mountains, blue-white clouds and patches of green and brown, but mostly tawny desert. We're looking west, across the Sahara. I'm writing this while everybody else is running around like a chicken with his head chopped off. I'm sitting on deck, listening to shouts and wild traffic and even some gunshots coming from ashore.

I can see farther east now—either we're turning, or we're rising fast and can see with a better perspective.

Where central Egypt was, there's a big, raw, dark hole.

The black must be the limestone underlying the desert. They've scraped off a rim of sandy margin enclosing the Nile valley, including us—and left the rest. And somehow, they're lifting it free of Earth.

No Quarthex flying around now. Nothing visible except that metallic blue smear of light high up in the air.

And beyond it—Earth, rising.

December 22

I skipped a day.

There was no time even to think yesterday. After I wrote the last entry, a crowd of Egyptians came down the quay, shuffling silently along, like the ones we saw back at Abu Simbel. Only there were thousands.

And leading them was a Quarthex. It carried a big disclike thing that made a humming sound. When the Quarthex lifted it, the pitch changed.

It made my eyes water, my skull ache. Like a hand squeezing my head, blurring the air.

Around me, everybody was writhing on the deck, moaning. Joanna, too.

By the time the Quarthex reached our ship I was the only one standing. Those yellow-shot, jittery eyes peered at me, giving nothing away. Then the angular head turned and went on. Pied piper, leading long trains of Egyptians.

Some of our friends from the ship joined at the end of the lines. Rigid, glassy-eyed faces. I shouted but nobody, not a single person in that procession, even looked up.

Joanna struggled to go with them. I threw her down and held her until the damned eerie parade was long past.

Now the ship's deserted. We've stayed aboard, out of pure fear.

Whatever the Quarthex did affects all but a few percent of those within range. A few crew stayed aboard, dazed but ok. Scared, hard to talk to.

Fewer at dinner.

The next morning, nobody.

We had to scavenge for food. The crew must've taken what was left aboard. I ventured into the market street nearby, but everything was closed up. Deserted. Only a few days ago we were buying caftans and alabaster sphinxes and beaten-bronze trinkets in the gaudy shops, and now it was stone cold dead. Not a sound, not a stray cat.

I went around to the back of what I remembered was a filthy corner cafe. I'd turned up my nose at it while we were shopping, certain there was a sure case of dysentery waiting inside . . . but now I was glad to find some days-old fruits and vegetables in a cabinet.

Coming back, I nearly ran into a bunch of Egyptian men who were marching through the streets. Spooks.

They had the look of police, but were dressed up like Mardi Gras—loincloths, big leather belts, bangles and beads, hair stiffened with wax. They carried sharp spears.

Good thing I was jumpy, or they'd have run right into me. I heard them coming and ducked into a grubby alley. They were systematically combing the area, searching the miserable apartments above the market. The honcho barked orders in a language I didn't understand—harsh, guttural, not like Egyptian.

I slipped away. Barely.

We kept out of sight after that. Stayed below deck and waited for nightfall.

Not that the darkness made us feel any better. There were fires ashore. Not in Aswan itself—the town was utterly black. Instead, orange dots sprinkled the distant hillsides. They were all over the scrub desert, just before the ramparts of the real desert that stretches—or did stretch—to east and west.

Now, I guess, there's only a few dozen miles of desert, before you reach—what?

I can't discuss this with Joanna. She has that haunted expression, from the time before her breakdown. She is drawn and silent. Stays in the room.

We ate our goddamn vegetables. Now we go to bed.

December 23

There were more of those patrols of Mardi Gras spooks today. They came along the quay, looking at the tour ships moored there, but for some reason they didn't come aboard.

We're alone on the ship. All the crew, the other tourists—all gone.

Around noon, when we were getting really hungry and I was mustering my courage to go back to the market street, I heard a roaring.

Understand, I hadn't heard an airplane in days. And those were jets. This buzzing, I suddenly realized, is a rocket or something, and it's in trouble.

I go out on the deck, checking first to see if the patrols are lurking around, and the roaring is louder. It's a plane with stubby little wings, coming along low over the water, burping and hacking and finally going dead quiet.

It nosed over and came in for a big splash. I thought the pilot was a goner, but the thing rode steady in the water for a while and the cockpit folded back and out jumps a man.

I yelled at him and he waved and swam for the ship. The plane sank.

He caught a line below and climbed up. An American, no less. But what he had to say was even more surprising.

He wasn't just some sky jockey from Cairo. He was an astronaut.

He was part of a rescue mission, sent up to try to stop the Quarthex. The others he'd lost contact with, although it looked like they'd all been drawn down toward the floating island that Egypt has become.

We're suspended about two Earth radii out, in a slowly widening orbit. There's a shield over us, keeping the air in and everything—cosmic rays, communications, spaceships—out.

The Quarthex somehow ripped off a layer of Egypt and are lifting it free of Earth, escaping with it. Nobody had ever guessed they had such power. Nobody Earthside knows what to do about it. The Quarthex who were outside Egypt at the time just lifted off in their ships and rendezvoused with this floating platform.

Ralph Blanchard is his name, and his mission was to fly under the slab of Egypt, in a fast orbital craft. He was supposed to see how they'd ripped the land free. A lot of it had fallen away.

There is an array of silvery pods under the soil, he says, and they must be enormous anti-grav units. The same kind that make the Quarthex ships fly, that we've been trying to get the secret of.

The pods are about a mile apart, making a grid. But between them, there are lots of Quarthex. They're building stuff, tilling soil, and so on—upside down! The gravity works opposite on the underside. That must be the way the whole thing is kept together—compressing it with artificial gravity from both sides. God knows what makes the shield above.

But the really strange thing is the Nile. There's one on the underside, too.

It starts at the underside of Alexandria, where *our* Nile meets—met—the Mediterranean. It then flows back, all the way along the underside, running through a Nile valley of its own. Then it turns up and around the edge of the slab, and comes over the lip of it a few hundred miles upstream of here.

The Quarthex have drained the region beyond the Aswan dam. Now the Nile flows in its old course. The big temples of Rameses II are perched on a hill high above the river, and Ralph was sure he saw Quarthex working on the site, taking it apart.

He thinks they're going to put it back where it was, before the dam was built in the 1960s.

Ralph was supposed to return to Orbital City with his data. He came in close for a final pass and hit the shield they have, the one that keeps the air in. His ship was damaged.

He'd been issued a suborbital craft, able to do reentries, in case he should penetrate the airspace. That saved him. There were other guys who hit the shield and cracked through, guys with conventional deepspace shuttle tugs and the like, and they fell like bricks.

We've talked all this over but no one has a good theory of what is going on. The best we can do is stay away from the patrols.

Meanwhile, Joanna scavenged through obscure bins of the ship, and turned up an entire case of Skivva, a cheap Egyptian beer. So after I finish this ritual entry—who knows, this might be in a history book someday, and as a good academic I should keep it up—I'll go share it out in one grand bust with Ralph and Joanna. It'll do her good. It'll do us both good. She's been rocky. As well,

> *Malt does more than Milton can*
> *To justify God's ways to man.*

December 24

This little diary was all I managed to take with us when the spooks came. I had it in my pocket.

I keep going over what happened. There was nothing I could do, I'm sure of that, and yet . . .

We stayed below decks, getting damned hungry again but afraid to go out. There was chanting from the distance. Getting louder. Then footsteps aboard. We retreated to the small cabins aft, third class.

The sounds got nearer. Ralph thought we should stand and fight but I'd seen those spears and hell, I'm a middle-aged man, no match for those maniacs.

Joanna got scared. It was like her breakdown. No, worse. The jitters built until her whole body seemed to vibrate, fingers digging into her hair like claws, eyes squeezed tight, face compressed as if to shut out the world.

There was nothing I could do with her, she wouldn't keep quiet. She ran out of the cabin we were hiding in, just rushed down the corridor screaming at them.

Ralph said we should use her diversion to get away and I said I'd stay, help her, but then I saw them grab her and hold her, not rough. It didn't seem as if they were going to do anything, just take her away.

My fear got the better of me then. It's hard to write this. Part of me says I should've stayed, defended her—but it was hopeless. You can't live up to your ideal self. The world of literature shows people summoning up courage, but there's a thin line between that and stupidity. Or so I tell myself.

The spooks hadn't seen us yet, so we slipped overboard, keeping quiet.

We went off the loading ramp on the river side, away from shore. Ralph paddled around to see the quay and came back looking worried. There were spooks swarming all over.

We had to move. The only way to go was across the river.

This shaky handwriting is from sheer, flat-out fatigue. I swam what seemed like forever. The water wasn't bad, pretty warm, but the current kept pushing us off course. Lucky thing the Nile is pretty narrow there, and there are rocky little stubs sticking out. I grabbed onto those and rested.

Nobody saw us, or at least they didn't do anything about it.

We got ashore looking like drowned rats. There's a big hill there, covered with ancient rock-cut tombs. I thought of taking shelter in one of them and started up the hill, legs wobbly under me, and then we saw a mob up top.

And a Quarthex, a big one with a shiny shell. It wore something over its head. Supposedly Quarthex don't wear clothes, but this one had a funny rig on. A big bird head, with a long narrow beak and flinty black eyes.

There was madness all around us. Long lines of people carrying burdens, chanting. Quarthex riding on those lifter units of theirs. All beneath the piercing, biting sun.

We hid for a while. I found that this diary, in its zippered leather case, made it through the river without a leak. I started writing this entry. Joanna said once that I'd retreated into books as a defense, in adolescence—she was full of psychoanalytical explanations, it was a hobby. She kept thinking that if she could figure herself out, then things would be all right. Well, maybe I did use words and books and a quiet, orderly life as a place to hide. So what? It was better than this "real" world around me right now. I thought of Joanna and what might be happening to her.

The Quarthex can—

(New Entry)

I was writing when the Quarthex came closer. I thought we were finished, but they didn't see us. Those huge heads turned all the time, the glittering black eyes scanning. Then they moved away. The chanting was a relentless, singsong drone that gradually faded.

We got away from there, fast.

I'm writing this during a short break. Then we'll move on.

No place to go but the goddamn desert.

December 25

Christmas.

I keep thinking about fat turkey stuffed with spicy dressing, crisp cranberries, a dry white wine, thick gravy—

No point in that. We found some food today in an abandoned construction site, bread at least a week old and some dried-up fruit. That was all.

Ralph kept pushing me on west. He wants to see over the edge, how they hold this thing together.

I'm not that damn interested, but I don't know where else to go. Just running on blind fear. My professorial instincts—like keeping this journal. It helps keep me sane. Assuming I still am.

Ralph says putting this down might have scientific value. If I can ever get it to anybody outside. So I keep on. Words, words, words. Much cleaner than this gritty, surreal world.

We saw people marching in the distance, dressed in loincloths again. It suddenly struck me that I'd seen that clothing before—in those marvelous wall paintings, in the tombs of the Valley of Kings. It's ancient dress.

Ralph thinks he understands what's happening. There was an all-frequencies broadcast from the Quarthex when they tore off this wedge we're on. Nobody understood much—it was in that odd semi-speech of theirs, all the words blurred and placed wrong, scrambled up. Something about their mission or destiny or whatever being to enhance the best in each world. About how they'd make a deal with the Egyptians to bring forth the unrealized promise of their majestic past and so on. And that meant isolation, so the fruit of ages could flower.

Ha. The world's great age begins anew, maybe—but Percy Bysshe Shelley never meant it like this.

Not that I care a lot about motivations right now. I spent the day thinking of Joanna, still feeling guilty. And hiking west in the heat and dust, hiding from gangs of glassy-eyed workers when we had to.

We reached the edge at sunset. It hadn't occurred to me,

but it's obvious—for there to be days and nights at all means they're spinning the slab we're on.

Compressing it, holding in the air, adding just the right rotation. Masters—of space/time and the river, yes.

The ground started to slope away. Not like going downhill, because there was nothing pulling you down the face of it. I mean, we *felt* like we were walking on level ground. But overhead the sky moved as we walked.

We caught up with the sunset. The sun dropped for a while in late afternoon, then started rising again. Pretty soon it was right overhead, high noon.

And we could see Earth, too, farther away than yesterday. Looking cool and blue.

We came to a wall of glistening metal tubes, silvery and rippling with a frosty blue glow. I started to get woozy as we approached. Something happened to gravity—it pulled your stomach as if you were spinning around. Finally we couldn't get any closer. I stopped, nauseated. Ralph kept on. I watched him try to walk toward the metal barrier, which by then looked like luminous icebergs suspended above barren desert.

He tried to walk a straight line, he said later. I could see him veer, his legs rubbery, and it looked as though he rippled and distended, stretching horizontally while some force compressed him vertically, an egg man, a plastic body swaying in tides of gravity.

Then he starting stumbling, falling. He cried out—a horrible, warped sound, like paper tearing for a long, long time. He fled. The sand clawed at him as he ran, strands grasping at his feet, trailing long streamers of glittering, luminous sand— but it couldn't hold him. Ralph staggered away, gasping, his eyes huge and white and terrified.

We turned back.

But coming away, I saw a band of men and women

marching woodenly along toward the wall. They were old, most of them, and diseased. Some had been hurt—you could see the wounds.

They were heading straight for the lip. Silent, inexorable.

Ralph and I followed them for a while. As they approached the wall, they started walking up off the sand—right into the air.

And over the tubes.

Just flying.

We decided to head south. Maybe the lip is different there. Ralph says the plan he'd heard, after the generals had studied the survey-mission results, was to try to open the shield at the ground, where the Nile spills over. Then they'd get people out by boating them along the river.

Could they be doing that, now? We hear roaring sounds in the sky sometimes. Explosions. Ralph is ironic about it all, says he wonders when the Quarthex will get tired of intruders and go back to the source—*all* the way back.

I don't know. I'm tired and worn down.

Could there be a way out? Sounds impossible, but it's all we've got.

Head south, to the Nile's edge.

We're hiding in a cave tonight. It's bitterly cold out here in the desert, and a sunburn is no help.

I'm hungry as hell. Some Christmas.

We were supposed to be back in Laguna Beach by now.

God knows where Joanna is.

December 26

I got away. Barely.

The Quarthex work in teams now. They've gridded off the desert and work across it systematically in those floating platforms. There are big tubes like cannon mounted on each end and a Quarthex scans it over the sands.

Ralph and I crept up to the mouth of the cave we were in and watched them comb the area. They worked out from the Nile. When a muzzle turned toward us I felt an impact like a warm, moist wave smacking into my face, like being in the ocean. It drove me to my knees. I reeled away. Threw myself farther back into the cramped cave.

It all dropped away then, as if the wave had pinned me to the ocean floor and filled my lungs with a sluggish liquid.

And in an instant was gone. I rolled over, gasping, and saw Ralph staggering into the sunlight, heading for the Quarthex platform. The projector was leveled at him so that it no longer struck the cave mouth. So I'd been released from its grip.

I watched them lower a rope ladder. Ralph dutifully climbed up. I wanted to shout to him, try to break the hold that thing had over him, but once again the better part of valor—I just watched. They carried him away.

I waited until twilight to move. Not having anybody to talk to makes it harder to control my fear.

God I'm hungry. Couldn't find a scrap to eat.

When I took out this diary I looked at the leather case and remembered stories of people getting so starved they'd eat their shoes. Suitably boiled and salted, of course, with a tangy sauce.

Another day or two and the idea might not seem so funny.

I've got to keep moving.

December 27

Hard to write. They got me this morning.

It grabs your mind. Like before. Squeezing in your head. But after a while it is better. Feels good. But a buzzing all the time, you can't think.

Picked me up while I was crossing an arroyo. Didn't have any idea they were around. A platform.

Took me to some others. All Egyptians. Caught like me.

Marched us to the Nile.

Plenty to eat.

Rested at noon.

Brought Joanna to me. She is all right. Lovely in the long draping dress the Quarthex gave her.

All around are the bird-headed ones. Ibis, I remember, the bird of the Nile. And dog-headed ones. Lion-headed ones.

Gods of the old times. The Quarthex are the gods of the old time. Of the greater empire.

We are the people.

Sometimes I can think, like now. They sent me away from the work gang on an errand. I am old, not strong. They are kind—give me easy jobs.

So I came to here. Where I hid this diary. Before they took my old uncomfortable clothes I put this little book into a crevice in the rock. Pen too.

Now writing helps. Mind clears some.

I saw Ralph, then lost track of him. I worked hard after the noontime. Sun felt good. I lifted pots, carried them where the foreman said.

The Quarthex-god with ibis head is building a fresh temple. Made from the stones of Aswan. It will be cool and deep, many pillars.

They took my dirty clothes. Gave me fresh loincloth, headband, sandals. Good ones. Better than my old clothes.

It is hard to remember how things were before I came here. Before I knew the river. Its flow. How it divides the world.

I will rest before I try to read what I have written in here before. The words are hard.

Days Later

I come back but can read only a little.

Joanna says you should not. The ibis will not like it if I do.

I remember I liked these words on paper, in my days before. I earned my food with them. Now they are empty. Must not have been true.

Do not need them any more.

Ralph, science. All words too.

Later

Days since I find this again. I do the good work, I eat, Joanna is there in the night. Many things. I do not want to do this reading.

But today another thing howled overhead. It passed over the desert like a screaming black bird, the falcon, and then fell, flames, big roar.

I remembered Ralph.

This book I remembered, came for it.

The ibis-god speaks to us each sunset. Of how the glory of our lives is here again. We are one people once more again yes after a long long time of being lost.

What the red sunset means. The place where the dead are buried in the western desert. To be taken in death close to the edge, so the dead will walk their last steps in this world, to the lip and over, to the netherworld.

There the lion-god will preserve them. Make them live again.

The Quarthex-gods have discovered how to revive the dead of any beings. They spread this among the stars.

But only to those who understand. Who deserve. Who bow to the great symmetry of life.

One face light, one face dark.

The sun lights the netherworld when for us it is night. There the dead feast and mate and laugh and live forever.

Ralph saw that. The happy land below. It shares the sun.

I saw Ralph today. He came to the river to see the falcon thing cry from the clouds. We all did.

It fell into the river and was swallowed and will be taken to the netherworld where it flows over the edge of the world.

Ralph was sorry when the falcon fell. He said it was a mistake to send it to bother us. That someone from the old dead time had sent it.

Ralph works in the quarry. Carving the limestone. He looks good, the sun has lain on him and made him strong and brown.

I started to talk of the time we met but he frowned.

That was before we understood, he says. Shook his head. So I should not speak of it.

The gods know of time and the river. They know.

I tire now.

Again

Joanna sick. I try help but no way to stop the bleeding from her.

In old time I would try to stop the stuff of life from leaving her. I would feel sorrow.

I do not now. I am calm.

Ibis-god prepares her. Works hard and good over her.

She will journey tonight. Walk the last trek. Over the edge of the sky and to the netherland.

It is what the temple carving says. She will live again forever.

Forever waits.

I come here to find this book to enter this. I remember sometimes how it was.

I did not know joy then. Joanna did not.

We lived but to no point. Just come-go-come-again.

Now I know what comes. The western death. The rising life.

The Quarthex-gods are right. I should forget that life. To hold on is to die. To flow forward is to live.

Today I saw the pharaoh. He came in radiant chariot, black horses before, bronze sword in hand. The sun was high above him. No shadow be cast.

Big and with red skin the pharaoh rode down the avenue of the kings. We the one people cheered.

His great head was mighty in the sun and his many arms waved in salute to his one people. He is so great the horses groan and sweat to pull him. His hard gleaming body is all armor for he will always be on guard against our enemies.

Like those who fall from the sky. Every day now more come down, dying fireballs to smash in the desert. All fools. Black rotting bodies. None will rise to walk west. They are only burned prey of the pharaoh.

The pharaoh rode three times to the avenue. We threw ourselves down to attract a glance. His huge glaring eyes regarded us and we cried out, our faces wet with joy.

He will speak for us in the netherworld. Sing to the undergods.

Make our westward walking path smooth.

I fall before him.

I bury this now. No more write in it.

This kind of writing is not for the world now. It comes from the old dead time when I knew nothing and thought everything.

I go to my eternity on the river.

Matter's End

> When Dr. Samuel Johnson felt himself getting tied up
> in an argument over Bishop Berkeley's ingenious
> sophistry to prove the nonexistence of matter, and
> that everything in the universe is merely ideal, he
> kicked a large stone and answered, "I refute it thus."
> Just what that action assured him of is not very obvious,
> but apparently he found it comforting.
>
> —Sir Arthur Eddington

India came to him first as a breeze like soured buttermilk, rich yet tainted. A door banged somewhere, sending gusts sweeping through the Bangalore airport, slicing through the 4 a.m. silences.

Since the Free State of Bombay had left India, Bangalore had become an international airport. Yet the damp caress seemed to erase the sterile signatures that made all big airports alike, even giving a stippled texture to the cool enamel glow of the fluorescents.

The moist air clasped Robert Clay like a stranger's sweaty palm. The ripe, fleshy aroma of a continent enfolded him, swarming up his nostrils and soaking his lungs with sullen spice. He put down his carry-on bag and showed the immi-

117

gration clerk his passport. The man gave him a piercing, ferocious stare—then mutely slammed a rubber stamp onto the pages and handed it back.

A hand snagged him as he headed toward baggage claim. "Professor Clay?" The face was dark olive with intelligent eyes riding above sharp cheekbones. A sudden white grin flashed as Clay nodded. "Ah, *good*. I am Dr. Sudarshan Patil. Please come this way."

Dr. Patil's tone was polite, but his hands impatiently pulled Clay away from the sluggish lines, through a battered wooden side door. The heavy-lidded immigration guards were carefully looking in other directions, hands held behind their backs. Apparently they had been paid off and would ignore this odd exit. Clay was still groggy from trying to sleep on the flight from London. He shook his head as Patil led him into the gloom of a baggage storeroom.

"Your clothes," Patil said abruptly.

"What?"

"They mark you as a Westerner. Quickly!"

Patil's hands, light as birds in the quilted soft light, were already plucking at his coat, his shirt. Clay was taken aback at this abruptness. He hesitated, then struggled out of the dirty garments, pulling his loose slacks down over his shoes. He handed his bundled clothes to Patil, who snatched them away without a word.

"You're welcome," Clay said. Patil took no notice, just thrust a wad of tan cotton at him. The man's eyes jumped at each distant sound in the storage room, darting, suspecting every pile of dusty bags.

Clay struggled into the pants and rough shirt. They looked dingy in the wan yellow glow of a single distant fluorescent tube.

"Not the reception I'd expected," Clay said, straightening

the baggy pants and pulling at the rough drawstring.

"These are not good times for scientists in my country, Dr. Clay," Patil said bitingly. His voice carried that odd lilt that echoed both the Raj and Cambridge.

"Who're you afraid of?"

"Those who hate Westerners and their science."

"They said in Washington—"

"We are about great matters, Professor Clay. Please cooperate, please."

Patil's lean face showed its bones starkly, as though energies pressed outward. Promontories of bunched muscle stretched a mottled canvas skin. He started toward a far door without another word, carrying Clay's overnight bag and jacket.

"Say, where're we—"

Patil swung open a sheet-metal door and beckoned. Clay slipped through it and into the moist wealth of night. His feet scraped on a dirty sidewalk beside a black tar road. The door hinge squealed behind them, attracting the attention of a knot of men beneath a vibrant yellow streetlight nearby.

The bleached fluorescence of the airport terminal was now a continent away. Beneath a line of quarter-ton trucks huddled figures slept. In the astringent street-lamp glow he saw a decrepit green Korean Tochat van parked at the curb.

"In!" Patil whispered.

The men under the streetlight started walking toward them, calling out hoarse questions.

Clay yanked open the van's sliding door and crawled into the second row of seats. A fog of unknown pungent smells engulfed him. The driver, a short man, hunched over the wheel. Patil sprang into the front seat and the van ground away, its low gear whining.

Shouts. A stone thumped against the van roof. Pebbles rattled at the back.

They accelerated, the engine clattering. A figure loomed up from the shifting shadows and flung muck against the window near Clay's face. He jerked back at the slap of it. "Damn!"

They plowed through a wide puddle of dirty rainwater. The engine sputtered and for a moment Clay was sure it would die. He looked out the rear window and saw vague forms running after them. Then the engine surged again and they shot away.

They went two blocks through hectic traffic. Clay tried to get a clear look at India outside, but all he could see in the starkly shadowed street were the crisscrossings of three-wheeled taxis and human-drawn rickshaws. He got an impression of incessant activity, even in this desolate hour. Vehicles leaped out of the murk as headlights swept across them and then vanished utterly into the moist shadows again.

They suddenly swerved around a corner beneath spreading, gloomy trees. The van jolted into deep potholes and jerked to a stop. "Out!" Patil called.

Clay could barely make out a second van at the curb ahead. It was blue and caked with mud, but even in the dim light would not be confused with their green one. A rotting fetid reek filled his nose as he got out the side door, as if masses of overripe vegetation loomed in the shadows. Patil tugged him into the second van. In a few seconds they went surging out through a narrow, brick-lined alley.

"Look, what—"

"Please, quiet," Patil said primly. "I am watching carefully now to be certain that we are not being followed."

They wound through a shantytown warren for several minutes. Their headlights picked up startled eyes that blinked from what Clay at first had taken to be bundles of rags lying against the shacks. They seemed impossibly small even to be children. Huddled against decaying tin lean-tos, the dim forms often did not stir even as the van splashed dirty water on them from potholes.

Clay began, "Look, I understand the need for—"

"I apologize for our rude methods, Dr. Clay," Patil said. He gestured at the driver. "May I introduce Dr. Singh?"

Singh was similarly gaunt and intent, but with bushy hair and a thin, pointed nose. He jerked his head aside to peer at Clay, nodded twice like a puppet on strings, and then quickly stared back at the narrow lane ahead. Singh kept the van at a steady growl, abruptly yanking it around corners. A wooden cart lurched out of their way, its driver swearing in a strident singsong.

"Welcome to India," Singh said with reedy solemnity. "I am afraid circumstances are not the best."

"Uh, right. You two are heads of the project, they told me at the NSF."

"Yes," Patil said archly, "the project which officially no longer exists and unofficially is a brilliant success. It is amusing!"

"Yeah," Clay said cautiously, "we'll see."

"Oh, you will see," Singh said excitedly. "We have the events! More all the time."

Patil said precisely, "We would not have suggested that your National Science Foundation send an observer to confirm our findings unless we believed them to be of the highest importance."

"You've seen proton decay?"

Patil beamed. "Without doubt."

"Damn."

"Exactly."

"What mode?"

"The straightforward pion and positron decay products."

Clay smiled, reserving judgment. Something about Patil's almost prissy precision made him wonder if this small, beleaguered team of Indian physicists might actually have brought it off. An immense long shot, of course, but possible. There were much bigger groups of particle physicists in Europe and the U.S. who had tried to detect proton decay using underground swimming pools of pure water. Those experiments had enjoyed all the benefits of the latest electronics. Clay had worked on the big American project in a Utah salt mine, before lean budgets and lack of results closed it down. It would be galling if this lone, under-funded Indian scheme had finally done it. Nobody at the NSF believed the story coming out of India.

Patil smiled at Clay's silence, a brilliant slash of white in the murk. Their headlights picked out small panes of glass stuck seemingly at random in nearby hovels, reflecting quick glints of yellow back into the van. The night seemed misty; their headlights forked ahead. Clay thought a soft rain had started outside, but then he saw that thousands of tiny insects darted into their headlights. Occasionally big ones smacked against the windshield.

Patil carefully changed the subject. "I . . . believe you will pass unnoticed, for the most part."

"I look Indian?"

"I hope you will not take offense if I remark that you do not. We requested an Indian, but your NSF said they did not have anyone qualified."

"Right. Nobody who could hop on a plane, anyway." Or *would*, he added to himself.

"I understand. You are a compromise. If you will put this on . . ." Patil handed Clay a floppy khaki hat. "It will cover your curly hair. Luckily, your nose is rather more narrow than

I had expected when the NSF cable announced they were sending a Negro."

"Got a lot of white genes in it, this nose," Clay said evenly.

"Please, do not think I am being racist. I simply wished to diminish the chances of you being recognized as a Westerner in the countryside."

"Think I can pass?"

"At a distance, yes."

"Be tougher at the site?"

"Yes. There are 'celebrants,' as they term themselves, at the mine."

"How'll we get in?"

"A ruse we have devised."

"Like that getaway back there? That was pretty slick."

Singh sent them jouncing along a rutted lane. Withered trees leaned against the pale stucco two-story buildings that lined the lane like children's blocks lined up not quite correctly. "Men in customs, they would give word to people outside. If you had gone through with the others, a different reception party would have been waiting for you."

"I see. But what about my bags?"

Patil had been peering forward at the gloomy jumble of buildings. His head jerked around to glare at Clay. "You were not to bring more than your carry-on bag!"

"Look, I can't get by on that. Chrissake, that'd give me just one change of clothes—"

"You left bags there?"

"Well, yeah, I had just one—"

Clay stopped when he saw the look on the two men's faces.

Patil said with strained clarity, "Your bags, they had identification tags?"

"Sure, airlines make you—"

"They will bring attention to you. There will be inquiries. The devotees will hear of it, inevitably, and know you have entered the country."

Clay licked his lips. "Hell, I didn't think it was so important."

The two lean Indians glanced at each other, their faces taking on a narrowing, leaden cast. "Dr. Clay," Patil said stiffly, "the 'celebrants' believe, as do many, that Westerners deliberately destroyed our crops with their biotechnology."

"Japanese companies' biologists did that, I thought," Clay said diplomatically.

"Perhaps. Those who disturb us at the Kolar gold mine make no fine distinctions between biologists and physicists. They believe that we are disturbing the very bowels of the earth, helping to further the destruction, bringing on the very end of the world itself. Surely you can see that in India, the mother country of religious philosophy, such matters are important."

"But your work, hell, it's not a matter of life or death or anything."

"On the contrary, the decay of the proton is precisely an issue of death."

Clay settled back in his seat, puzzled, watching the silky night stream by, cloaking vague forms in its shadowed mysteries.

2

Clay insisted on the telephone call. A wan winter sun had already crawled partway up the sky before he awoke, and the two Indian physicists wanted to leave immediately. They had stopped while still in Bangalore, holing up in the cramped apartment of one of Patil's graduate students. As Clay took his first sip of tea, two other students had turned up with his bag, retrieved at a cost he never knew.

Clay said, "I promised I'd call home. Look, my family's worried. They read the papers, they know the trouble here."

Shaking his head slowly, Patil finished a scrap of curled brown bread that appeared to be his only breakfast. His movements had a smooth liquid inertia, as if the sultry morning air oozed like jelly around him. They were sitting at a low table that had one leg too short; the already rickety table kept lurching, slopping tea into their saucers. Clay had looked for something to prop up the leg, but the apartment was bare, as though no one lived here. They had slept on pallets beneath a single bare bulb. Through the open windows, bare of frames or glass, Clay had gotten fleeting glimpses of the neighborhood—rooms of random clutter, plaster peeling off slumped walls, revealing the thin steel cross-ribs of the buildings, stained windows adorned with gaudy pictures of many-armed gods, already sun-bleached and frayed. Children yelped and cried below, their voices reflected among the odd angles and apertures of the tangled streets, while carts rattled by and bare feet slapped the stones. Students had apparently stood guard last night, though Clay had never seen more than a quick motion in the shadows below as they arrived.

"You ask much of us," Patil said. By morning light his walnut-brown face seemed gullied and worn. Lines radiated from his mouth toward intense eyes.

Clay sipped his tea before answering. A soft, strangely sweet smell wafted through the open window. They sat well back in the room so nobody could see in from the nearby buildings. He heard Singh tinkering downstairs with the van's engine.

"Okay, it's maybe slightly risky. But I want my people to know I got here all right."

"There are few telephones here."

"I only need one."

"The system, often it does not work at all."

"Gotta try."

"Perhaps you do not understand—"

"I understand damn well that if I can't even reach my people, I'm not going to hang out here for long. And if I don't see that your experiment works right, nobody'll believe you."

"And your opinion depends upon . . . ?"

Clay ticked off points on his fingers. "On seeing the apparatus. Checking your raw data. Running a trial case to see your system response. Then a null experiment—to verify your threshold level on each detector." He held up five fingers. "The works."

Patil said gravely, "Very good. We relish the opportunity to prove ourselves."

"You'll get it." Clay hoped to himself that they were wrong, but he suppressed that. He represented the faltering forefront of particle physics, and it would be embarrassing if a backwater research team had beaten the world. Still, either way, he would end up being the expert on the Kolar program, and that was a smart career move in itself.

"Very well. I must make arrangements for the call, then. But I truly—"

"Just do it. Then we get down to business."

The telephone was behind two counters and three doors at a Ministry for Controls office. Patil did the bribing and cajoling inside and then brought Clay in from the back of the van. He had been lying down on the back seat so he could not be seen easily from the street.

The telephone itself was a heavy black plastic thing with a

rotary dial that clicked like a sluggish insect as it whirled. Patil had been on it twice already, clearing international lines through Bombay. Clay got two false rings and a dead line. On the fourth try he heard a faint, somehow familiar buzzing. Then a hollow, distant click.

"Angy?"

"Daddy, is that you?" Faint rock music in the background.

"Sure, I just wanted to let you know I got to India okay."

"Oh, Mommy will be so glad! We heard on the TV last night that there's trouble over there."

Startled, Clay asked, "What? Where's your mother?"

"Getting groceries. She'll be *so* mad she missed your call!"

"You tell her I'm fine, okay? But what trouble?"

"Something about a state leaving India. Lots of fighting, John Trimble said on the news."

Clay never remembered the names of news announcers; he regarded them as faceless nobodies reading prepared scripts, but for his daughter they were the voice of authority. "Where?"

"Uh, the lower part."

"There's nothing like that happening here, honey. I'm safe. Tell Mommy."

"People have ice cream there?"

"Yeah, but I haven't seen any. You tell your mother what I said, remember? About being safe?"

"Yes, she's been worried."

"Don't worry, Angy. Look, I got to go." The line popped and hissed ominously.

"I miss you, Daddy."

"I miss you double that. No, squared."

She laughed merrily. "I skinned my knee today at recess. It bled so much I had to go to the nurse."

"Keep it clean, honey. And give your mother my love."

"She'll be *so* mad."

"I'll be home soon."

She giggled and ended with the joke she had been using lately. "G'bye, Daddy. It's been real."

Her light laugh trickled into the static, a grace note from a bright land worlds away. Clay chuckled as he replaced the receiver. She cut the last word of "real nice" to make her goodbyes hip and sardonic, a mannerism she had heard on television somewhere. An old joke; he had heard that even "groovy" was coming back in.

Clay smiled and pulled his hat down further and went quickly out into the street where Patil was waiting. India flickered at the edge of his vision, the crowds a hovering presence.

3

They left Bangalore in two vans. Graduate students drove the green Tochat from the previous night. He and Patil and Singh took the blue one, Clay again keeping out of sight by lying on the back seat. The day's raw heat rose around them like a shimmering lake of light.

They passed through lands leached of color. Only gray stubble grew in the fields. Trees hung limply, their limbs bowing as though exhausted. Figures in rags huddled for shade. A few stirred, eyes white in the shadows, as the vans ground past. Clay saw that large boles sat on the branches like gnarled knots with brown sheaths wrapped around the underside.

"Those some of the plant diseases I heard about?" he asked.

Singh pursed his lips. "I fear those are the pouches like

those of wasps, as reported in the press." His watery eyes regarded the withered, graying trees as Patil slowed the car.

"Are they dangerous?" Clay could see yellow sap dripping from the underside of each.

"Not until they ripen," Singh said. "Then the assassins emerge."

"They look pretty big already."

"They are said to be large creatures, but of course there is little experience."

Patil downshifted and they accelerated away with an occasional sputtering misfire. Clay wondered whether they had any spare spark plugs along. The fields on each side of the road took on a dissolute and shredded look. "Did the genetech experiments cause this?" he asked.

Singh nodded. "I believe this emerged from the European programs. First we had their designed plants, but then pests found vulnerability. They sought strains which could protect crops from the new pests. So we got these wasps. I gather that now some error or mutation has made them equally excellent at preying on people and even cows."

Clay frowned. "The wasps came from the Japanese aid, didn't they?"

Patil smiled mysteriously. "You know a good deal about our troubles, sir."

Neither said anything more. Clay was acutely conscious that his briefing in Washington had been detailed technical assessments, without the slightest mention of how the Indians themselves saw their problems. Singh and Patil seemed either resigned or unconcerned; he could not tell which. Their sentences refracted from some unseen nugget, like seismic waves warping around the earth's core.

"I would not worry greatly about these pouches," Singh

said after they had ridden in silence for a while. "They should not ripen before we are done with our task. In any case, the Kolar fields are quite barren, and afford few sites where the pouches can grow."

Clay pointed out the front window. "Those round things on the walls—more pouches?"

To his surprise, both men burst into merry laughter. Gasping, Patil said, "Examine them closely, Doctor Clay. Notice the marks of the species which made them."

Patil slowed the car and Clay studied the round, circular pads on the whitewashed vertical walls along the road. They were brown and matted and marked in a pattern of radial lines. Clay frowned and then felt enormously stupid: the thick lines were handprints.

"Drying cakes, they are," Patil said, still chuckling.

"Of what?"

"Dung, my colleague. We use the cow here, not merely slaughter it."

"What for?"

"Fuel. After the cakes dry, we stack them—see?" They passed a plastic-wrapped tower. A woman was adding a circular, annular tier of thick dung disks to the top, then carefully folding the plastic over it. "In winter they burn nicely."

"For heating?"

"And cooking, yes."

Seeing the look on Clay's face, Singh's eyes narrowed and his lips drew back so that his teeth were bright stubs. His eyebrows were long brush strokes that met the deep furrows of his frown. "Old ways are still often preferable to the new."

Sure, Clay thought, the past of cholera, plague, infanticide. But he asked with neutral politeness, "Such as?"

"Some large fish from the Amazon were introduced into our principal river three years ago to improve fishing yields."

"The Ganges? I thought it was holy."

"What is more holy than to feed the hungry?"

"True enough. Did it work?"

"The big fish, yes. They are delicious. A great delicacy."

"I'll have to try some," Clay said, remembering the thin vegetarian curry he had eaten at breakfast.

Singh said, "But the Amazon sample contained some minute eggs which none of the proper procedures eliminated. They were of a small species—the candiru, is that not the name?" he inquired politely of Patil.

"Yes," Patil said, "a little being who thrives mostly on the urine of larger fish. Specialists now believe that perhaps the eggs were inside the larger species, and so escaped detection."

Patil's voice remained calm and factual, although while he spoke he abruptly swerved to avoid a goat that spontaneously ambled onto the rough road. Clay rocked hard against the van's door, and Patil then corrected further to stay out of a gratuitous mud hole that seemed to leap at them from the rushing foreground. They bumped noisily over ruts at the road's edge and bounced back onto the tarmac without losing speed. Patil sat ramrod straight, hands turning the steering wheel lightly, oblivious to the wrenching effects of his driving.

"Suppose, Professor Clay, that you are a devotee," Singh said. "You have saved to come to the Ganges for a decade, for two. Perhaps you even plan to die there."

"Yeah, okay." Clay could not see where this was leading.

"You are enthused as you enter the river to bathe. You are perhaps profoundly affected. An intense spiritual moment. It is not uncommon to merge with the river, to inadvertently urinate into it."

Singh spread his hands as if to say that such things went without saying.

131

"Then the candiru will be attracted by the smell. It mistakes this great bountiful largess, the food it needs, as coming from a very great fish indeed. It excitedly swims up the stream of uric acid. Coming to your urethra, it swims like a snake into its burrow, as far up as it can go. You will see that the uric flow velocity will increase as the candiru makes its way upstream, inside you. When this tiny fish can make no further progress, some trick of evolution tells it to protrude a set of sidewise spines. So intricate!"

Singh paused a moment in smiling tribute to this intriguing facet of nature.

Clay nodded, his mouth dry.

"These embed deeply in the walls and keep the candiru close to the source of what it so desires." Singh made short, delicate movements, his fingers jutting in the air. Clay opened his mouth, but said nothing.

Patil took them around a team of bullocks towing a wooden wagon and put in, "The pain is intense. Apparently there is no good treatment. Women—forgive this indelicacy—must be opened to get at the offending tiny fish before it swells and blocks the passage completely, having gorged itself insensate. Some men have an even worse choice. Their bladders are already engorged, having typically not been much emptied by the time the candiru enters. They must decide whether to attempt the slow procedure of poisoning the small thing and waiting for it to shrivel and withdraw its spines. However, their bladders might burst before that, flooding their abdomens with urine and of course killing them. If there is not sufficient time . . ."

"Yes?" Clay asked tensely.

"Then the penis must be chopped off," Singh said, "with the candiru inside."

Through a long silence Clay rode, swaying as the car wove

through limitless flat spaces of parched fields and ruined brick walls and slumped whitewashed huts. Finally he said hoarsely, "I . . . don't blame you for resenting the . . . well, the people who brought all this on you. The devotees—"

"They believe this apocalyptic evil comes from the philosophy which gave us modern science."

"Well, look, whoever brought over those fish—"

Singh's eyes widened with surprise. A startled grin lit his face like a sunrise.

"Oh no, Professor Clay! We do not blame the errors, or else we would have to blame equally the successes!"

To Clay's consternation, Patil nodded sagely.

He decided to say nothing more. Washington had warned him to stay out of political discussions, and though he was not sure if this was such, or if the lighthearted way Singh and Patil had related their story told their true attitude, it seemed best to just shut up. Again Clay had the odd sensation that here the cool certainties of Western biology had become diffused, blunted, crisp distinctions rendered into something beyond the constraints of the world outside, all blurred by the swarming, dissolving currents of India. The tin-gray sky loomed over a plain of ripe rot. The urgency of decay here was far more powerful than the abstractions that so often filled his head, the digitized iconography of sputtering, splitting protons.

4

The Kolar gold fields were a long, dusty drive from Bangalore. The sway of the van made Clay sleepy in the back, jet lag pulling him down into fitful, shallow dreams of muted voices, shadowy faces, and obscure purpose. He awoke frequently amid the dry smells, lurched up to see dry farmland stretching to the horizon, and collapsed again to bury his face in the pillow he had made by wadding up a shirt.

They passed through innumerable villages that, after the first few, all seemed alike with their scrawny children, ramshackle sheds, tin roofs, and general air of sleepy dilapidation. Once, in a narrow town, they stopped as rickshaws and carts backed up. An emaciated cow with pink paper tassels on its horns stood square in the middle of the road, trembling. Shouts and honks failed to move it, but no one ahead made the slightest effort to prod it aside.

Clay got out of the van to stretch his legs, ignoring Patil's warning to stay hidden, and watched. A crowd collected, shouting and chanting at the cow but not touching it. The cow shook its head, peering at the road as if searching for grass, and urinated powerfully. A woman in a red sari rushed into the road, knelt, and thrust her hand into the full stream. She made a formal motion with her other hand and splashed some urine on her forehead and cheeks. Three other women had already lined up behind her, and each did the same. Disturbed, the cow waggled its head and shakily walked away. Traffic started up, and Clay climbed back into the van. As they ground out of the dusty town, Singh explained that holy bovine urine was widely held to have positive health effects.

"Many believe it settles stomach troubles, banishes headaches, even improves fertility," Singh said.

"Yeah, you could sure use more fertility." Clay gestured at the throngs that filled the narrow clay sidewalks.

"I am not so Indian that I cannot find it within myself to agree with you, Professor Clay," Singh said.

"Sorry for the sarcasm. I'm tired."

"Patil and I are already under a cloud simply because we

are scientists, and therefore polluted with Western ideas."

"Can't blame Indians for being down on us. Things're getting rough."

"But you are a black man. You yourself were persecuted by Western societies."

"That was a while back."

"And despite it you have risen to a professorship."

"You do the work, you get the job." Clay took off his hat and wiped his brow. The midday heat pressed sweat from him.

"Then you do not feel alienated from Western ideals?" Patil put in.

"Hell no. Look, I'm not some sharecropper who pulled himself up from poverty. I grew up in Falls Church, Virginia. Father's a federal bureaucrat. Middle class all the way."

"I see," Patil said, eyes never leaving the rutted road. "Your race bespeaks an entirely different culture, but you subscribe to the program of modern rationalism."

Clay looked at them quizzically. "Don't you?"

"As scientists, of course. But that is not all of life."

"Um," Clay said.

A thousand times before he had endured the affably condescending attention of whites, their curious eyes searching his face. No matter what the topic, they somehow found a way to inquire indirectly after his *true* feelings, his *natural* emotions. And if he waved away these intrusions, there remained in their heavy-lidded eyes a subtle skepticism, doubts about his authenticity. Few gave him space to simply be a suburban man with darker skin, a man whose interior landscape was populated with the same icons of Middle America as their own. Hell, his family name came from slaves, given as a tribute to Henry Clay, a nineteenth-century legislator. He had never expected to run into stereotyping in India, for chrissakes.

Still, he was savvy enough to lard his talk with some homey touches, jimmy things up with collard greens and black-eyed peas and street jive. It might put them at ease.

"I believe a li'l rationality could help," he said.

"Um." Singh's thin mouth twisted doubtfully. "Perhaps you should regard India as the great chessboard of our times, Professor. Here we have arisen from the great primordial agrarian times, fashioned our gods from our soil and age. Then we had orderly thinking, with all its assumptions, thrust upon us by the British. Now they are all gone, and we are suspended between the miasmic truths of the past, and the failed strictures of the present."

Clay looked out the dirty window and suppressed a smile. Even the physicists here spouted mumbo jumbo. They even appeared solemnly respectful of the devotees, who were just crazies like the women by the cow. How could anything solid come out of such a swamp? The chances that their experiment was right dwindled with each lurching, damp mile.

They climbed into the long range of hills before the Kolar fields. Burned-tan grass shimmered in the prickly heat. Sugarcane fields and rice paddies stood bone dry. In the villages, thin figures shaded beneath awnings, canvas tents, lean-tos, watched them pass. Lean faces betrayed only dim, momentary interest, and Clay wondered if his uncomfortable disguise was necessary outside Bangalore.

Without stopping they ate their lunch of dried fruit and thin, brown bread. In a high hill town, Patil stopped to refill his water bottle at a well. Clay peered out and saw down an alley a gang of stick-figure boys chasing a dog. They hemmed it in, and the bedraggled hound fled yapping from one side of their circle to the other. The animal whined at each rebuff and twice lost its footing on the cobblestones, sprawling, only to scramble up again and rush on. It was a cruel game, and the boys were strangely silent, playing without laughter. The dog was tiring; they drew in their circle.

A harsh edge to the boys' shouts made Clay slide open the van door. Several men were standing beneath a rust-scabbed sheet-metal awning nearby, and their eyes widened when they saw his face. They talked rapidly among themselves. Clay hesitated. The boys down the alley rushed the dog. They grabbed it as it yapped futilely and tried to bite them. They slipped twine around its jaws and silenced it. Shouting, they hoisted it into the air and marched off.

Clay gave up and slammed the door. The men came from under the awning. One rapped on the window. Clay just stared at them. One thumped on the door. Gestures, loud talk.

Patil and Singh came running, shouted something. Singh pushed the men away, chattering at them while Patil got the van started. Singh slammed the door in the face of a man with wild eyes. Patil gunned the engine and they ground away.

"They saw me and—"

"Distrust of outsiders is great here," Singh said. "They may be connected with the devotees, too."

"Guess I better keep my hat on."

"It would be advisable."

"I don't know, those boys—I was going to stop them pestering that dog. Stupid, I guess, but—"

"You will have to avoid being sentimental about such matters," Patil said severely.

"Uh—sentimental?"

"The boys were not playing."

"I don't—"

"They will devour it," Singh said.

Clay blinked. "Hindus eating meat?"

"Hard times. I am really quite surprised that such an animal has survived this long," Patil said judiciously. "Dogs are uncommon. I imagine it was wild, living in the countryside, and ventured into town in search of garbage scraps."

The land rose as Clay watched the shimmering heat bend and flex the seemingly solid hills.

5

They pulled another dodge at the mine. The lead green van veered off toward the main entrance, a cluster of concrete buildings and conveyer assemblies. From a distance, the physicists in the blue van watched a ragtag group envelop the van before it had fully stopped.

"Devotees," Singh said abstractedly. "They search each vehicle for evidence of our research."

"Your graduate students, the mob'll let them pass?"

Path peered through binoculars. "The crowd is administering a bit of a pushing about," he said in his oddly cadenced accent, combining lofty British diction with a singsong lilt.

"Damn, won't the mine people get rid—"

"Some mine workers are among the crowd, I should imagine," Patil said. "They are beating the students."

"Well, can't we—"

"No time to waste." Singh waved them back into the blue van. "Let us make use of this diversion."

"But we could—"

"The students made their sacrifice for you. Do not devalue it, please."

Clay did not take his eyes from the nasty knot of confusion until they lurched over the ridgeline. Patil explained that they had been making regular runs to the main entrance for months now, to establish a pattern that drew devotees away from the secondary entrance.

"All this was necessary, and insured that we could bring in a foreign inspector," Patil concluded. Clay awkwardly thanked him for the attention to detail. He wanted to voice his embarrassment at having students roughed up simply to provide him cover, but something in the offhand manner of the two Indians made him hold his tongue.

The secondary entrance to the Kolar mine was a wide, tin-roofed shed like a low aircraft hangar. Girders crisscrossed it at angles that seemed to Clay dictated less by the constraints of mechanics than by the whims of the construction team. Cables looped among the already rusting steel struts and sang low notes in the rot-tinged wind that brushed his hair.

Monkeys chattered and scampered high in the struts. The three men walked into the shed, carrying cases. The cables began humming softly. The weave above their heads tightened with pops and sharp cracks. Clay realized that the seemingly random array was a complicated hoist that had started to pull the elevator up from miles beneath their feet. The steel lattice groaned as if it already knew how much work it had to do.

When it arrived, he saw that the elevator was a huge rattling box that reeked of machine oil. Clay lugged his cases in. The walls were broad wooden slats covered with chicken wire. Heat radiated from them. Patil stabbed a button on the big control board and they dropped quickly. The numbers of the levels zipped by on an amber digital display. A single dim yellow bulb cast shadows onto the wire. At the fifty-third level the bulb went out. The elevator did not stop.

In the enveloping blackness Clay felt himself lighten, as if the elevator was speeding up.

"Do not be alarmed," Patil called. "This frequently occurs."

Clay wondered if he meant the faster fall or the light bulb. In the complete dark, he began to see blue phantoms leaping out from nowhere.

Abruptly he became heavy—and thought of Einstein's *Gedanken* experiment, which equated a man in an accelerating elevator to one standing on a planet. Unless Clay could see outside, check that the massive earth raced by beyond as it clasped him further into its depths, in principle he could be in either situation. He tried to recall how Einstein had reasoned from an imaginary elevator to deduce that matter curved space-time, and could not.

Einstein's elegant proof was impossibly far from the pressing truth of *this* elevator. Here Clay plunged in thick murk, a weight of tortured air prickling his nose, making sweat pop from his face. Oily, moist heat climbed into Clay's sinuses.

And he was not being carried aloft by this elevator, but allowed to plunge into heavy, primordial darkness—Einstein's vision in reverse. No classical coolness separated him from the press of a raw, random world. That European mindscape—Galileo's crisp cylinders rolling obediently down inclined planes, Einstein's dispassionate observers surveying their smooth geometries like scrupulous bank clerks—evaporated here like yesterday's stale champagne. Sudden anxiety filled his throat. His stomach tightened and he tasted acrid gorge. He opened his mouth to shout, and as if to stop him, his own knees sagged with suddenly returning weight, physics regained.

A rattling thump—and they stopped. He felt Patil slam aside the rattling gate. A sullen glow beyond bathed an ornate brass shrine to a Hindu god. They came out into a steepled room of carved rock. Clay felt a breath of slightly cooler air from a cardboard-mouthed conduit nearby.

"We must force the air down from above." Patil gestured. "Otherwise this would read well over a hundred and ten Fahrenheit." He proudly pointed to an ancient battered British thermometer, whose mercury stood at ninety-eight.

They trudged through several tunnels, descended another few hundred feet on a ramp, and then followed gleaming railroad tracks. A white bulb every ten meters threw everything into exaggerated relief, shadows stabbing everywhere. A brown cardboard sign proclaimed from the ceiling:

FIRST EVER COSMIC RAY
NEUTRINO INTERACTION
RECORDED HERE IN APRIL 1965

For over forty years, teams of devoted Indian physicists had labored patiently inside the Kolar gold fields. For half a century, India's high mountains and deep mines had made important cosmic-ray experiments possible with inexpensive instruments. Clay recalled how a joint Anglo-Indian-Japanese team had detected that first neutrino, scooped it from the unending cosmic sleet that penetrated even to this depth. He thought of unsung Indian physicists sweating here, tending the instruments and tracing the myriad sources of background error. Yet they themselves were background for the original purpose of the deep holes: Two narrow cars clunked past, full of chopped stone.

"Some still work this portion," Patil's clear voice cut through the muffled air. "Though I suspect they harvest little."

Pushing the rusty cars were four wiry men, so sweaty that the glaring bulbs gave their sliding muscles a hard sheen like living stone. They wore filthy cloths wrapped around their heads, as if they needed protection against the low ceiling rather than the heat. As Clay stumbled on, he felt that there might be truth to this, because he sensed the mass above as a precarious judgment over them all, a sullen presence. Einstein's crisp distinctions, the clean certainty of the *Gedanken* experiments, meant nothing in this blurred air.

They rounded an irregular curve and met a niche neatly cut off by a chain-link fence.

PROTON STABILITY EXPERIMENT
TATA INSTITUTE OF FUNDAMENTAL
RESEARCH, BOMBAY
80th Level Heathcote Shaft, KFG
2300 meters depth

These preliminaries done, the experiment itself began abruptly. Clay had expected some assembly rooms, an office, refrigerated 'scope cages. Instead, a few meters ahead the tunnel opened in all directions. They stood before a huge bay roughly cleaved from the brown rock.

And filling the vast volume was what seemed to be a wall as substantial as the rock itself. It was an iron grid of rusted pipe. The pipes were square, not round, and dwindled into the distance. Each had a dusty seal, a pressure dial, and a number painted in white. Clay estimated them to be at least a hundred feet long. They were stacked Lincoln-log fashion. He walked to the edge of the bay and looked down. Layers of pipe tapered away below to a distant floodlit floor and soared to meet the gray ceiling above.

"Enormous," he said.

"We expended great effort in scaling up our earlier apparatus," Singh said enthusiastically.

"As big as a house."

Patil said merrily, "An American house, perhaps. Ours are smaller."

A woman's voice nearby said, "And nothing lives in this iron house, Professor Clay."

Clay turned to see a willowy Indian woman regarding him with a wry smile. She seemed to have come out of the shadows, a brown apparition in shorts and a scrupulously white blouse, appearing full-blown where a moment before there had been nothing. Her heavy eyebrows rose in amusement.

"Ah, this is Mrs. Buli," Patil said.

"I keep matters running here, while my colleagues venture into the world," she said.

Clay accepted her coolly offered hand. She gave him one quick, well-defined shake and stepped back. "I can assist your assessment, perhaps."

"I'll need all your help," he said sincerely. The skimpy surroundings already made him wonder if he could do his job at all.

"Labor we have," she said. "Equipment, little."

"I brought some cross-check programs with me," he said.

"Excellent," Mrs. Buli said. "I shall have several of my graduate students assist you, and of course I offer my full devotion as well."

Clay smiled at her antique formality. She led him down a passage into the soft fluorescent glow of a large data-taking room. It was crammed with terminals and a bank of disk drives, all meshed by the usual cable spaghetti. "We keep our computers cooler than our staff, you see," Mrs. Buli said with a small smile.

They went down a ramp, and Clay could feel the rock's steady heat. They came out onto the floor of the cavern. Thick I-beams roofed the stone box.

"Over a dozen lives, that was the cost of this excavation," Singh said.

"That many?"

"They attempted to save on the cost of explosives," Patil said with a stern look.

"Not that such will matter in the long run," Singh said mildly. Clay chose not to pursue the point.

Protective bolts studded the sheer rock, anchoring crossbeams that stabilized the tower of pipes. Scaffolding covered some sections of the blocky, rusty pile. Blasts of compressed air from the surface a mile above swept down on them from the ceiling, flapping Clay's shirt.

Mrs. Buli had to shout, the effort contorting her smooth face. "We obtained the pipes from a government program that attempted to improve the quality of plumbing in the cities. A failure, I fear. But a godsend for us."

Patil was pointing out electrical details when the air conduits wheezed into silence. "Hope that's temporary," Clay said in the sudden quiet.

"A minor repair, I am sure," Patil said.

"These occur often," Singh agreed earnestly.

Clay could already feel prickly sweat oozing from him. He wondered how often they had glitches in the circuitry down here, awash in pressing heat, and how much that could screw up even the best diagnostics.

Mrs. Buli went on in a lecturer's singsong. "We hired engineering students—there are many such, an oversupply—to thread a single wire down the bore of each pipe. We sealed each, then welded them together to make lengths of a hundred feet. Then we filled them with argon and linked them with a high-voltage line. We have found that a voltage of 280 keV . . ."

Clay nodded, filing away details, noting where her description differed from that of the NSF. The Kolar group had continuously modified their experiment for decades, and this latest enormous expansion was badly documented. Still, the principle was simple. Each pipe was held at high voltage, so that when a charged particle passed through, a spark leaped. A particle's path was followed by counting the segments of triggered pipes. This mammoth stack of iron was a huge Geiger counter.

He leaned back, nodding at Buli's lecture, watching a team of men at the very top. A loud clang rang through the chasm. Sparks showered, burnt-orange and blue. The garish plumes silhouetted the welders and sent cascades of sparks down through the lattice of pipes. For an instant Clay imagined he was witnessing cosmic rays sleeting down through the towering house of iron, illuminating it with their short, sputtering lives.

"—and I am confident that we have seen well over fifty true events," Mrs. Buli concluded with a jaunty upward tilt of her chin.

"What?" Clay struggled back from his daydreaming. "That many?"

She laughed, a high tinkling. "You do not believe!"

"Well, that is a lot."

"Our detecting mass is now larger," Mrs. Buli said.

"Last we heard it was five hundred tons," Clay said carefully. The claims wired to the NSF and the Royal Society had been skimpy on details.

"That was years ago," Patil said. "We have redoubled our efforts, as you can see."

"Well, to see that many decays, you'd have to have a hell of a lot of observing volume," Clay said doubtfully.

"We can boast of five *thousand* tons, Professor Clay," Mrs. Buli said.

"Looks it," Clay said laconically to cover his surprise. It would not do to let them think they could overwhelm him with magnitudes. Question was, did they have the telltale events?

The cooling air came on with a thump and *whoosh*. Clay breathed it in deeply, face turned up to the iron house where protons might be dying, and sucked in swarming scents of the parched countryside miles above.

6

He knew from the start that there would be no eureka moment. Certainty was the child of tedium.

He traced the tangled circuitry for two days before he trusted it. "You got to open the sack 'fore I'll believe there's a cat in there," he told Mrs. Buli, and then had to explain that he was joking.

Then came a three-day trial run, measuring the exact sputter of decay from a known radioactive source. System response was surprisingly good. He found their techniques needlessly Byzantine, but workable. His null checks of the detectors inside the pipes came up goose-egg clean.

Care was essential. Proton decay was rare. The Grand Unified Theories which had enjoyed such success in predicting new particles had also sounded a somber note through all of physics. Matter was mortal. But not very mortal, compared with the passing flicker of a human lifetime.

The human body had about 10^{29} neutrons and protons in it. If only a tiny fraction of them decayed in a human lifetime, the radiation from the disintegration would quickly kill everyone of cancer. The survival of even small life forms implied that the protons inside each nucleus had to survive an average of nearly a billion billion years.

So even before the Grand Unified Theories, physicists knew that protons lived long. The acronym for the theories was GUTs, and a decade earlier graduate students like Clay had worn T-shirts with insider jokes like IT TAKES GUTS TO DO PARTICLE PHYSICS. But proving that there was some truth to the lame nerd jests took enormous effort.

The simplest of the GUTs predicted a proton lifetime of about 10^{31} years, immensely greater than the limit set by the existence of life. In fact, it was far longer even than the age of the universe, which was only a paltry 2×10^{10} years old.

One could check this lifetime by taking one proton and watching it for 10^{31} years. Given the short attention span of humans, it was better to assemble 10^{31} protons and watch them for a year, hoping one would fizzle.

Physicists in the United States, Japan, Italy, and India had done that all through the 1980s and 1990s. And no protons had died.

Well, the theorists had said, the mathematics must be more complicated. They discarded certain symmetry groups and thrust others forward. The lifetime might be 10^{32} years, then.

The favored method of gathering protons was to use those in water. Western physicists carved swimming pools six stories deep in salt mines and eagerly watched for the characteristic blue pulse of dying matter. Detecting longer lifetimes meant waiting longer, which nobody liked, or adding more protons. Digging bigger swimming pools was easy, so attention had turned to the United States and Japan . . . but still, no protons died. The lifetime exceeded 10^{32} years.

The austerity of the 1990s had shut down the ambitious experiments in the West. Few remembered this forlorn experiment in Kolar, wedded to watching the cores of iron rods for the quick spurt of decay. When political difficulties cut off contact, the already beleaguered physicists in the West assumed the Kolar effort had ceased.

But Kolar was the deepest experiment, less troubled by the hail of cosmic rays that polluted the Western data. Clay came to appreciate that as he scrolled through the myriad event-plots in the Kolar computer cubes.

There were 9×10^9 recorded decays of all types. The system rejected obvious garbage events, but there were many subtle enigmas. Theory said that protons died because the quarks that composed them could change their identities. A seemingly capricious alteration of quarky states sent the proton asunder, spitting forth a zoo of fragments. Neutrons were untroubled by this, for in free space they decayed anyway, into a proton and electron. Matter's end hinged, finally, on the stability of the proton alone.

Clay saw immediately that the Kolar group had invested years in their software. They had already filtered out thousands of phantom events that imitated true proton decay. There were eighteen ways a proton could die, each with a different signature of spraying light and particle debris.

The delicate traceries of particle paths were recorded as flashes and sparkles in the house of iron outside. Clay searched through endless graphic printouts, filigrees woven from digital cloth.

"You will find we have pondered each candidate event," Mrs. Buli said mildly on the sixth day of Clay's labors.

"Yeah, the analysis is sharp," he said cautiously. He was surprised at the high level of the work but did not want to concede anything yet.

"If any ambiguity arose, we discarded the case."

"I can see that."

"Some pions were not detected in the right energy range, so of course we omitted those."

"Good."

Mrs. Buli leaned over to show him a detail of the cross-checking program, and he caught a heady trace of wildflowers. Her perfume reminded him abruptly that her sari wrapped over warm, ample swells. She had no sagging softness, no self-indulgent bulgings. The long oval of her face and her ample lips conveyed a fragile sensuality . . .

He wrenched his attention back to physics and stared hard at the screen.

Event vertices were like time-lapse photos of traffic accidents, intersections exploding, screaming into shards. The crystalline mathematical order of physics led to riots of incandescence. And Clay was judge, weighing testimony after the chaos.

7

He had insisted on analyzing the several thousand preliminary candidates himself, as a double blind against the Kolar group's software. After nine days, he had isolated sixty-seven events that looked like the genuine article.

Sixty-five of his agreed with Mrs. Buli's analysis. The two holdouts were close, Clay had to admit.

"Nearly on the money," he said reflectively as he stared at the Kolar software's array.

"You express such values," Mrs. Buli said. "Always a financial analogy."

"Just a way of speaking."

"Still, let us discard the two offending events."

"Well, I'd be willing—"

"No, no, we consider only the sixty-five." Her almond eyes gave no hint of slyness.

"They're pretty good bets, I'd say." Her eyebrows arched. "Only a manner of speech."

"Then you feel they fit the needs of theory."

Her carefully balanced way of phrasing made him lean forward, as if to compensate for his judge's role. "I'll have to consider all the other decay modes in detail. Look for really obscure processes that might mimic the real thing."

She nodded. "True, there is need to study such."

Protons could die from outside causes, too. Wraithlike neutrinos spewed forth by the sun penetrated even here, shattering protons. Murderous muons lumbered through as cosmic rays, plowing furrows of exploding nuclei.

Still, things looked good. He was surprised at their success, earned by great labor. "I'll be as quick about it as I can."

"We have prepared a radio link that we can use, should the desire come."

"Huh? What?"

"In case you need to reach your colleagues in America."

"Ah, yes."

To announce the result, he saw. To get the word out. But why the rush?

It occurred to him that they might doubt whether he himself would get out at all.

8

They slept each night in a clutch of tin lean-tos that cowered down a raw ravine. Laborers from the mine had slept there in better days, and the physicists had gotten the plumbing to work for an hour each night. The men slept in a long shed, but gave Clay a small wooden shack. He ate thin, mealy gruel with them each evening, carefully dropping purification tablets in his water, and was rewarded with untroubled bowels. He lost weight in the heat of the mine, but the nights were cool and the breezes that came then were soft with moisture.

The fifth evening, as they sat around a potbellied iron stove in the men's shed, Patil pointed to a distant corrugated metal hut and said, "There we have concealed a satellite dish. We can knock away the roof and transmit, if you like."

Clay brightened. "Can I call home?"

"If need be."

Something in Patil's tone told him a frivolous purpose was not going to receive their cooperation.

"Maybe tomorrow?"

"Perhaps. We must be sure that the devotees do not see us reveal it."

"They think we're laborers?"

"So we have convinced them, I believe."

"And me?"

"You would do well to stay inside."

"Um. Look, got anything to drink?"

Patil frowned. "Has the water pipe stopped giving?"

"No, I mean, you know—a drink. Gin and tonic, wasn't that what the Brits preferred?"

"Alcohol is the devil's urine," Patil said precisely.

"It won't scramble my brains."

"Who can be sure? The mind is a tentative instrument."

"You don't want any suspicion that I'm unreliable, that it?"

"No, of course not," Singh broke in anxiously.

"Needn't worry," Clay muttered. The heat below and the long hours of tedious work were wearing him down. "I'll be gone soon's I can get things wrapped up."

"You agree that we are seeing the decays?"

"Let's say things're looking better."

Clay had been holding back even tentative approval. He had expected some show of jubilation. Patil and Singh simply sat and stared into the flickering coals of the stove's half-open door.

Slowly Patil said, "Word will spread quickly."

"Soon as you transmit it on that dish, sure."

Singh murmured, "Much shall change."

"Look, you might want to get out of here, go present a paper—"

"Oh no, we shall remain," Singh said quickly.

"Those devotees could give you trouble if they find—"

"We expect that this discovery, once understood, shall have great effects," Patil said solemnly. "I much prefer to witness them from my home country."

The cadence and mood of this conversation struck Clay as odd, but he put it down to the working conditions. Certainly they had sacrificed a great deal to build and run this experiment amid crippling desolation.

"This result will begin the final renunciation of the materialistic worldview," Singh said matter-of-factly.

"Huh?"

"In peering at the individual lives of mere particles, we employ the reductionist hammer," Patil explained. "But nature is not like a salamander, cut into fragments."

"Or if it were," Singh added, "once the salamander is so sliced, try to make it do its salamander walk again." A broad white grin split the gloom of nightfall.

"The world is an implicate order, Dr. Clay. All parts are hinged to each other."

Clay frowned. He vaguely remembered a theory of

quantum mechanics which used that term—"implicate order," meaning that a deeper realm of physical theory lay beneath the uncertainties of wave mechanics. Waves that took it into their heads to behave like particles, and the reverse—these were supposed to be illusions arising from our ignorance of a more profound theory. But there was no observable consequence of such notions, and to Clay such mumbo jumbo from theorists who never got their hands dirty was empty rhapsodizing. Still, he was supposed to be the diplomat here.

He gave a judicial nod. "Yeah, sure—but when the particles die, it'll all be gone, right?"

"Yes, in about 10^{34} years," Patil said. "But the *knowledge* of matter's mortality will spread as swiftly as light, on the wind of our transmitter."

"So?"

"You are an experimentalist, Dr. Clay, and thus—if you will forgive my putting it so—addicted to cutting the salamander." Patil made a steeple of his fingers, sending spindly shadows rippling across his face. "The world we study is conditioned by our perceptions of it. The implied order is partially from our own design."

"Sure, quantum measurement, uncertainty principle, all that." Clay had sat through all the usual lectures about this stuff and didn't feel like doing so again. Not in a dusty shed with his stomach growling from hunger. He sipped at his cup of weak Darjeeling and yawned.

"Difficulties of measurement reflect underlying problems," Patil said. "Even the Westerner Plato saw that we perceive only imperfect modes of the true, deeper world."

"What deeper world?" Clay sighed despite himself.

"We do not know. We *cannot* know."

"Look, we make our measurements, we report. Period."

Amused, Singh said, "And that is where matters end?"

Patil said, "Consensual reality, that is your 'real' world, Professor Clay. But our news may cause that bland, unthinking consensus to falter."

Clay shrugged. This sounded like late-night college bullshit sessions among boozed-up science nerds. Patty-cake pantheism, quantum razzle-dazzle, garbage philosophy. It was one thing to be open-minded and another to let your brains fall out. Was *every*body on this wrecked continent a booga-booga type? He had to get out.

"Look, I don't see what difference—"

"Until the curtain of seeming surety is swept away," Singh put in.

"Surety?"

"This world—this universe!—has labored long under the illusion of its own permanence." Singh spread his hands, animated in the flickering yellow glow. "We might die, yes, the sun might even perish—but the universe went on. Now we prove otherwise. There cannot help but be profound reactions."

He thought he saw what they were driving at. "A Nobel Prize, even."

To his surprise, both men laughed merrily. "Oh no," Patil said, arching his eyebrows. "No such trifles are expected!"

9

The boxy meeting room beside the data bay was packed. From it came a subdued mutter, a fretwork of talk laced with anticipation.

Outside, someone had placed a small chalky statue of a grinning elephant. Clay hesitated, stroked it. Despite the heat of the mine, the elephant was cool.

"The workers just brought it down," Mrs. Buli explained with a smile. "Our Hindu god of auspicious beginnings."

"Or endings," Patil said behind her. "Equally."

Clay nodded and walked into the trapped, moist heat of the room. Everyone was jammed in, graduate students and laborers alike, their dhotis already showing sweaty crescents. Clay saw the three students the devotees had beaten and exchanged respectful bows with them.

Perceiving some need for ceremony, he opened with lengthy praise for the endless hours they had labored, exclaiming over how startled the world would be to learn of such a facility. Then he plunged into consideration of each candidate event, his checks and counter-checks, vertex corrections, digital-array flaws, mean free paths, ionization rates, the artful programming that deflected the myriad possible sources of error. He could feel tension rising in the room as he cast the events on the inch-thick wall screen, calling them forth from the files in his cubes. Some he threw into 3-D, to show the full path through the cage of iron that had captured the death rattle of infinity.

And at the end, all cases reviewed, he said quietly, "You have found it. The proton lifetime is very nearly 10^{34} years."

The room burst into applause, wide grins and wild shouts as everyone pressed forward to shake his hand.

10

Singh handled the message to the NSF. Clay also constructed a terse though detailed summary and sent it to the International Astronomical Union for release to the worldwide system of observatories and universities.

Clay knew this would give a vital assist to his career. With the Kolar team staying here, he would be their only spokesman. And this was very big, media-mesmerizing news indeed.

The result was important to physicists and astronomers alike, for the destiny of all their searches ultimately would be sealed by the faint failures of particles no eye would ever see. In 10^{34} years, far in the depths of space, the great celestial cities, the galaxies, would be ebbing. The last red stars would flicker, belch, and gutter out. Perhaps life would have clung to them and found a way to persist against the growing cold. Cluttered with the memorabilia of the ages, the islands of mute matter would turn at last to their final conqueror—not entropy's still hand, but this silent sputter of protons.

Clay thought of the headlines: UNIVERSE TO END. What would *that* do to harried commuters on their way to work?

He watched Singh send the stuttering messages via the big satellite dish, the corrugated tin roof of the shed pulled aside, allowing him to watch burnt-gold twilight seep across the sky. Clay felt no elation, as blank as a drained capacitor. He had gone into physics because of the sense it gave of grasping deep mysteries. He could look at bridges and trace the vectored stability that ruled them. When his daughter asked why the sky was blue, he actually knew, and could sketch out a simple answer. It had never occurred to him to fear flying, because he knew the Bernoulli equation for the pressure that held up the plane.

But this result . . .

Even the celebratory party that evening left him unmoved. Graduate students turned out in their best khaki. Sitar music swarmed through the scented air, ragas thumping and

156

weaving. He found his body swaying to the refractions of tone and scale.

"It is a pity you cannot learn more of our country," Mrs. Buli remarked, watching him closely.

"Right now I'm mostly interested in sleep."

"Sleep is not always kind." She seemed wry and distant in the night's smudged humidity. "One of our ancient gods, Brahma, is said to sleep—and we are what he dreams."

"In that case, for you folks maybe he's been having a nightmare lately."

"Ah yes, our troubles. But do not let them mislead you about India. They pass."

"I'm sure they will," Clay replied, dutifully diplomatic.

"You were surprised, were you not, at the outcome?" she said piercingly.

"Uh, well, I had to be skeptical."

"Yes, for a scientist certainty is built on deep layers of doubt."

"Like my daddy said, in the retail business deal with everybody, but count your change."

She laughed. "We have given you a bargain, perhaps!"

He was acutely aware that his initial doubts must have been obvious. And what unsettled him now was not just the hard-won success here, but their strange attitude toward it.

The graduate students came then and tried to teach him a dance. He did a passable job, and a student named Venkatraman slipped him a glass of beer, forbidden vice. It struck Clay as comic that the Indian government spent much energy to suppress alcohol but did little about the population explosion. The students all laughed when he made a complicated joke about booze, but he could not be sure whether they meant it. The music seemed to quicken, his heart thumping to keep up with it. They addressed him as Clay*ji,* a term of respect, and asked his opinion of what they might do next with the experiment. He shrugged, thinking 'Nother *job,* sahib? and suggested using it as a detector for neutrinos from supernovas. That had paid off when the earlier generation of neutrino detectors picked up the 1987 supernova.

The atom bomb, the 1987 event, now this—particle physics, he realized uncomfortably, was steeped in death. The sitar slid and rang, and Mrs. Buli made arch jokes to go with the spicy salad. Still, he turned in early.

11

To be awakened by a soft breeze. A brushing presence, sliding cloth . . . He sensed her sari as a luminous fog. Moonlight streaming through a lopsided window cast shimmering auras through the cloth as she loomed above him. Reached for him. Lightly flung away his sticky bedclothes.

"I—"

A soft hand covered his mouth, bringing a heady savor of ripe earth. His senses ran out of him and into the surrounding dark, coiling in air as he took her weight. She was surprisingly light, though thick-waisted, her breasts like teacups compared with the full curves of her hips. His hands slid and pressed, finding a delightful slithering moisture all over her, a sheen of vibrancy. Her sari evaporated. The high planes of her face caught vagrant blades of moonlight, and he saw a curious tentative, expectant expression there as she wrapped him in soft pressures. Her mouth did not so much kiss his as enclose it, formulating an argument of sweet rivulets that trickled into his porous self. She slipped into place atop him, a slick clasp that melted him up into her, a perfect fit, slick with dark insistence. He closed his eyes, but the glow diffused through his eyelids, and he could see her hair fanning through the air like motion underwater, her luxuriant weight bucking, trembling as her nails scratched his shoulders, musk rising smoky from them both. A silky muscle milked him at each heart-thump. Her velvet mass orbited above their fulcrum, bearing down with feathery demands, and he remembered brass icons, gaudy Indian posters, and felt above him Kali strumming in fevered darkness. She locked legs around him, squeezing him up into her surprisingly hard muscles, grinding, drawing forth, pushing back. She cried out with great heaves and lungfuls of the thickening air, mouth going slack beneath hooded eyes, and he shot sharply up into her, a convulsion that poured out all the knotted aches in him, delivering them into the tumbled steamy earth—

12

—and next, with no memories between, he was stumbling with her . . . down a gully . . . beneath slanting silvery moonlight.

"What—what's—"

"Quiet!" She shushed him like a schoolmarm.

He recognized the rolling countryside near the mine. Vague forms flitted in the distance. Wracked cries cut the night.

"The devotees," Mrs. Buli whispered as they stumbled on. "They have assaulted the mine entrance."

"How'd we—"

"You were difficult to rouse," she said with a sidelong glance.

Was she trying to be amusing? The sudden change from mysterious super-charged sensuality back to this clipped, formal professionalism disoriented him.

"Apparently some of our laborers had a grand party. It alerted the devotees to our presence, some say. I spoke to a laborer while you slept, however, who said that the devotees knew of your presence. They asked for you."

"Why me?"

"Something about your luggage and a telephone call home."

Clay gritted his teeth and followed her along a path that led among the slumped hills, away from their lodgings. Soon the mine entrance was visible below. Running figures swarmed about it like black gnats. Ragged chants erupted from them. A *waarrrk waarrrk* sound came from the hangar, and it was some moments until Clay saw long chains of human bodies hanging from the rafters, swinging themselves in unison.

"They're pulling down the hangar," he whispered.

"I despair for what they have done inside."

He instinctively reached for her and felt the supple warmth he had embraced seemingly only moments before. She turned and gave him her mouth again.

"We—back there—why'd you come to me?"

"It was time. Even we feel the joy of release from order, Professor Clay."

"Well, sure . . ." Clay felt illogically embarrassed, embracing a woman who still had the musk of the bed about her, yet who used his title. "But . . . how'd I get here? Seems like—"

"You were immersed. Taken out of yourself."

"Well, yeah, it was good, fine, but I can't remember anything."

She smiled. "The best moments leave no trace. That is a signature of the implicate order."

Clay breathed in the waxy air to help clear his head. More mumbo jumbo, he thought, delivered by her with an open, expectant expression. In the darkness it took a moment to register that she had fled down another path.

"Where'll we go?" he gasped when he caught up.

"We must get to the vans. They are parked some kilometers away."

"My gear—"

"Leave it."

He hesitated a moment, then followed her. There was nothing irreplaceable. It certainly wasn't worth braving the mob below for the stuff.

They wound down through bare hillsides dominated by boulders. The sky rippled with heat lightning. Puffy clouds scudded quickly in from the west, great ivory flashes working among them. The ground surged slightly.

"Earthquake?" he asked.

"There were some earlier, yes. Perhaps that has excited the devotees further tonight, put their feet to running."

There was no sign of the physics team. Pebbles squirted from beneath his boots—he wondered how he had managed to get them on without remembering it—and recalled again her hypnotic sensuality. Stones rattled away down into narrow dry washes on each side. Clouds blotted out the moonglow, and they had to pick their way along the trail.

Clay's mind spun with plans, speculations, jittery anxiety. Mrs. Buli was now his only link to the Western fragment of India, and he could scarcely see her in the shadows. She moved with liquid grace, her sari trailing, sandals slapping. Suddenly she crouched down. "More."

Along the path came figures bearing lanterns. They moved silently in the fitful silvery moonlight. There was no place to hide, and the party had already seen them.

"Stand still," she said. Again the crisp Western diction, yet her ample hips swayed slightly, reminding him of her deeper self.

Clay wished he had a club, a knife, anything. He made himself stand beside her, hands clenched. For once his blackness might be an advantage.

The devotees passed, eyes rapt. Clay had expected them to be singing or chanting mantras or rubbing beads—but not shambling forward as if to their doom. The column barely glanced at him. In his baggy cotton trousers and formless shirt, he hoped he was unremarkable. A woman passed nearby, apparently carrying something across her back. Clay blinked. Her hands were nailed to the ends of a beam, and she carried it proudly, palms bloody, half crucified. Her face was serene, eyes focused on the roiling sky. Behind her was a man bearing a plate. Clay thought the shambling figure carried marbles on the dish until he peered closer and saw an iris, and realized the entire plate was packed with eyeballs. He gasped and faces turned toward him. Then the man was gone along the path, and Clay waited, holding his breath against a gamy stench he could not name. Some muttered to themselves, some carried religious artifacts, beads and statuettes and drapery, but none had the fervor of the devotees he had seen before. The ground trembled again.

And out of the dark air came a humming. Something struck a man in the line and he clutched at his throat, crying hoarsely. Clay leaped forward without thinking. He pulled the man's hands away. Lodged in the narrow of the throat was something like an enormous cockroach with fluttering wings. It had already embedded its head in the man. Spiky legs furiously scrabbled against the soiled skin to dig deeper. The man coughed and shouted weakly, as though the thing was already blocking his throat.

Clay grabbed its hind legs and pulled. The insect wriggled with surprising strength. He saw the hind stinger too late. The sharp point struck a hot jolt of pain into his thumb. Anger boiled in him. He held on despite the pain and yanked the thing free. It made a sucking sound coming out. He hissed with revulsion and violently threw it down the hillside.

The man stumbled, gasping, and then ran back down the path, never even looking at them. Mrs. Buli grabbed Clay, who was staggering around in a circle, shaking his hand. "I will cut it!" she cried.

He held still while she made a precise crosscut and drained the blood.

"What . . . what *was* that?"

"A wasp-thing from the pouches that hang on our trees."

"Oh yeah. One of those bio tricks."

"They are still overhead."

Clay listened to the drone hanging over them. Another devotee shrieked and slapped the back of his neck. Clay numbly watched the man run away. His hand throbbed, but he could feel the effects ebbing. Mrs. Buli tore a strip from her sari and wrapped his thumb to quell the bleeding.

All this time, devotees streamed past them in the gloom. None took the slightest notice of Clay. Some spoke to themselves.

"Western science doesn't seem to bother 'em much now," Clay whispered wryly.

Mrs. Buli nodded. The last figure to pass was a woman who limped, sporting an arm that ended not in a hand but in a spoon, nailed to a stub of cork.

He followed Mrs. Buli into enveloping darkness. "Who were they?"

"I do not know. They spoke seldom and repeated the same words. Dharma and samsara, terms of destiny."

"They don't care about us?"

"They appear to sense a turning, a resolution." In the fitful moonglow her eyes were liquid puzzles.

"But they destroyed the experiment."

"I gather that knowledge of your Western presence was like the wasp-things. Irritating, but only a catalyst, not the cause."

"What *did* make them—"

"No time. Come."

They hurriedly entered a thin copse of spindly trees that lined a streambed. Dust stifled his nose and he breathed through his mouth. The clouds raced toward the horizon with unnatural speed, seeming to flee from the west. Trees swayed before an unfelt wind, twisting and reaching for the shifting sky.

"Weather," Mrs. Buli answered his questions. "Bad weather."

They came upon a small crackling fire. Figures crouched around it, and Clay made to go around, but Mrs. Buli walked straight toward it. Women squatted, poking sticks into the flames. Clay saw that something moved on the sticks. A momentary shaft of moonlight showed the oily skin of snakes, tiny eyes crisp as crystals, the shafts poking from yawning white mouths that still moved. The women's faces of stretched yellow skin anxiously watched the blackening, sizzling snakes, turning them. The fire hissed as though raindrops fell upon it, but Clay felt nothing wet, just the dry rub of a fresh abrading wind. Smoke wrapped the women in gray wreaths, and Mrs. Buli hurried on.

So much, so fast. Clay felt rising in him a leaden conviction born of all he had seen in this land. So many people, so much pain—how could it matter? The West assumed that the individual was important, the bedrock of all. That was why

the obliterating events of the West's own history, like the
Nazi Holocaust, by erasing humans in such numbing numbers, cast grave doubt on the significance of any one. India
did something like that for him. Could a universe which produced so many bodies, so many minds in shadowed torment,
care a whit about humanity? Endless, meaningless duplica-
tion of grinding pain . . .

A low mutter came on the wind, like a bass theme
sounding up from the depths of a dusty well.

Mrs. Buli called out something he could not understand.
She began running, and Clay hastened to follow. If he lost her
in these shadows, he could lose all connection.

Quickly they left the trees and crossed a grassy field rutted
by ancient agriculture and prickly with weeds. On this flat
plain he could see that the whole sky worked with twisted
light, a colossal electrical discharge feathering into more
branches than a gnarled tree. The anxious clouds caught blue
and burnt-yellow pulses and seemed to relay them, like the
countless transformers and capacitors and voltage drops that
made a worldwide communications net, carrying staccato
messages laced with crackling punctuations.

"The vans," she panted.

Three brown vans crouched beneath a canopy of thin
trees, further concealed beneath khaki tents that blended in
with the dusty fields. Mrs. Buli yanked open the door of the
first one. Her fingers fumbled at the ignition.

"The key must be concealed," she said quickly.

"Why?" he gasped, throat raw.

"They are to be always with the vans."

"Uh-huh. Check the others."

She hurried away. Clay got down on his knees, feeling the
lip of the van's undercarriage. The ground seemed to heave
with inner heat, dry and rasping, the pulse of the planet. He

finished one side of the van and crawled under, feeling along the rear axle. He heard a distant plaintive cry, as eerie and forlorn as the call of a bird lost in fog.

"Clay*ji?* None in the others."

His hand touched a small slick box high up on the axle. He plucked it from its magnetic grip and rolled out from under.

"If we drive toward the mine," she said, "we can perhaps find others."

"Others, hell. Most likely we'll run into devotees."

"Well, I—"

Figures in the trees. Flitting, silent, quick.

"Get in."

"But—"

He pushed her in and tried to start the van. Running shapes in the field. He got the engine started on the third try and gunned it. They growled away. Something hard shattered the back window into a spider web, but then Clay swerved several times and nothing more hit them.

After a few minutes his heart-thumps slowed, and he turned on the headlights to make out the road. The curves were sandy and he did not want to get stuck. He stamped on the gas.

Suddenly great washes of amber light streamed across the sky, pale lances cutting the clouds. "My God, what's happening?"

"It is more than weather."

Her calm, abstracted voice made him glance across the seat. "No kidding."

"No earthquake could have collateral effects of this order."

He saw by the dashboard lights that she wore a lapis lazuli necklace. He had felt it when she came to him, and now its deep blues seemed like the only note of color in the deepening folds of night.

"It must be something far more profound."

"What?"

The road narrowed straight through a tangled terrain of warped trees and oddly shaped boulders. Something rattled against the windshield like hail, but Clay could see nothing.

"We have always argued, some of us, that the central dictate of quantum mechanics is the interconnected nature of the observer and the observed."

The precise, detached lecturer style again drew his eyes to her. Shadowed, her face gave away no secrets.

"We always filter the world," she said with dreamy momentum, "and yet are linked to it. How much of what we see is in fact taught us, by our bodies, or by the consensus reality that society trains us to see, even before we can speak for ourselves?"

"Look, that sky isn't some problem with my eyes. It's *real*. Hear that?" Something big and soft had struck the door of the van, rocking it.

"And we here have finished the program of materialistic science, have we not? We flattered the West by taking it seriously. As did the devotees."

Clay grinned despite himself. It was hard to feel flattered when you were fleeing for your life.

Mrs. Buli stretched lazily, as though relaxing into the clasp of the moist night. "So we have proven the passing nature of matter. What fresh forces does that bring into play?"

"Huh!" Clay spat back angrily. "Look here, we just sent word out, reported the result. How—"

"So that by now millions, perhaps billions of people know that the very stones that support them must pass."

"So what? Just some theoretical point about subnuclear

physics, how's that going to—"

"Who is to say? What avatar? The point is that we were believed. Certain knowledge, universally correlated, surely has some impact—"

The van lurched. Suddenly they jounced and slammed along the smooth roadway. A bright plume of sparks shot up behind them, brimming firefly yellow in the night.

"Axle's busted!" Clay cried. He got the van stopped. In the sudden silence, it registered that the motor had gone dead.

They climbed out. Insects buzzed and hummed in the hazy gloom.

The roadway was still straight and sure, but on all sides great blobs of iridescent water swelled up from the ground, making colossal drops. The trembling half-spheres wobbled in the frayed moonlight. Silently, softly, the bulbs began to detach from the foggy ground and gently loft upward. Feathery luminescent clouds above gathered on swift winds that sheared their edges. These billowing, luxuriant banks snagged the huge teardrop shapes as they plunged skyward.

"I . . . I don't . . ."

Mrs. Buli turned and embraced him. Her moist mouth opened a redolent interior continent to him, teeming and blackly bountiful, and he had to resist falling inward, a tumbling silvery bubble in a dark chasm.

"The category of perfect roundness is fading," she said calmly.

Clay looked at the van. The wheels had become ellipses. At each revolution they had slammed the axles into the roadway, leaving behind long scratches of rough tar.

He took a step.

She said, "Since we can walk, the principle of pivot and lever, of muscles pulling bones, survives."

"How . . . this doesn't . . ."

"But do our bodies depend on roundness? I wonder." She carefully lay down on the blacktop.

The road straightened precisely, like joints in an aged spine popping as they realigned.

Angles cut their spaces razor-sharp, like axioms from Euclid.

Clouds merged, forming copious tinkling hexagons.

"It is good to see that some features remain. Perhaps these are indeed the underlying Platonic beauties."

"What?" Clay cried.

"The undying forms," Mrs. Buli said abstractly. "Perhaps that one Western idea was correct after all."

Clay desperately grasped the van. He jerked his arm back when the metal skin began flexing and reshaping itself.

Smooth glistening forms began to emerge from the rough, coarse earth. Above the riotous, heaving land the moon was now a brassy cube. Across its face played enormous black cracks like mad lightning.

Somewhere far away his wife and daughter were in this, too. *G'bye, Daddy. It's been real.*

Quietly the land began to rain upward. Globs dripped toward the pewter, filmy continent swarming freshly above. Eons measured out the evaporation of ancient sluggish seas.

His throat struggled against torpid air. "Is . . . Brahma . . . ?"

"Awakening?" came her hollow voice, like an echo from a distant gorge.

"What happens . . . to . . . us?"

His words diffracted away from him. He could now see acoustic waves, wedges of compressed, mute atoms crowding in the exuberant air. Luxuriant, inexhaustible riches burst from beneath the ceramic certainties he had known.

"Come." Her voice seeped through the churning ruby air.

Centuries melted between them as he turned. A being he recognized without conscious thought spun in liquid air.

Femina, she was now, and she drifted on the new wafting currents. He and she were made of shifting geometric elements, molecular units of shape and firm thrust. A wan joy spread through him.

Time that was no time did not pass, and he and she and the impacted forces between them were pinned to the forever moment that cascaded through them, all of them, the billions of atomized elements that made them, all, forever.

Immersion

Africa came to them in air thick with smells. In the dry, prickly heat was a promise of the primitive, of ancient themes beyond knowing.

Warily Kelly gazed out at the view beyond the formidable walls. "We're safe here from the animals?"

"I imagine so. Those walls are high and there are guard canines. Wirehounds, I believe."

"Good." She smiled in a way that he knew implied a secret was about to emerge. "I really urged you to come here to get you away from Helsinki."

"Not to study chimpanzees?"

"Oh, that might be useful—or better still, fun," she said with wifely nonchalance. "My main consideration was that if you had stayed in Helsinki you might be dead."

He stopped looking at the striking scenery. She was serious. "You think they would . . . ?"

"They could, which is a better guide to action than trying to guess woulds."

"I see." He didn't, but he had learned to trust her judgment in matters of the world. "You think Imperial Industrie would . . . ?"

"Knock you off for undermining their case? Sure. But they'd be careful."

"But the case is over. Settled."

He had made a successful sociometric prediction of political and economic trends in central Europe. His reputation was powerful enough to cause a fall in certain product markets. Economics increasingly resembled fashion: Commodities racheted like hemlines.

Imperial Industrie had lost considerably—a fortune, even for a world-wrapping corporation. They had accused him of manipulating the markets, but he had in all honesty merely tried to test his new model of sociohistory. His reputation among econometric circles was enough to circulate the predictions. Imperial Industrie, he thought, was simply being childish. Reason would prevail there soon enough.

"You intend to make more predictions, don't you?" she asked.

"Well, once I get some better parameter fixes—"

"There. Then they can lose again. Imperial doesn't like losing."

"You exaggerate." He dismissed the subject with a wave of his hand.

Then too, he thought, perhaps he did need a vacation. To be on a rough, natural world—he had forgotten, in the years buried in Helsinki, how vivid wild things could be. Greens and yellows leaped out, after decades amid steel and glitter.

Here the sky yawned impossibly deep, unmarked by the graffiti of aircraft, wholly alive to the flapping wonder of birds. Bluffs and ridges looked like they had been shaped hastily with a putty knife. Beyond the station walls he could see a sole tree thrashed by an angry wind. Its topknot finally blew off in a pocket of wind, fluttering and fraying over somber flats like a fragmenting bird. Distant, eroded mesas had yellow streaks down their shanks which, as they met the forest, turned a burnt orange tinge that suggested the rot of rust. Across the valley, where the chimps ranged, lay a dusky canopy hidden behind low gray clouds and raked by winds. A thin, cold rain fell there and Leon wondered what it was like to cower beneath the sheets of moisture, without hope of shelter or warmth. Perhaps Helsinki's utter predictability was better, but he wondered, breathing in the tangy air.

He pointed to the distant forest. "We're going there?" He liked this fresh place, though the jungle was foreboding. It had been a long time since he had even worked with his hands, alongside his father, back on the farm.

"Don't start judging."

"I'm anticipating."

She grinned. "You always have a longer word for it, no matter what I say."

"The treks look a little, well—touristy."

"Of course. We're tourists."

The land here rose up into peaks as sharp as torn tin. In the thick trees beyond, mist broke on gray, smooth rocks. Even here, high up the slope of an imposing ridge, the Excursion Station was hemmed in by slimy, thick-barked trees standing in deep drifts of dead, dark leaves. With rotting logs half buried in the wet layers, the air swarmed so close it was like breathing damp opium.

Kelly stood, her drink finished. "Let's go in, socialize."

He followed dutifully and right away knew it was a mistake. Most of the indoor stim-party crowd was dressed in rugged safari-style gear. They were ruddy folk, faces flushed with excitement or perhaps just enhancers. Leon waved away the bubbleglass-bearing waiter; he disliked the way it dulled his wits. Still, he smiled and tried to make small talk.

This turned out to be not merely small, but microscopic. "Where are you from? Oh, *Helsinki*—What's it like? We're from (fill in the city)—have you ever heard of it?" Of course he had not.

Most were Primitivists, drawn by the unique experience available here. It seemed to him that every third word in their conversation was *natural* or *vital,* delivered like a mantra.

"What a *relief* to be away from straight lines," a thin man said.

"Um, how so?" Leon said, trying to seem interested.

"Well, of course straight lines don't exist in nature. They have to be put there by humans." He sighed. "I love to be free of straightness!"

Leon instantly thought of pine needles; strata of metamorphic rock; the inside edge of a half-moon; spider-woven silk strands; the line along the top of a breaking ocean wave; crystal patterns; white quartz lines on granite slabs; the far horizon of a vast calm lake; the legs of birds; spikes of cactus; the arrow dive of a raptor; trunks of young, fast-growing trees; wisps of high windblown clouds; ice cracks; the two sides of the V of migrating birds; icicles.

"Not so," he said, but no more.

His habit of laconic implication was trampled in the headlong talk, of course; the enhancers were taking hold. They all chattered on, excited by the prospect of immersing themselves in the lives of the creatures roaming the valleys below. He listened, not commenting, intrigued. Some wanted to share the world view of herd animals, others of hunters, some of birds. They spoke as though they were entering some athletic event, and that was not his view at all. Still, he stayed silent.

He finally escaped with Kelly into the small park beside the Excursion Station, designed to make guests familiar with local conditions before their treks or immersions. There were whole kraals of domestic stock. The unique assets, the genetically altered and enhanced animals, were nowhere near, of course.

He stopped and stared at the kraals and thought again about sociohistory. His mind kept diving at it from many angles. He had learned to just stand aside and let his thoughts run.

Animals. Was there a clue here? Despite millennia of trying, humans had domesticated few animals. To be domesticated, wild beasts had to have an entire suite of traits. Most had to be herd animals, with instinctive submission patterns which humans could co-opt. They had to be placid; herds that bolt at a strange sound and can't tolerate intruders are hard to keep. Finally, they had to be willing to breed in captivity. Most humans didn't want to court and copulate under the watchful gaze of others, and neither did most animals.

So here there were sheep and goats and cows, slightly adapted by biotechnology but otherwise unremarkable. Except for the chimps. They were unique artifacts of this preservation deep in the rugged laboratory of central Africa. A wirehound came sniffing, checking them out, muttering an unintelligible apology. "Interesting," he remarked to Kelly, "that Primitivists still want to be protected from the wild, by the domesticated."

"Well, of course. This fellow is *big*."

"Not sentimental about the natural state? We were once just another type of large mammal."

"The natural state might be a pleasant place to visit, but . . ."

"Right, wouldn't want to live there. Still, I want to try the chimps."

"What? An immersion?" Her eyebrows lifted in mild alarm.

"As long as we're here, why not?"

"I don't . . . well, I'll think about it."

"You can bail out at any time, they say."

She nodded, pursed her lips. "Um."

"We'll *feel* at home—the way chimps do."

"You believe everything you read in a brochure?"

"I did some research. It's a well-developed tech."

Her lips had a skeptical tilt. "Um."

He knew by now better than to press her. Let time do his work.

The canine, quite large and alert, snuffled at his hand and slurred, "Goood naaaght, suuur." He stroked it. In its eyes he saw a kinship, an instant rapport that he did not need to think about. For one who dwelled in his head so much, this was a welcome rub of reality.

Significant evidence, he thought. *We have a deep past together.* Perhaps that was why he wanted to immerse in a chimp. To go far back, peering beyond the vexing state of being human.

"We're certainly closely related, yes," Expert Specialist Ruben said. He was a big man, tanned and muscular and casually confident. He was both a safari guide and immersion specialist, with a biology background. He did research using immersion techniques, but keeping the Station going soaked up most of his time, he said. "Chimp-riding is the best immersion available."

Leon looked skeptical. *Pan troglodytes* had hands with thumbs, the same number of teeth as humans, no tails, but he had never felt great empathy for them, seen behind bars in a zoo.

Ruben waved a big hand at the landscape below the Station. "We hope to make them more useful. We haven't tried training them much, beyond research purposes. Remember, they're supposed to be kept wild. The original UN grant stipulated that."

"Tell me about your research," Leon said. In his experience, no scientist ever passed up a chance to sing his own song. He was right.

They had taken human DNA and chimp DNA—Ruben said, waxing enthusiastically on—then unzipped the double-helix strands in both. Linking one human strand with a chimp strand made a hybrid.

Where the strands complemented, the two then tightly bound in a partial, new double helix. Where they differed, bonding between the strands was weak, intermittent, with whole sections flapping free.

Then they spun the watery solutions in a centrifuge, so the weak sections ripped apart. Closely linked DNA was 98.2 percent of the total. Chimps were startlingly like humans. Less than 2 percent different—yet they lived in forests and invented nothing.

The typical difference between individual people's DNA was a tenth of a percentage point, Ruben said. Roughly, then, chimps were twenty times more different from humans than particular people differed among themselves—genetically. But genes were like levers, supporting vast weights by pivoting about a small fulcrum.

"But we don't *come* from them. We parted company, genetically, six million years ago."

"Do they think like us?" Leon asked.

"Best way to tell is an immersion," Ruben said. "Very best way."

He smiled invitingly, and Leon wondered if Ruben got a commission on immersions. His sales pitch was subtle, shaped for an academic's interest—but still a sales pitch.

Ruben had already made the vast stores of data on chimp movements, population dynamics, and behaviors available to Leon. It was a rich source and with some math modeling might be fertile ground for a simple description, using a truncated version of sociohistory.

"Describing the life history of a species mathematically is one thing," Kelly said. "But living in it . . ."

"Come now," Leon said. Even though he knew the entire Excursion Station was geared to sell the guests safaris and immersions, he was intrigued. " 'I need a change,' you said. 'Get out of stuffy old Helsinki,' you said."

Ruben said warmly, "It's completely safe."

Kelly smiled at Leon tolerantly. "Oh, all right."

He spent the morning studying the chimp data banks. The mathematician in him pondered how to represent their dynamics with a trimmed-down sociohistory. The marble of fate rattling down a cracked slope. So many paths, variables . . .

In the afternoons they took several treks. Kelly did not like the dust and heat and they saw few animals. "What self-respecting beast would want to be seen with these over-dressed Primitivists?" she said. The others could never stop talking; that kept the animals away.

He liked the atmosphere and relaxed into it as his mind kept on working. He thought about this as he stood on the sweeping veranda, drinking pungent fruit juice as he watched a sunset. Kelly stood beside him silently. Raw Africa made it clear that the Earth was an energy funnel, he thought. At the bottom of the gravitational well, Earth captured for use barely a tenth of a percent of the sunlight that fell. Nature built organic molecules with a star's energy. In turn, plants were prey for animals, who could harvest roughly a tenth of the plant's stored energy. Grazers were themselves prey to meat-eaters, who could use about a tenth of the flesh-stored energy. So, he estimated, only about one part in a hundred thousand of a star's lancing energy wound up in the predators.

Wasteful! Yet nowhere had a more efficient engine evolved. Why not? Predators were invariably more intelligent than their prey, and they sat atop a pyramid of very steep slopes. Omnivores had a similar balancing act. Out of that rugged landscape had come humanity.

That fact *had* to matter greatly in any sociohistory. The chimps, then, were essential to finding the ancient keys to the human psyche.

Kelly said, "I hope immersion isn't, well, so hot and sticky."

"Remember, you'll see the world through different eyes."

She snorted. "Just so I can come back whenever I want and have a nice hot bath."

"Compartments"? Kelly shied back. "They look more like caskets."

"They have to be snug, Madam."

ExSpec Ruben smiled amiably—which, Leon sensed, probably meant he wasn't feeling amiable at all. Their conversation had been friendly, the staff here was respectful of the noted Dr. Mattick, but, after all, basically he and Kelly were just more tourists. Paying for a bit of primitive fun, all couched in proper scholarly terms, but—tourists.

"You're kept in fixed status, all body systems running slow but normal," the ExSpec said, popping out the padded networks for inspection. He ran through the controls, emergency procedures, safeguards.

"Looks comfortable enough," Kelly observed begrudgingly.

"Come on," Leon chided. "You promised we would do it."

"You'll be meshed into our systems at all times," Ruben said.

"Even your data library?" Leon asked.

"Sure thing."

The team of ExSpecs booted them into the stasis compartments with deft, sure efficiency. Tabs, pressors, magnetic pickups plated onto his skull to pick up thoughts directly. The very latest tech.

"Ready? Feeling good?" Ruben asked with his professional smile.

Leon was not feeling good (as opposed to feeling well) and he realized part of it was this ExSpec. He had always distrusted bland, assured people. Something about this one bothered him, but he could not say why. Oh well; Kelly was probably right. He needed a vacation. What better way to get out of yourself?

"Good, yes. Ready, yes."

The suspension tech suppressed neuromuscular responses. The customer lay dormant, only his mind engaged with the chimp.

Magnetic webs capped over his cerebrum. Through electromagnetic inductance they interwove into layers of the brain. They routed signals along tiny thread-paths, suppressing many brain functions and blocking physiological processes. All this, so that the massively parallel circuitry of the brain could be inductively linked out, thought by thought. Then it was transmitted to chips embedded in the chimp subject. Immersion.

The technology had ramified throughout the world, quite famously. The ability to distantly manage minds had myriad uses. The suspension tech, however, found its own odd applications.

In certain European classes, women were wedded, then suspended for all but a few hours of the day. Their wealthy husbands awoke them from freeze-frame states only for social and sexual purposes. For more than a half century, the wives experienced a heady whirlwind of places, friends, parties, vacations, passionate hours—but their total accumulated time was only a few years. Their husbands died in what seemed to the wives like short order indeed. They left a wealthy widow of perhaps thirty. Such women were highly sought, and not only for their money. They were uniquely sophisticated, seasoned by a long "marriage." Often, these widows returned the favor, wedding freeze-frame husbands whom they revived for similar uses.

All this Leon had taken with the sophisticated veneer he had cultivated in Helsinki. So he thought his immersion would be comfortable, interesting, the stuff of stim-party talk.

He had thought that he would in some sense *visit* another, simpler, mind.

He did not expect to be swallowed whole.

A good day. Plenty of grubs to eat in a big moist log. Dig them out with my nails, fresh tangy sharp crunchy.

Biggest, he shoves me aside. Scoops out plenty rich grubs. Grunts. Glowers.

My belly rumbles. I back off and eye Biggest. He's got pinched-up face, so I know not to fool with him.

I walk away, I squat down. Get some picking from a fem. She finds some fleas, cracks them in her teeth.

Biggest rolls the log around some to knock a few grubs loose, finishes up. He's strong. Fems watch him. Over by the trees a bunch of fems chatter, suck their teeth. Everybody's sleepy now in early afternoon, lying in the shade. Biggest, though, he waves at me and Hunker and off we go.

Patrol. Strut tall, step out proud. I like it fine. Better than humping even.

Down past the creek and along to where the hoof smells are. That's the shallow spot. We cross and go into the trees sniff-sniffing and there are two Strangers.

They don't see us yet. We move smooth, quiet. Biggest picks up a branch and we do too. Hunker is sniffing to see who these Strangers are and he points off to the hill. Just like I thought, they're Hillies. The worst. Smell bad.

Hillies come onto our turf. Make trouble. We make it back.

We spread out. Biggest, he grunts and they hear him. I'm already moving, branch held up. I can run pretty far without going all-four. The Strangers cry out, big-eyed. We go fast and then we're on them.

They have no branches. We hit them and kick and they grab at us. They are tall and quick. Biggest slams one to the ground. I hit that one so Biggest knows real well I'm with him. Hammer hard, I do. Then I go quick to help Hunker.

His Stranger has taken his branch away. I club the Stranger. He sprawls. I whack him good and Hunker jumps on him and it is wonderful.

The Stranger tries to get up and I kick him solid. Hunker grabs back his branch and hits again and again with me helping hard.

Biggest, his Stranger gets up and starts to run. Biggest whacks his ass with the branch, roaring and laughing.

Me, I got my skill. Special. I pick up rocks. I'm the best thrower, better than Biggest even.

Rocks are for Strangers. My buddies, them I'll scrap

with, but never use rocks. Strangers, though, they deserve to get rocks in the face. I love to bust a Stranger that way.

I throw one clean and smooth and catch the Stranger on the leg. He stumbles and I smack him good with a sharp-edged rock, in the back. He runs fast then and I can see he's bleeding. Stranger leaves drops in the dust.

Biggest laughs and slaps me and I know I'm in good with him.

Hunker is clubbing his Stranger. Biggest takes my club and joins in. The blood all over the Stranger sings warm in my nose and I jump up and down on him. We keep at it like that a long time. Not worried about the other Stranger coming back. Strangers are brave sometime but they know when they have lost.

The Stranger stops moving. I give him one more kick.

No reaction. Dead maybe.

We scream and dance and holler out our joy.

Leon shook his head to clear it. That helped a little.

"You were that big one?" Kelly asked. "I was the female, over by the trees."

"Sorry, I couldn't tell."

"It was . . . different, wasn't it?"

He laughed dryly. "Murder usually is."

"When you went off with the, well, leader—"

"My chimp thinks of him as 'Biggest.' We killed another chimp."

They were in the plush reception room of the immersion facility. Leon stood and felt the world tilt a little and then right itself. "I think I'll stick to historical research for a while."

Kelly smiled sheepishly. "I . . . I rather liked it." He

thought a moment, blinked. "So did I," he said, surprising himself.

"Not the murder—"

"No, of course not. But . . . the *feel*."

She grinned. "Can't get that in Helsinki, Professor."

He spent two days coasting through cool lattices of data in the formidable Station library. It was well-equipped and allowed interfaces with several senses. He patrolled through cool, digital labyrinths.

In the vector spaces portrayed on huge screens, the research data was covered with thick, bulky protocols and scabs of security precautions. All were easily broken or averted, of course, but the chunky abstracts, reports, summaries, and crudely processed statistics still resisted easy interpretation. Occasionally some facets of chimp behavior were carefully hidden away in appendices and sidebar notes, as though the biologists in the lonely outpost were embarrassed by it. Some *was* embarrassing: mating behavior, especially. How could he use this?

He navigated through the 3-D maze and cobbled together his ideas. Could he follow a strategy of analogy?

Chimps shared nearly all their genes with humans, so chimp dynamics should be a simpler version of human dynamics. Could he then analyze chimp troop interactions as a reduced case of sociohistory?

At sunset of the next day he sat with Kelly watching blood-red shafts spike through orange-tinged clouds. Africa was gaudy beyond good taste and he liked it. The food was tangy, too. His stomach rumbled in anticipation of dinner.

He remarked to Kelly, "It's tempting, using chimps to build a sort of toy model of sociohistory."

"But you have doubts."

"They're like us in . . . only they have, well, uh . . ."

"Base, animalistic ways?" She smirked, then kissed him. "My prudish Leon."

"We have our share of beastly behaviors, I know. But we're a lot smarter too."

Her eyelids dipped in a manner he knew by now suggested polite doubt. "They live intensely, you'll have to give them that."

"Maybe we're smarter than we need to be anyway."

"What?" This surprised her.

"I've been reading up on evolution. Plainly, the human brain was an evolutionary overshoot—far more capable than a competent hunter-gatherer needed. To get the better of animals, it would have been enough to master fire and simple stone tools. Such talents alone would have made people the lords of creation, removing selection pressure to change. Instead, all evidence from the brain itself said that change accelerated. The human cerebral cortex added mass, stacking new circuitry atop older wiring. That mass spread over the lesser areas like a thick new skin."

"Considering the state of the world, I'd say we need all the brains we can get," she said skeptically.

"From that layer came musicians and engineers, saints and savants," he finished with a flourish. One of Kelly's best points was her willingness to sit still while he waxed professorially long-winded, even on vacation. "And all this evolutionary selection happened in just a few million years."

Kelly snorted prettily. "Look at it from the woman's point of view. It happened, despite putting mothers in desperate danger in childbirth."

"Uh, how?"

"From those huge baby heads. They're hard to get out. We women are still paying the price for your brains—and for ours."

He chuckled. She always had a special spin on a subject that made him see it fresh. "Then why was it selected for, back then?"

Kelly smiled enigmatically. "Maybe men and women alike found intelligence sexy in each other."

"Really?"

Her sly smile. "How about us?"

"Have you ever watched very many 3-D stars? They don't feature brains, my dear."

"Remember the animals we saw in the Madrid Senso-Zoo? The mating exhibit? It could be that for early humans, brains were like peacock tails, or moose horns—display items, to attract the females. Runaway sexual selection."

"I see, an overplayed hand of otherwise perfectly good cards." He laughed. "So being smart is just a bright ornament."

"Works for me," she said, giving him a wink.

He watched the sunset turn to glowering, ominous crimson, oddly happy. Sheets of light worked across the sky among curious, layered clouds. "Ummm . . ." Kelly murmured.

"Yes?"

"Maybe this is a way to use the research the ExSpecs are doing too. Learn who we were—and therefore who we are."

"Intellectually, it's a jump. In social ways, though, the gap could be less."

Kelly looked skeptical. "You think chimps are only a bit further back in a social sense?"

"Ummm. I wonder if in logarithmic time we might scale from chimps to us, now?"

"A big leap. To do anything you'll need more experience with them." She eyed him. "You like immersion, don't you?"

"Well, yes. It's just . . ."

"What?"

"That ExSpec Ruben, he keeps pushing immersions—"

"That's his job."

"—and he knew who I was."

"So?" She spread her hands and shrugged.

"You're normally the suspicious one. Why should an ExSpec know an obscure mathematician?"

"He looked you up. Data dumps on incoming guests are standard. And in some circles you're hardly obscure. Plenty of people back in Helsinki line up to see you."

"And some would like to see me dead. Say, you're supposed to be the ever-vigilant one." He grinned. "Shouldn't you be encouraging my caution?"

"Paranoia isn't caution. Time spent on nonthreats subtracts from vigilance."

By the time they went in for dinner she had talked him into more immersions.

Hot day in the sun. Dust makes me snort.

That Biggest, he walks by, gets respect right away. Fems and guys alike, they stick out their hands.

Biggest touches them, taking time with each, letting them know he is there. The world is all right.

I reach out to him too. Makes me feel good. I want to be like Biggest, to be big, be as big as him, be *him*.

Fems don't give him any trouble. He wants one, she goes. Hump right away. He's Biggest.

Most males, they don't get much respect. Fems don't want to do with them as much as they do with Biggest. The little males, they huff and throw sand and all that but everybody knows they're not going to be much. No chance they could ever be like Biggest. They don't like that but they are stuck with it.

Me, I'm pretty big. I get respect. Some, anyway.

All the guys like stroking. Petting. Grooming. Fems give it to them and they give it back.

Guys get more though. After it, they're not so gruff.

I'm sitting getting groomed and all of a sudden I smell something. I don't like it. I jump up, cry out. Biggest, he takes notice. Smells it too.

Strangers. Everybody starts hugging each other. Strong smell, plenty of it. Lots of Strangers. The wind says they are near, getting nearer.

They come running down on us from the ridge. Looking for fems, looking for trouble.

I run for my rocks. I always have some handy. I fling one at them, miss. Then they are in among us. It's hard to hit them, they go so fast.

Four Strangers, they grab two fems. Drag them away.

Everybody howling, crying. Dust everywhere.

I throw rocks. Biggest leads the guys against the Strangers.

They turn and run off. Just like that. Got the two fems though and that's bad.

Biggest mad. He pushes around some of the guys, makes noise. He not looking so good now, he let the Strangers in.

Those Strangers bad. We all hunker down, groom each other, pet, make nice sounds.

Biggest, he come by, slap some of the fems. Hump some. Make sure everybody know he's still Biggest.

He don't slap me. He know better than to try. I growl at him when he come close and he pretend not to hear.

Maybe he not so Big any more, I'm thinking.

He stayed with it this time. After the first crisis, when the Stranger chimps came running through, he sat and let himself get groomed for a long time. It really did calm him.

Him? Who was he?

This time he could fully sense the chimp mind. Not below him—that was an evolutionary metaphor—but *around* him. A swarming scattershot of senses, thoughts, fragments like leaves blowing by him in a wind.

And the wind was *emotion*. Blustering gales, howling and whipping in gusts, raining thoughts like soft hammer blows.

These chimps thought poorly, in the sense that he could get only shards, like human musings chopped by a nervous editor. But chimps *felt* intensely.

Of course, he thought—and he could think, nestled in the hard kernel of himself, wrapped in the chimp mind. *Emotions told it what to do, without thinking. Quick reactions demanded that. Strong feeling amplified subtle clues into strong imperatives. Blunt orders from Mother Evolution.*

He saw now that the belief that high order mental experiences like emotion were unique to people was . . . simply conceited. These chimps shared much of the human world view. A theory of chimp sociohistory could be valuable.

He gingerly separated himself from the dense, pressing chimp mind. He wondered if the chimp knew he was here. Yes, it did—dimly. But somehow this did not bother the chimp. He integrated it into his blurred, blunt world. Leon was somewhat like an emotion, just one of many fluttering by and staying a while, then wafting away.

Could he be more than that? He tried getting the chimp to lift its right arm—and it was like lead. He struggled for a while that way with no success. Then he realized his error. He could not overpower this chimp, not as a kernel in a much larger mind.

He thought about this as the chimp groomed a female, picking carefully through coarse hair. The strands smelled good, the air was sweet, the sun stroked him with blades of generous warmth . . .

Emotion. Chimps didn't follow instructions because that simply lay beyond them. They could not understand directions in the human sense. Emotions—those they knew. He had to be an emotion, not a little general giving orders.

He sat for a while simply being this chimp. He learned—or rather, he felt. The troop groomed and scavenged food, males eyeing the perimeter, females keeping close to the young. A lazy calm descended over him, carrying him effortlessly through warm moments of the day. Not since he was a boy had he felt anything like this. A slow, graceful easing, as though there were no time at all, only slices of eternity.

In this mood, he could concentrate on a simple movement—raising an arm, scratching—and create the desire to do it. His chimp responded. To make it happen, he had to *feel* his way toward a goal. Sail before the emotion wind.

Catching a sweet scent on the air. Leon thought about what food that might signal. His chimp meandered upwind, sniffed, discarded the clue as uninteresting. Leon could now smell the reason why: fruit, true, sweet, yes—but inedible for a chimp.

Good. He was learning. And he was integrating himself into the deep recesses of this chimp-mind.

Watching the troop, he decided to name the prominent chimps, to keep them straight: Agile the quick one, Sheelah the sexy one, Grubber the hungry one . . . But what was his own name? His he dubbed Ipan. Not very original, but that was its main characteristic, *I as Pan troglodytes*.

Grubber found some bulb-shaped fruit and the others drifted over to scavenge. The hard fruit smelled a little too young (how did he know that?) but some ate it anyway.

And which of these was Kelly? They had asked to be immersed in the same troop, so one of these—he forced himself to count, though somehow the exercise was like moving heavy weights in his mind—these twenty-two was her. How could he tell? He ambled over to several females who were using sharp-edged stones to cut leaves from branches. They tied the strands together so they could carry food.

Leon peered into their faces. Mild interest, a few hands held out for stroking, an invitation to groom. No glint of recognition in their eyes.

He watched a big fem, Sheelah, carefully wash sand-covered fruit in a creek. The troop followed suit; Sheelah was a leader of sorts, a female lieutenant to Biggest.

She ate with relish, looked around. There was grain growing nearby, past maturity, ripe tan kernels already scattered in the sandy soil. Concentrating, Leon could tell from the faint bouquet that this was a delicacy. A few chimps squatted and picked grains from the sand, slow work. Sheelah did the same, and then stopped, gazing off at the creek. Time passed, insects buzzed. After a while she scooped up sand and kernels and walked to the brook's edge. She tossed it all in. The sand sank, the kernels floated. She skimmed them off and gulped them down, grinning widely.

An impressive trick. The other chimps did not pick up on her kernel-skimming method. Fruit washing was conceptually easier, he supposed, since the chimp could keep the fruit the whole time. Kernel-skimming demanded throwing away the food first, then rescuing it—a harder mental jump.

He thought about her and in response Ipan sauntered over her way. He peered into Sheelah's eyes—and she winked at him. Kelly! He wrapped hairy arms around her in a burst of sweaty love.

"Pure animal love," she said over dinner. "Refreshing."
Leon nodded. "I like being there, living that way."
"I can *smell* so much more."

"Fruit tastes differently when they bite into it." He held up a purple bulb, sliced into it, forked it into his mouth. "To me, this is almost unbearably sweet. To Ipan, it's pleasant, a little peppery. I suppose chimps have been selected for a sweet tooth. It gets them more fast calories."

"I can't think of a more thorough vacation. Not just getting away from home, but getting away from your species."

He eyed the fruit. "And they're so, so . . ."

"Horny?"

"Insatiable."

"You didn't seem to mind."

"My chimp, Ipan? I bail out when he gets into his hump-them-all mood."

She eyed him. "Really?"

"Don't you bail out?"

"Yes, but I don't expect men to be like women."

"Oh?" he said stiffly.

"I've been reading in the ExSpec's research library, while you toy with chimp social movements. Women invest heavily in their children. Men can use two strategies—parental investment, plus 'sow the oats.' " She lifted an eyebrow. "Both must have been selected for in our evolution, because they're both common."

"Not with *me*."

To his surprise, she laughed. "I'm talking in general. My point is: The chimps are much more promiscuous than we are. The males run everything. They help out the females who are carrying their children, I gather, but then they shop around elsewhere *all* the time."

Leon switched into his professional mode; it was decidedly more comfortable, when dealing with such issues. "As the specialists say, they are pursuing a mixed reproductive strategy."

"How polite."

"Polite plus precise."

Of course, he couldn't really be sure Kelly bailed out of Sheelah when a male came by for a quick one. (They were always quick too—thirty seconds or less.) *Could* she exit the chimp mind that quickly? He required a few moments to extricate himself. Of course, if she saw the male coming, guessed his intentions . . .

He was surprised at himself. What role did jealousy have when they were inhabiting other bodies? Did the usual moral code make any sense? Yet to talk this over with her was . . . embarrassing.

He was still the country boy, like it or not.

Ruefully he concentrated on his meal of local "roamerfleisch," which turned out to be an earthy, dark meat in a stew of tangy vegetables. He ate heartily and in response to Kelly's rather obviously amused silence said, "I'd point out that chimps understood commerce too. Food for sex, betrayal of the leader for sex, spare my child for sex, grooming for sex, just about anything for sex."

"It does seem to be their social currency. Short and decidedly not sweet. Just quick lunges, strong sensations, then boom—it's over."

He nodded. "The males need it, the females use it."

"Ummm, you've been taking notes."

"If I'm going to model chimps as a sort of simplified people, then I must."

"Model chimps?" came the assured tones of ExSpec Ruben. "They're not model citizens, if that's what you mean." He gave them a sunny smile and Leon guessed this was more of the obligatory friendliness of this place.

Leon smiled mechanically. "I'm trying to find the variables that could describe chimp behavior."

"You should spend a lot of time with them," Ruben said,

sitting at the table and holding up a finger to a waiter for a drink. "They're subtle creatures."

"I agree," said Kelly. "Do you ride them very much?"

"Some, but most of our research is done differently now." Ruben's mouth twisted ruefully. "Statistical models, that sort of thing. I got this touring idea started, using the immersion tech we had developed earlier, to make money for the project. Otherwise, we'd have had to close."

"I'm happy to contribute," Leon said.

"Admit it—you like it," Kelly said, amused.

"Well, yes. It's . . . different."

"And good for the staid Professor Mattick to get out of his shell," she said.

Ruben beamed. "Be sure you don't take chances out there. Some of our customers think they're superchimps or something."

Kelly's eyes flickered. "What danger is there? Our bodies are in slowtime, back here."

Ruben said, "You're strongly linked. A big shock to a chimp can drive a back-shock in your own neurological systems."

"What sort of shock?" Leon asked.

"Death, major injury."

"In that case," Kelly said to Leon, "I really do not think you should immerse."

Leon felt irked. "Come on! I'm on vacation, not in prison."

"Any threat to you—"

"Just a minute ago you were rhapsodizing about how good for me it was."

"You're too important to—"

"There's really very little danger," Ruben came in smoothly. "Chimps don't die suddenly, usually."

"And I can bail out when I see danger coming," Leon added.

"But *will* you? I think you're getting a taste for adventure."

She was right, but he wasn't going to concede the point. If he wanted a little escape from his humdrum mathematician's routine, so much the better. "I like being out of Helsinki's endless corridors."

Ruben gave Kelly a confident smile. "And we haven't lost a tourist yet."

"How about research staff?" she shot back.

"Well, that was a most unusual—"

"What happened?"

"A chimp fell off a ledge. The human operator couldn't bail out in time and she came out of it paralyzed. The shock of experiencing death through immersion is known from other incidents to prove fatal. But we have systems in place to short-circuit—"

"What else?" she persisted.

"Well, there was one difficult episode. In the early days, when we had simple wire fences." The ExSpec shifted uneasily. "Some predators got in."

"What sort of predators?"

"A primate-pack hunter, Carnopapio grandis. We call them raboons, genetically derived in an experiment two decades ago. They took baboon DNA—"

"How did they get in?" Kelly insisted.

"They're somewhat like a wild hog, with hooves that double as diggers. Carnivores, though. They smelled game— our corralled animals. Dug under the fences."

Kelly eyed the high, solid walls. "These are adequate?"

"Certainly. They're from a genetic experiment. Someone tried to make a predator by raising the earlier baboon stock up onto two legs."

Kelly said dryly, "Evolutionary gambling."

Ruben didn't catch the edge in her voice. "Like most

bipedal predators, the forelimbs are shortened and the head carries forward, balanced by a thick tail they use for signaling to each other. They prey on the biggest herd animals, the gigantelope—another experiment—and eat only the richest meat."

"Why attack humans, then?" she asked.

"They take targets of opportunity too. Chimps, even. When they got into the compound, they went for adult humans, not children—a very selective strategy."

Kelly shivered. "You look at this very . . . objectively."

"I'm a biologist."

"I never knew it could be so interesting," Leon said to defuse her apprehension.

Ruben beamed. "Not as involving as higher mathematics, I'm sure."

Kelly's mouth twisted with wry skepticism. "Do you mind if guests carry weapons inside the compound?"

He had a glimmering of an idea about the chimps, a way to use their behaviors in building a simple toy model of sociohistory. He might be able to use the statistics of chimp troop movements, the ups and downs of their shifting fortunes.

He talked it over with Kelly and she nodded, but beneath it she seemed worried. Since Ruben's remark she was always tut-tutting about safety. He reminded her that she had earlier urged him to do more immersions. "This is a vacation, remember?" he said more than once.

Her amused sidewise glances told him that she also didn't buy his talk about the toy modeling. She thought he just liked romping in the woods. "A country boy at heart," she chuckled.

So the next morning he skipped a planned trek to view the

vast gigantelope herds. He immediately went to the immersion chambers and slipped under. To get some solid work done, he told himself.

The chimps slept in trees and spent plenty of time grooming each other. For the lucky groomer a tick or louse was a treat. With enough, they could get high on some peppery-tasting alkaloid. He suspected the careful stroking and combing of his hair by Kelly was a behavior selected because it improved chimp hygiene. It certainly calmed Ipan, also.

Then it struck him: Chimps groomed rather than vocalizing. Only in crises and when agitated did they call and cry, mostly about breeding, feeding, or self-defense.

They were like people who could not release themselves through the comfort of talk.

And they needed comfort. The core of their social life resembled human societies under stress—in tyrannies, in prisons, in city gangs. Nature red in tooth and claw, yet strikingly like troubled people.

But there were "civilized" behaviors here too. Friendships, grief, sharing, buddies-in-arms who hunted and guarded turf together. Their old got wrinkled, bald, and toothless, yet were still cared for.

Their instinctive knowledge was prodigious. They knew how to make a bed of leaves as dusk fell, high up in trees. They could climb with grasping feet. They felt, cried, mourned—without being able to parse these into neat grammatical packages, so the emotions could be managed, subdued. Instead, emotions drove them.

Hunger was the strongest. They found and ate leaves, fruit, insects, even fair-sized animals. They loved caterpillars.

Each moment, each small enlightenment, sank him deeper into Ipan. He began to sense the subtle nooks and crannies of the chimp mind. Slowly, he gained more cooperative control.

That morning a female found a big tree and began banging it. The hollow trunk boomed like a drum and all the foraging party rushed forward to beat it too, grinning wildly at the noise. Ipan joined in and Leon felt the burst of joy, seethed in it.

Later, coming on a waterfall after a heavy rain, they seized vines and swung among trees—out over the foaming water, screeching with joy as they performed twists and leaps from vine to vine. Like children in a new playground. Leon got Ipan to make impossible moves, wild tumbles and dives, propelling him forward with abandon—to the astonishment of the other chimps.

They were violent in their sudden, peevish moments—in hustling available females, in working out their perpetual dominance hierarchy, and especially in hunting. A successful hunt brought enormous excitement—hugging, kissing, pats. As the troop descended to feed the forest rang with barks, screeches, hoots, and pants. Leon joined the tumult, sang, danced with Sheelah/Kelly.

In some matters he had to restrain his feelings. Rats they ate head first. Larger game they smashed against rocks. They devoured the brains first, a steaming delicacy. Leon gulped—metaphorically, but with Ipan echoing the impulse—and watched, screening his reluctance. Ipan had to eat, after all.

At the scent of predators, he felt Ipan's hair stand on end. Another tangy bouquet made Ipan's mouth water. He gave no mercy to food, even if it was still walking. Evolution in action; those chimps who had showed mercy in the past ate less and left fewer descendants. Those weren't represented here anymore.

For all its excesses, he found the chimps' behavior hauntingly familiar. Males gathered often for combat, for pitching rocks, for blood sports, to work out their hierarchy. Females networked and formed alliances. There were trades of favors for loyalty, alliances, kinship bonds, turf wars, threats and displays, protection rackets, a hunger for "respect," scheming subordinates, revenge—a social world enjoyed by many people that history had judged "great." Much like an emperor's court, in fact.

Did people long to strip away their clothing and conventions, bursting forth as chimps?

Leon felt a flush of revulsion, so strong Ipan shook and fidgeted. Humanity's lot *had* to be different, not this primitive horror.

He could use this, certainly, as a test bed for a full theory. Learn from our nearest genetic neighbors. Then humankind would be self-knowing, captains of themselves. He would build in the imperatives of the chimps, but go far beyond—to true, deep sociohistory.

"I don't see it," Kelly said at dinner.

"But they're so much like us!" He put down his spoon. "We're a brainy chimp—that's a valuable insight. We can probably train them to work for us, do housekeeping."

"I wouldn't have them messing up *my* house."

Adult humans weighed little more than chimps, but were far weaker. A chimp could lift five times more than a well-conditioned man. Human brains were three or four times more massive than a chimp's. A human baby a few months old already had a brain larger than a grown chimp. People had different brain architecture, as well.

But was that the whole story? Give chimps bigger brains and speech, ease off on the testosterone, saddle them with more inhibitions, spruce them up with a shave and a haircut, teach them to stand securely on hind legs—and you had deluxe-model chimps that would look and act rather human. They might pass in a crowd without attracting notice.

Leon said curtly, "Look, my point is that they're close enough to us to make a sociohistory model work."

"To make anybody believe that, you'll have to show that they're intelligent enough to have intricate interactions."

"What about their foraging, their hunting?" he persisted.

"Ruben says they couldn't even be trained to do work around this Excursion Station."

"I'll show you what I mean. Let's master their methods together."

"What method?"

"The basic one. Getting enough to eat."

She bit into a steak of a meaty local grazer, suitably processed and "fat-flensed for the fastidious urban palate," as the brochure had it. Chewing with unusual ferocity, she eyed him. "You're on. Anything a *chimp* can do, I can do better."

Kelly waved at him from within Sheelah. *Let the contest begin.*

The troop was foraging. He let Ipan meander and did not try to harness the emotional ripples that lapped through the chimp mind. He had gotten better at it, but at a sudden smell or sound he could lose his grip. And guiding the blunt chimp mind through anything complicated was like moving a puppet with rubber strings.

Sheelah/Kelly waved and signed to him. *This way.*

They had worked out a code of a few hundred words, using finger and facial gestures, and their chimps seemed to go along with these fairly well. Chimps had a rough language, mixing grunts and shrugs and finger displays. These conveyed immediate meanings, but not in the usual sense of sentences. Mostly they just set up associations.

Tree, fruit, go, Kelly sent. They ambled their chimps over to a clump of promising spindly trunks, but the bark was too slick to climb.

The rest of the troop had not even bothered. *They have forest smarts we lack,* Leon thought ruefully.

What there? he signed to Sheelah/Kelly.

Chimps ambled up to mounds, gave them the once-over, and reached out to brush aside some mud, revealing a tiny tunnel. *Termites,* Kelly signed.

Leon analyzed the situation as chimps drifted in. Nobody seemed in much of a hurry. Sheelah winked at him and waddled over to a distant mound.

Apparently termites worked outside at night, then blocked the entrances at dawn. Leon let his chimp shuffle over to a large tan mound, but he was riding it so well now that the chimp's responses were weak. Leon/Ipan looked for cracks, knobs, slight hollows—and yet when he brushed away some mud, found nothing. Other chimps readily unmasked tunnels. Had they memorized the hundred or more tunnels in each mound?

He finally uncovered one. Ipan was no help. Leon could control, but that blocked up the wellsprings of deep knowledge within the chimp.

The chimps deftly tore off twigs or grass stalks near their mounds. Leon carefully followed their lead. His twigs and grass didn't work. The first lot was too pliant, and when he tried to work them into a twisting tunnel, they collapsed and buckled. He switched to stiffer ones, but those caught on the tunnel walls, or snapped off. From Ipan came little help. Leon had managed him a bit too well.

He was getting embarrassed. Even the younger chimps had no trouble picking just the right stems or sticks. Leon watched a chimp nearby drop a stick that seemed to work. He then picked it up when the chimp moved on. He felt welling up from Ipan a blunt anxiety, mixing frustration and hunger. He could *taste* the anticipation of luscious, juicy termites.

He set to work, plucking the emotional strings of Ipan. This job went even worse. Vague thoughts drifted up from Ipan, but Leon was in control of the muscles now, and that was the bad part.

He quickly found that the stick had to be stuck in about ten centimeters, turning his wrist to navigate it down the twisty channel. Then he had to gently vibrate it. Through Ipan he sensed that this was to attract termites to bite into the stick.

At first he did it too long and when he drew the stick out it was half gone. Termites had bitten cleanly through it. So he had to search out another stick and that made Ipan's stomach growl.

The other chimps were through termite-snacking while Leon was still fumbling for his first taste. The nuances irked him. He pulled the stick out too fast, not turning it enough to ease it past the tunnel's curves. Time and again he fetched forth the stick, only to find that he had scraped the luscious termites off on the walls. Their bites punctured his stick, until it was so shredded he had to get another. The termites were dining better than he.

He finally caught the knack, a fluid slow twist of the wrist, gracefully extracting termites, clinging like bumps. Ipan licked them off eagerly. Leon liked the morsels, filtered through chimp taste buds.

Not many, though. Others of the troop were watching his skimpy harvest, heads tilted in curiosity, and he felt humiliated.

The hell with this, he thought.

He made Ipan turn and walk into the woods. Ipan resisted, dragging his feet. Leon found a thick limb, snapped it off to carrying size, and went back to the mound.

No more fooling with sticks. He whacked the mound solidly. Five more and he had punched a big hole. Escaping termites he scooped up by the delicious handful.

So much for subtlety! he wanted to shout. He tried writing a note for her in the dust but it was hard, forcing the letters out through his suddenly awkward hands. Chimps could handle a stick to fetch forth grubs, but marking a surface was somehow not a ready talent. He gave up.

Sheelah/Kelly came into view, proudly carrying a reed swarming with white-bellied termites. These were the best, a chimp gourmet delicacy. *I better,* she signed.

He made Ipan shrug and signed, *I got more.*

So it was a draw.

Later Kelly reported to him that among the troop he was known now as Big Stick. The name pleased him immensely.

At dinner he felt elated, exhausted, and not in the mood for conversation. Being a chimp seemed to suppress his speech centers. It took some effort to ask ExSpec Ruben about immersion technology. Usually he accepted the routine technomiracles, but understanding chimps meant understanding how he experienced them.

"The immersion hardware puts you in the middle of a chimp's posterior cingulate gyrus," Ruben said over dessert. "Just 'gyrus' for short. That's the brain's center for mediating emotions and expressing them through action."

"*The* brain?" Kelly asked. "What about ours?"

Ruben shrugged. "Same general layout. Chimps' are smaller, without a big cerebrum."

Leon leaned forward, ignoring his steaming cup of Kaf.

"This 'gyrus,' it doesn't give direct motor control?"

"No, we tried that. It disorients the chimp so much, when you leave, it can't get itself back together."

"So we're more subtle," Kelly said.

"We have to be. In chimp males, the pilot light is always on in neurons that control action and aggression—"

"That's why they're more violence-prone?" she asked.

"We think so. It parallels structures in our own brains."

"Really? Men's neurons?" Kelly looked doubtful.

"Human males have higher activity levels in their temporal limbic systems, deeper down in the brain—evolutionarily older structures."

"So why not put me into that level?" Leon asked.

"We place the immersion chips into the gyrus area because we can reach it from the top, surgically. The temporal limbic is way far down, impossible to implant a chip and net."

Kelly frowned. "So chimp males—"

"Are harder to control. Professor Mattick here is running his chimp from the backseat, so to speak."

"Whereas Kelly is running hers from a control center that, for female chimps, is more central?" Leon peered into the distance. "I was handicapped!"

Kelly grinned. "You have to play the hand you're dealt."

"It's not fair."

"Big Stick, biology is destiny."

The troop came upon rotting fruit. Fevered excitement ran through them.

The smell was repugnant and enticing at the same time and at first he did not understand why. The chimps rushed to the overripe bulbs of blue and sickly green, popping open the skins, sucking out the juice.

Tentatively, Leon tried one. The hit was immediate. A

warm feeling of well-being kindled up in him. Of course—the fruity esters had converted into—alcohol! The chimps were quite deliberately setting about getting drunk.

He "let" his chimp follow suit. He hadn't much choice in the matter.

Ipan grunted and thrashed his arms whenever Leon tried to turn him away from the teardrop fruit. And after a while, Leon didn't want to turn away either. He gave himself up to a good, solid drunk. He had been worrying a lot lately, agitated in his chimp, and . . . this was completely natural, wasn't it?

Then a pack of raboons appeared, and he lost control of Ipan.

They come fast. Running two-legs, no sound. Their tails twitch, talking to each other.

Five circle left. They cut off Esa.

Biggest thunder at them. Hunker runs to nearest and it spikes him with its fore-puncher.

I throw rocks. Hit one. It yelps and scurries back. But others take its place. I throw again and they come and the dust and yowling are thick and the others of them have Esa. They cut her with their punch-claws. Kick her with sharp hooves.

Three of them carry her off.

Our fems run, afraid. We warriors stay.

We fight them. Shrieking, throwing, biting when they get close. But we cannot reach Esa.

Then they go. Fast, running on their two hoofed legs. Furling their tails in victory. Taunting us.

We feel bad. Esa was old and we loved her.

Fems come back, nervous. We groom ourselves and know that the two-legs are eating Esa somewhere.

Biggest come by, try to pat me. I snarl.

He Biggest! This thing he should have stopped.

His eyes get big and he slap me. I slap back at him. He slam into me. We roll around in dust. Biting, yowling. Biggest strong, strong and pound my head on ground.

Other warriors, they watch us, not join in.

He beat me. I hurt. I go away.

Biggest starts calming down the warriors. Fems come by and pay their respects to Biggest. Touch him, groom him, feel him the way he likes. He mounts three of them real quick. He feeling Biggest all right.

Me, I lick myself. Sheelah come groom me. After a while I feel better. Already forgotten Esa.

I not forget Biggest beat me though. In front of everybody. Now I hurt, Biggest get grooming.

He let them come and take Esa. He Biggest, he should stop them.

Someday I be all over him. On his back.

Someday I be Bigger.

"When did you bail out?" Kelly asked.

"After Biggest stopped pounding on me . . . uh, on Ipan."

They were relaxing in brilliant sun beside a swimming pool. The heady smells of the forest seemed to awaken in Leon the urge to be down there again, in the valleys of dust and blood. He trembled, took a deep breath. The fighting had been so involving he hadn't wanted to leave, despite the pain. Immersion had a hypnotic quality.

"I know how you feel," she said. "It's easy to totally identify with them. I left Sheelah when those raboons came close. Pretty scary."

"Why did anybody develop them?"

"Plans for using raboons as game, to hunt, Ruben said. Something new and challenging."

"*Hunting?* Business will exploit any throwback primitivism to—" He had been about to launch into a little lecture on how far humanity had come, when he realized that he didn't believe it anymore. "Um."

"You've always thought of people as cerebral. No sociohistory could work if it didn't take into account our animal selves."

"Our worst sins are all our own, I fear." He had not expected that his experiences here would shake him so. This was sobering.

"Not at all." Kelly gave him a lofty look. "I've been reading some of the Station background data on our room computer. Genocide occurs in wolves and chimps alike. Murder is widespread. Ducks and orangutans rape. Even ants have organized warfare and slave raids. Chimps have at least as good a chance of being murdered as do humans, Ruben says. Of all the hallowed hallmarks—speech, art, technology, and the rest—the one which comes most obviously from animal ancestors was genocide."

"You've been learning from Ruben."

"It was a good way to keep an eye on him."

"Better to be suspicious than sorry?"

"Of course," she said blandly. "Can't let Africa soften our brains."

"Well, luckily, even if we are superchimps, throughout human society, communication blurs distinctions between Us and Them."

"So?"

"That blunts the deep impulse to genocide."

She laughed again, this time rather to his annoyance. "You haven't understood history very well. Smaller groups still kill each other off with great relish. In Bosnia, during the reign of Omar the Impaler—"

"I concede, there are small-scale tragedies by the dozens. But on the scale where sociohistory might work, averaging over populations of many millions—"

"What makes you so sure numbers are any protection?" she asked pointedly.

"Well—without further work, I have nothing to say."

She smiled. "How uncharacteristic."

"Until I have a real, working theory."

"One that can allow for widespread genocide?"

He saw her point then. "You're saying I really need this 'animal nature' part of humans."

"I'm afraid so. 'Civilized man' is a contradiction in terms. Scheming, plots, Sheelah grabbing more meat for her young, Ipan wanting to do in Biggest—those things happen in fancy urban nations. They're just better disguised."

"I don't follow."

"People use their intelligence to hide motives. Consider ExSpec Ruben. He made a comment about your working on a 'theory of history' the other evening."

"So?"

"Who told him you were?"

"I don't think I—ah, you think he's checking up on us?"

"He already knows."

"We're just tourists here."

She graced him with an unreadable smile. "I do love your endless, naive way of seeing the world."

Later, he couldn't decide whether she had meant that as a compliment.

Ruben invited him to try a combat sport the Station offered, and Leon accepted. It was an enhanced swordplay using levitation through electrostatic lifters. Leon was slow and inept. Using his own body against Ruben's swift moves made him long for the sureness and grace of Ipan.

Ruben always opened with a traditional posture: one foot forward, his prod-sword making little circles in the air. Leon poked through Ruben's defense sometimes, but usually spent all his lifter energy eluding Ruben's thrusts. He did not enjoy it nearly as much as Ruben. The dry African air seemed to steal energy from him too, whereas Ipan reveled in it.

He did learn bits and pieces about chimps from Ruben, and from trolling through the vast Station library. The man seemed a bit uneasy when Leon probed the data arrays, as though Ruben somehow owned them and any reader was a thief. Or at least that was what Leon took to be the origin of the unease.

He had never thought about animals very much, though he had grown up among them on the farm. Yet he came to feel that they, too, had to be understood.

Catching sight of itself in a mirror, a dog sees the image as another dog. So did cats, fish, or birds. After a while they get used to the harmless image, silent and smell-free, but they did not see it as themselves.

Human children had to be about two years old to do better. Chimps took a few days to figure out that they were looking at themselves. Then they preened before it shamelessly, studied their backs, and generally tried to see themselves differently, even putting leaves on their backs like hats and laughing at the result.

So they could do something other animals could not—get outside themselves, and look back.

They plainly lived in a world charged with echoes and reminiscences. Their dominance hierarchy was a frozen record of past coercion. They remembered termite mounds, trees to drum, useful spots where large water-sponge leaves fell, or grain matured.

All this fed into the toy model he had begun building in his notes—a chimp sociohistory. It used their movements, rivalries, hierarchies, patterns of eating, and mating and dying. Territory, resources, and troop competition for them. He found a way to factor into his equations the biological baggage of dark behaviors. Even the worst, like delight in torture and easy exterminations of other species for short-term gain. All these the chimps had. Just like today's newspaper.

At a dance that evening he watched the crowd with fresh vision.

Flirting was practice mating. He could see it in the sparkle of eyes, the rhythms of the dance. The warm breeze wafting up from the valley brought smells of dust, rot, life. An animal restlessness moved in the room.

He quite liked dancing and Kelly was a lush companion tonight. Yet he could not stop his mind from sifting, analyzing, taking the world before him apart into mechanisms.

The nonverbal template humans used for attract/approach strategies apparently descended from a shared mammalian heritage, Kelly had pointed out. He thought of that, watching the crowd at the bar.

A woman crosses a crowded room, hips swaying, eyes resting momentarily on a likely man, then coyly looking away just as she apparently notices his regard. A standard opening move: *Notice me.*

The second is *I am harmless.* A hand placed palm up on a table or knee. A shoulder shrug, derived from an ancient vertebrate reflex, signifying helplessness. Combine that with a tilted head, which displays the vulnerability of the neck. These commonly appeared when two people drawn to each other have their first conversation—all quite unconsciously.

Such moves and gestures are subcortical, emerging far

below in a swamp of primordial circuitry . . . which had survived until now, because it worked.

Did such forces shape history more than trade balances, alliances, treaties? He looked at his own kind and tried to see it through chimp eyes.

Though human females matured earlier, they did not go on to acquire coarse body hair, bony eye ridges, deep voices, or tough skin. Males did. And women everywhere strove to stay young looking. Cosmetics makers freely admitted their basic role: *We don't sell products; we sell hope.*

Competition for mates was incessant. Male chimps sometimes took turns with females in estrus. They had huge testicles, implying that reproductive advantage had come to those males who produced enough to overwhelm their rivals' contributions. Human males had proportionally smaller testicles.

But humans got their revenge where it mattered. Of all primates, humans had the largest penises.

All primates had separated out as species many millions of years ago. In DNA-measured time, chimps lay six million years from humans. He mentioned to Kelly that only 4 percent of mammals formed pair bonds, were monogamous. Primates rated a bit higher, but not much. Birds were much better at it.

She sniffed. "Don't let all this biology go to your head."

"Oh no, I won't let it get that far."

"You mean it belongs in lower places?"

"Madam, you'll have to be the judge of that."

"Ah, you and your single-entendre humor."

Later that evening, with her, he had ample opportunity to reflect upon the truth that, while it was not always great to be human, it was tremendous fun being a mammal.

They spent a last day immersed in their chimps, sunning

themselves beside a gushing stream. The plane would pick them up early the next morning; Helsinki waited. They packed and entered the immersion capsule and sank into a last reverie. Sun, sweet air, the lassitude of the primitive . . .

Until Biggest started to mount Sheelah.

Leon/Ipan sat up, his head foggy. Sheelah was shrieking at Biggest. She slapped him.

Biggest had mounted Sheelah before. Kelly had bailed out, her mind returning to her body in the capsule.

Something was different now. Ipan hurried over and signed to Sheelah, who was throwing pebbles at Biggest. *What?*

She moved her hands rapidly, signing. *No go.*

She could not bail out. Something was wrong back at the capsule. He could go back himself, tell them.

Leon made the little mental flip that would bail him out.

Nothing happened.

He tried again. Sheelah threw dust and pebbles, backing away from Biggest. Nothing.

No time to think. He stepped between Sheelah and Biggest.

The massive chimp frowned. Here was Ipan, buddy Ipan, getting in the way. Denying him a fem. Biggest seemed to have forgotten the challenge and beating of the day before.

First he tried bellowing, eyes big and white. Then Biggest shook his arms, fists balled.

Leon made his chimp stand still. It took every calming impulse he could muster.

Biggest swung his fist like a club.

Ipan ducked. Biggest missed.

Leon was having trouble controlling Ipan, who wanted to flee. Sheets of fear shot up through the chimp mind, hot yellows in the blue-black depths.

Biggest charged forward, slamming Ipan back. Leon felt the jolt, a stabbing pain in his chest. He toppled backward. Hit hard.

Biggest yowled his triumph. Waved his arms at the sky.

Biggest would get on top, he saw. Beat him again.

Suddenly he felt a deep, raw hatred.

From that red seethe he felt his grip on Ipan tighten. He was riding both with and within the chimp, feeling its raw red fear, overrunning that with an iron rage. Ipan's own wrath fed back into Leon. The two formed a concert, anger building as if reflected from hard walls.

He might not be the same kind of primate, but he knew Ipan. Neither of them was going to get beaten again. And Biggest was not going to get Sheelah/Kelly.

He rolled to the side. Biggest hit the ground where he had been.

Ipan leaped up and kicked Biggest. Hard, in the ribs. Once, twice. Then in the head.

Whoops, cries, dust, pebbles—Sheelah was still bombarding them both. Ipan shivered with boiling energy and backed away.

Biggest shook his dusty head. Then he curled and rolled easily up to his feet, full of muscular grace, face a constricted mask. The chimp's eyes widened, showing white and red.

Ipan yearned to run. Only Leon's rage held him in place.

But it was a static balance of forces. Ipan blinked as Biggest shuffled warily forward, the big chimp's caution a tribute to the damage Ipan had inflicted.

I need some advantage, Leon thought, looking around. He could call for allies. Hunker paced nervously nearby.

Something told Leon that would be a losing strategy. Hunker was still a lieutenant to Biggest. Sheelah was too small to make a decisive difference. He looked at the other chimps, all chattering anxiously—and decided. He picked up a rock.

Biggest grunted in surprise. Chimps didn't use rocks against each other. Rocks were only for repelling invaders. He was violating a social code.

Biggest yelled, waved to the others, pounded the ground, huffed angrily. Then he charged.

Leon threw the rock hard. It hit Biggest in the chest, knocked him down.

Biggest came up fast, madder than before. Ipan scurried back, wanting desperately to run. Leon felt control slipping from him—and saw another rock. Suitable size, two paces back. He let Ipan turn to flee, then stopped and looked at the stone. Ipan didn't want to hold it. Panic ran through him.

Leon poured his rage into the chimp, forced the long arms down. Hands grabbed at the stone, fumbled, got it. Sheer anger made Ipan turn to face Biggest, who was thundering after him. To Leon, Ipan's arm came up in achingly slow motion. He leaned heavily into the pitch. The rock smacked Biggest in the face.

Biggest staggered. Blood ran into his eyes. Ipan caught the iron scent of it, riding on a prickly stench of outrage.

Leon made his trembling Ipan stoop down. There were some shaped stones nearby, made by the fems to trim leaves from branches. He picked up one with a chipped edge.

Biggest waved his head, dizzy.

Ipan glanced at the sober, still faces of his troop. No one had used a rock against a troop member, much less Biggest. Rocks were for Strangers.

A long, shocked silence stretched. The chimps stood rooted, Biggest grunted and peered in disbelief at the blood that spattered into his upturned hand.

Ipan stepped forward and raised the jagged stone, edge held outward. Crude, but a cutting edge.

Biggest flared his nostrils and came at Ipan. Ipan swept the rock through the air, barely missing Biggest's jaw.

Biggest's eyes widened. He huffed and puffed, threw dust, howled. Ipan simply stood with the rock and held his ground. Biggest kept up his anger-display for a long while, but he did not attack.

The troop watched with intense interest. Sheelah came and stood beside Ipan. It would have been against protocols for a female to take part in male-dominance rituals.

Her movement signaled that the confrontation was over. But Hunker was having none of that. He abruptly howled, pounded the ground, and scooted over to Ipan's side.

Leon was surprised. With Hunker maybe he could hold the line against Biggest. He was not fool enough to think that this one standoff would put Biggest to rest. There would be other challenges and he would have to fight them. Hunker would be a useful ally.

He realized that he was thinking in the slow, muted logic of Ipan himself. He *assumed* that the pursuit of chimp status-markers was a given, the great goal of his life.

This revelation startled him. He had known that he was diffusing into Ipan's mind, taking control of some functions from the bottom up, seeping through the deeply buried, walnut-sized gyrus. It had not occurred to him that the chimp would diffuse into *him*. Were they now married to each other in an interlocked web that dispersed mind and self?

Hunker stood beside him, eyes glaring at the other chimps, chest heaving. Ipan felt the same way, madly pinned to the moment. Leon realized that he would have to do something, break this cycle of dominance and submission which ruled Ipan at the deep, neurological level.

He turned to Sheelah. *Get out?* he signed.

No. No. Her chimp face wrinkled with anxiety.

Leave. He waved toward the trees, pointed to her, then him.

She spread her hands in a gesture of helplessness.

It was infuriating. He had so much to say to her and he had to funnel it through a few hundred signs. He chippered in a high-pitched voice, trying vainly to force the chimp lips and palate to do the work of shaping words.

It was no use. He had tried before, idly, but now he wanted to badly and none of the equipment worked. It couldn't. Evolution had shaped brain and vocal chords in parallel. Chimps groomed, people talked.

He turned back and realized that he had forgotten entirely about the status-setting. Biggest was glowering at him. Hunker stood guard, confused at his new leader's sudden loss of interest in the confrontation—and to gesture at a mere fem too.

Leon reared up as tall as he could and waved the stone. This produced the desired effect. Biggest inched back a bit and the rest of the troop edged closer. Leon made Ipan stalk forward boldly. By this time it did not take much effort, for Ipan was enjoying this enormously.

Biggest retreated. Fems inched around Biggest and approached Ipan.

If only I could leave him to the fems' delights, Leon thought.

He tried to bail out again. Nothing. The mechanism wasn't working back at the Excursion Station. And something told him that it wasn't going to get fixed.

He gave the edged stone to Hunker. The chimp seemed surprised but took it. Leon hoped the symbolism of the gesture would penetrate in some fashion because he had no time left to spend on chimp politics. Hunker hefted the rock and looked at Ipan. Then he cried in a rolling, powerful voice, tones rich in joy and triumph.

Leon was quite happy to let Hunker distract the troop. He took Sheelah by the arm and led her into the trees. No one followed.

He was relieved. If another chimp had tagged along, it would have confirmed his suspicions. Ruben might be keeping track.

Still, he reminded himself, absence of evidence is not evidence of absence.

The humans came swiftly, with clatter and booms.

He and Sheelah had been in the trees a while. At Leon's urging they had worked their way a few klicks away from the troop. Ipan and Sheelah showed rising anxiety at being separated from their troop. His teeth chattered and eyes jerked anxiously at every suspicious movement. This was natural, for isolated chimps were far more vulnerable.

The humans landing did not help.

Danger, Leon signed, cupping an ear to indicate the noise of fliers landing nearby.

Sheelah signed, *Where go?*

Away.

She shook her head vehemently. *Stay here. They get us.*

They would indeed, but not in the sense she meant. Leon cut her off curtly, shaking his head. *Danger*. They had never intended to convey complicated ideas with their signs and now he felt bottled up, unable to tell her his suspicions.

Leon made a knife-across-throat gesture. Sheelah frowned.

He bent down and made Ipan take a stick. In soft loam he wrote:

IMPERIAL INDUSTRIE AGENTS. WANT US DEAD.

Sheelah looked dumbfounded. Kelly had probably been operating under the assumption that the failure to bail out was a temporary error. It had lasted too long for that. The landing of people in noisy, intrusive fashion confirmed his hunch. No ordinary team would disturb the animals so much. And nobody would come after them directly. They would fix the immersion apparatus, where the real problem was.

THEY KEEP US HERE, KILL US, BLAME ON ANIMALS.

He had better arguments to back up his case, the slow accumulation of small details in Ruben's behavior. That, and the guess that letting them die in an "accident" while immersed in a chimp was plausible enough to escape an investigation.

The humans went about their noisy business. They were enough, though, to make his case. Sheelah's eyes narrowed, the big brow scowled. *Where?* she signed.

He had no sign for so abstract an idea, so he scribbled with the stick, AWAY. Indeed, he had no plan.

I'LL CHECK, she wrote in the dirt. She set off toward the noise of humans deploying on the valley floor below. To a chimp the din was a dreadful clanking irritation. Leon was not going to let her out of his sight. He followed her. She waved him back but he shook his head and stuck behind her. She gave up and let him follow.

They stayed in bushes until they could get a view of the landing party below. A skirmish line was forming up a few hundred meters away. They were encircling the area where the troop had been. Leon squinted. Chimp eyesight was not good for distance. Humans had been hunters once, and one could tell by the eyes alone.

He thought abstractly about the fact that nearly everybody

needed eye aids by the age of forty. Either civilization was hard on eyes, or maybe humans in prehistory had not lived long enough for eye trouble to rob them of game. Either conclusion was sobering.

The two chimps watched the humans calling to one another and in the middle of them Leon saw Ruben. That confirmed it. That, and that each man and woman carried a weapon.

Beneath his fear he felt something strong, dark.

Ipan trembled, watching humans, a strange awe swelling in his mind. Humans seemed impossibly tall in the shimmering distance, moving with stately, swaying elegance.

Leon floated above the surge of emotion, fending off its powerful effects. The reverence for those distant, tall figures came out of the chimp's dim past.

That surprised him until he thought it over. After all, animals were reared and taught by adults much smarter and stronger. Most species were like chimps, spring-loaded by evolution to work in a dominance hierarchy. Awe was adaptive.

When they met lofty humans with overwhelming power, able to mete out punishment and rewards—literally life and death—something like religious fervor arose in them. Dim, fuzzy, but strong.

Atop that warm, tropical emotion floated a sense of satisfaction at simply being. His chimp was happy to be a chimp, even when seeing a being of clearly superior power and thought.

Ironic, Leon thought. His chimp had just disproved another supposedly human earmark: their self-congratulatory distinction of being the only animal that congratulated itself.

He jerked himself out of his abstractions. How human, to ruminate even when in mortal danger.

CAN'T FIND US ELECTRONICALLY, he scratched in the sand.

MAYBE RANGE IS SHORT, she wrote.

RUBEN SABOTAGED LINK, he printed. She bit her lip, nodded.

Go. We go, he signed.

Sheelah nodded and they crept quickly away. Ipan was reluctant to leave the presence of the revered humans, his steps dragging.

They used chimp modes of patrolling. He and Kelly let their chimps take over, experts at silent movement, careful of every twig. Once they had left the humans behind the chimps grew even more cautious. Chimps had few enemies but the faint scent of a single predator could change the feel of every moment in the wild.

Ipan climbed tall trees and sat for hours surveying open land ahead before venturing forth. He weighed the evidence of pungent droppings, faint prints, bent branches.

They angled down the long slope of the valley and kept in the forest. Leon had only glanced at the big color-coded map of the area all guests received and had trouble recalling much of it. Once he recognized one of the distant, beak-shaped peaks he got his bearings. Kelly spotted a stream snaking down into the main river and that gave them further help, but still they did not know which way lay the Excursion Station. Or how far.

That way? Leon signed, pointing over the distant ridge.

No. That, Kelly insisted.

Far, not.

Why?

The worst part of it all was that they could not talk. He could not say clearly that the technology of immersion worked best at reasonably short range, less than a hundred klicks, say. And it made sense to keep the subject chimps within easy flier distance. Certainly Ruben and the others had gotten to the troop quickly.

Is. He persisted.

Not. She pointed down the valley. *Maybe there.*

He could only hope Kelly got the general idea. Their signs were scanty and he began to feel a broad, rising irritation. Chimps felt and sensed strongly, but they were so *limited.*

Ipan expressed this by tossing limbs and stones, banging on tree trunks. It didn't help much. The need to speak was like a pressure he could not relieve and Kelly felt it too. Sheelah chippered and grunted in frustration.

Beneath his mind he felt the smoldering presence of Ipan. They had never been together this long before and urgency welled up between the two canted systems of mind. Their uneasy marriage was showing greater strains.

Sit. Quiet. She did. He cupped a hand to his ear.

Bad come?

No. Listen—In frustration Leon pointed to Sheelah herself. Blank incomprehension in the chimp's face. He scribbled in the dust, LEARN FROM CHIMPS. Sheelah's mouth opened and she nodded.

They squatted in the shelter of prickly bushes and listened to the sounds of the forest. Scurryings and murmurs came through strongly as Leon relaxed his grip on the chimp. Dust hung in slanted cathedral light, pouring down from the forest canopy in rich yellow shafts. Scents purled up from the forest floor, chemical messengers telling Ipan of potential foods, soft loam for resting, bark to be chewed. Leon gently lifted Ipan's head to gaze across the valley at the peaks . . . musing . . . and felt a faint tremor of resonance.

To Ipan the valley came weighted with significance beyond words. His troop had imbued it with blunt emotions, attached to clefts where a friend fell and died, where the troop found a hoard of fruits, where they met and fought two big cats. It was an intricate landscape suffused with feeling, the chimp mechanism of memory.

Leon faintly urged Ipan to think beyond the ridgeline and felt in response a diffuse anxiety. He bore in on that kernel—and an image burst into Ipan' s mind, fringed in fear. A rectangular bulk framed against a cool sky. The Excursion Station.

There. He pointed for Kelly.

Ipan had simple, strong, apprehensive memories of the place. His troop had been taken there, outfitted with the implants which allowed them to be ridden, then deposited back in their territory.

Far, Kelly signed.

We go?

Hard. Slow.

No stay here. They catch.

Kelly looked as skeptical as a chimp could look. *Fight?*

Did she mean fight Ruben here? Or fight once they reached the Excursion Station? *No here. There.*

Kelly frowned but accepted this. He had no real plan, only the idea that Ruben was ready for chimps out here, and might not be so prepared for them at the Station. There he and Kelly might gain the element of surprise. How, he had no idea.

They studied each other, each trying to catch a glimmer of the other in an alien face. She stroked his earlobe, Kelly's fond calming gesture. Sure enough, it made him tingle. But he could say so little . . . The moment crystallized for him the hopelessness of their situation.

Ruben plainly was trying to kill Leon and Kelly through

Ipan and Sheelah. What would become of their own bodies? The shock of experiencing death through immersion was known to prove fatal. Their bodies would fail from neurological shock, without ever regaining consciousness.

He saw a tear run down Sheelah's cheek. She knew how hopeless matters were too. He swept her up in his arms and, looking at the distant mountains, was surprised to find tears in his own eyes as well.

He had not counted on the river. Men, animals—these problems he had considered. They ventured down to the surging waters where the forest gave the nearest protection and the stream broadened, making the best place to ford.

But the hearty river that chuckled and frothed down the valley was impossible to swim.

Or rather, for Ipan to swim. Leon had been coaxing his chimp onward, carefully pausing when his muscles shook or when he wet himself from anxiety. Kelly was having similar trouble and it slowed them. A night spent up in high branches soothed both chimps, but now at midmorning all the stressful symptoms returned, as Ipan put one foot into the river. Cool, swift currents.

Ipan danced back onto the narrow beach, yelping in dread.

Go? Kelly/Sheelah signed.

Leon calmed his chimp and they tried to get it to attempt swimming. Sheelah displayed only minor anxiety. Leon plumbed the swampy depths of Ipan's memory and found a cluster of distress, centered around a dim remembrance of nearly drowning when a child. When Sheelah helped him he fidgeted, then bolted from the water again.

Go! Sheelah waved long arms upstream and downstream and shook her head angrily.

Leon guessed that she had reasonably clear chimp-memories of the river, which had no easier crossings than this. He shrugged, lifted his hands palm up.

A big herd of gigantelope grazed nearby and some were crossing the river for better grass beyond. They tossed their great heads, as if mocking the chimps. The river was not deep, but to Ipan it was a wall. Leon, trapped by Ipan's solid fear, seethed and could do nothing.

Sheelah paced the shore. She huffed in frustration and looked at the sky, squinting. Her head snapped around in surprise. Leon followed her gaze. A flier was swooping down the valley, coming this way.

Ipan beat Sheelah to the shelter of trees, but not by much. Luckily the gigantelope herd provided a distraction for the flyer. They cowered in bushes as the machine hummed overhead in a circular search pattern. Leon had to quell Ipan's mounting apprehension by envisioning scenes of quiet and peace and food while he and Sheelah groomed each other.

The flier finally went away. They would have to minimize their exposure on open grasslands now.

They foraged for fruit. His mind revolved uselessly and a sour depression settled over him. He was quite neatly caught in a trap, a pawn in politics. Worse, Kelly was in it too. He was no man of action. *Nor a chimp of action, either,* he thought dourly.

As he brought a few overripe bunches of fruit back to their bushes overlooking the river, he heard cracking noises. He crouched down and worked his way uphill and around the splintering sounds. Sheelah was stripping branches from the trees. When he approached she waved him on impatiently, a common chimp gesture remarkably like a human one.

She had a dozen thick branches lined up on the ground. She went to a nearby spindly tree and peeled bark from it in long strips. The noise made Ipan uneasy. Predators would be curious at this unusual sound. He scanned the forest for danger.

Sheelah came over to him, slapped him in the face. She wrote with a stick on the ground, RAFT.

Leon felt particularly stupid as he pitched in. Of course. Had his chimp immersion made him more stupid? Did the effect worsen with time? Even if he got out of this, would he be the same? Many questions, no answers. He forgot about them and worked.

They lashed branches together with bark, crude but serviceable. They found two small fallen trees and used them to anchor the edge of the raft. *I,* Sheelah pointed, and demonstrated pulling the raft.

First, a warm-up. Ipan liked sitting on the raft in the bushes. Apparently the chimp could not see the purpose of the raft yet. Ipan stretched out on the deck of saplings and gazed up into the trees as they swished in the warm winds.

They carried the awkward plane of branches down to the river after another mutual grooming session. The sky was filled with birds but he could see no fliers.

They hurried. Ipan was skeptical about stepping onto the raft when it was halfway into the water, but Leon called up memories filled with warm feeling, and this calmed the quick-tripping heart he could feel knocking in the chimp veins.

Ipan sat gingerly on the branches. Sheelah cast off.

She pushed hard but the river swept them quickly downstream. Alarm spurted in Ipan.

Leon made Ipan close his eyes. That slowed the breathing, but anxiety skittered across the chimp mind like heat lightning forking before a storm. The raft's rocking motion actually helped, making Ipan concentrate on his queasy stomach. Once his eyes flew open when a floating log smacked into the raft, but the dizzying sight of water all around made him squeeze them tight immediately.

Leon wanted to help her, but he knew from the trip-hammer beating of Ipan's heart that panic hovered near. He could not even see how she was doing. He had to sit blind and feel her shoving the raft along.

She panted noisily, struggling to keep it pointed against the river's tug. Spray splashed onto him. Ipan jerked, yelped, pawed anxiously with his feet, as if to run.

A sudden lurch. Sheelah' s grunt cut off with a gurgle and he felt the raft spin away on rising currents. A sickening spin . . .

Ipan jerked clumsily to his feet. Eyes jumped open.

Swirling water, the raft unsteady. He looked down and the branches were coming apart. Panic consumed him. Leon tried to promote soothing images but they blew away before winds of fright.

Sheelah came paddling after the raft but it was picking up speed. Leon made Ipan gaze at the far shore but that was all he could do before the chimp started yelping and scampering on the raft, trying to find a steady place.

It was no use. The branches broke free of their bindings and chilly water swept over the deck. Ipan screamed. He leaped, fell, rolled, jumped up again.

Leon gave up any idea of control. The only hope lay in seizing just the right moment. The raft split down the middle and his half veered heavily to the left. Ipan started away from the edge and Leon fed that, made the chimp step further. In two bounds he took the chimp off the deck and into the water—toward the far shore.

Ipan gave way then to pure blind panic. Leon let the legs and arms thrash—but to each he gave a push at the right moment. He could swim, Ipan couldn't.

The near-aimless flailing held Ipan's head out of water most of the time. It even gained a little headway. Leon kept focused on the convulsive movements, ignoring the cold water—and then Sheelah was there, her jaws agape.

She grabbed him by the scruff of the neck and shoved him toward shore. Ipan tried to grapple with her, climb up her. Sheelah socked him in the jaw. He gasped. She pulled him toward shore.

Ipan was stunned. This gave Leon a chance to get the legs moving in a thrusting stroke. He worked at it, single-minded among the rush and gurgle, chest heaving . . . and after a seeming eternity, felt pebbles beneath his feet. Ipan scrambled up onto the rocky beach on his own.

He let the chimp slap himself and dance to warm up. Sheelah emerged dripping and bedraggled and Ipan swept her up in his thankful arms.

Walking was work and Ipan wasn't having any.

Leon tried to make the chimp cover ground, but now they had to ascend difficult gullies, some mossy and rough. They stumbled, waded, climbed, and sometimes just crawled up the slopes of the valley. The chimps found animal trails, which helped a bit.

Ipan stopped often for food or just to gaze idly into the distance. Soft thoughts flitted like moths through the foggy mind, buoyant on liquid emotional flows which eddied to their own pulse.

Chimps were not made for extended projects. They made slow progress. Night came and they had to climb trees, snagging fruit on the way.

Ipan slept, but Leon did not. Could not.

Their lives were just as much at risk here as the chimps', but the slumbering minds he and Kelly attended had always lived this way. To the chimps, the forest night seeped through as a quiet rain of information, processed as they slept. Their minds keyed vagrant sounds to known non-threats, leaving slumber intact.

Leon did not know the subtle signs of danger and so mistook every rustle and tremor in the branches as danger approaching on soft feet. Sleep came against his will.

In dawn's first pale glow Leon awoke with a snake beside him. It coiled like a green rope around a descending branch, getting itself into striking position. It eyed him and Leon tensed.

Ipan drifted up from his own profound slumber. He saw the snake but did not react with a startled jerk, as Leon feared he might.

A long moment passed between them and Ipan blinked just once. The snake became utterly motionless and Ipan' s heart quickened but he did not move. Then the snake uncoiled and glided away, and the unspoken transaction was done. Ipan was unlikely prey, this green snake did not taste good, and chimps were smart enough to be about other business.

When Sheelah awoke they went down to a nearby chuckling stream for a drink, scavenging leaves and a few crunchy insects on the way. Both chimps nonchalantly peeled away fat black land leeches which had attached to them in the night. The thick, engorged worms sickened Leon, but Ipan pulled them off with the same casualness Leon would have retying loosened shoelaces.

Ipan drank and Leon reflected that the chimp felt no need to clean himself. Normally Leon showered twice a day, before breakfast and before dinner, and felt ill at ease if he sweated, but here he wore the shaggy body comfortably. Had his frequent cleansings been a health measure, like the chimps' grooming? Or a rarified, civilized habit? He dimly remembered that as a boy he had gone for days in happy, sweaty pleasure, and had disliked baths and showers. Somehow Ipan returned him to a simpler sense of self, at ease in the grubby world.

His comfort did not last long. They sighted raboons uphill.

Ipan had picked up the scent, but Leon did not have access to the part of the chimp brain that made scent-picture associations. He had only known that something disturbed Ipan, wrinkling the knobby nose. The sight at short range jolted him.

Thick hindquarters, propelling them in brisk steps. Short forelimbs, ending in sharp claws. Their large heads seemed to be mostly teeth, sharp and white above slitted, wary eyes. A thick brown pelt covered them, growing bushy in the heavy tail they used for balance.

Days before, from the safety of a high tree, Ipan had watched some rip and devour the soft tissues of a gigantelope out on the grasslands. These came sniffing, working downslope in a skirmish line, five of them. Sheelah and Ipan trembled at the sight. They were downwind of the raboons and so beat a retreat in silence.

There were no tall trees here, just brush and saplings. Leon and Sheelah angled away downhill and got some distance, and then saw ahead a clearing. Ipan picked up the faint tang of other chimps, wafting from across the clearing.

He waved to her: *Go.* At the same moment a chorus rose behind them. The raboons had smelled them.

Their wheezing grunts came echoing through the thick bushes. Down the slope there was even less cover, but bigger trees lay beyond. They could climb those.

Ipan and Sheelah hurried across the broad tan clearing on

all fours but they were not quick. Snarling raboons burst into the grass behind them. Leon scampered into the trees—and directly into the midst of a chimp troop.

There were several dozen, startled and blinking. He yelled incoherently, wondering how Ipan would signal to them.

The nearest large male turned, bared teeth, and shrieked angrily. The entire pack took up the call, whooping and snatching up sticks and rocks, throwing them—at Ipan. A pebble hit him on the chin, a branch on the thigh. He fled, Sheelah already a few steps ahead of him.

The raboons came charging across the clearing. In their claws they held small, sharp stones. They looked big and solid but they slowed at the barrage of screeches and squawks coming from the trees.

Ipan and Sheelah burst out into the grass of the clearing and the chimps came right after them. The raboons skidded to a halt.

The chimps saw the raboons but they did not stop or even slow. They still came after Ipan and Sheelah with murderous glee.

The raboons stood frozen, their claws working uneasily.

Leon realized what was happening and picked up a branch as he ran, calling hoarsely to Sheelah. She saw and copied him. He ran straight at the raboons, waving the branch. It was an awkward, twisted old limb, useless, but it looked big. Leon wanted to seem like the advance guard of some bad business.

In the rising cloud of dust and general chaos the raboons saw a large party of enraged chimps emerging from the forest. They bolted.

Squealing, they ran at full stride into the far trees,

Ipan and Sheelah followed, running with the last of their strength. By the time Ipan reached the first trees, he looked back and the chimps had stopped halfway, still screeching their vehemence.

He signed to Sheelah, *Go,* and they cut away at a steep angle, heading uphill.

Ipan needed food and rest to stop his heart from lurching at every minor sound. Sheelah and Ipan clutched each other, high in a tree, and crooned and petted.

Leon needed time to think. Who was keeping their bodies alive at the Station? It would be smart to let them stay out here, in danger, saying to the rest of the staff that the two odd tourists wanted a really long immersion.

His thinking triggered jitters in Ipan, so he dropped that mode. Better to think abstractly. And there was plenty out here that needed understanding.

The biotechnicians who planted chimps and gigantelope and the rest here had tinkered with the raboons. The wild days of explosive biotech, in the first years of the twencen, had allowed just about anything. Capabilities soon thereafter, in the twentens, had allowed the biotech tinkerers to see if they could turn a more distant primate relative, the baboon, into something like humans. A perverse goal, it seemed to Leon, but believable. Scientists loved to monkey with matters.

The work had gotten as far as pack-hunting behavior. But raboons had no tools beyond crudely edged stones, occasionally used to cut meat once they had brought it down.

In another few million years, under evolution's raw rub, they might be as smart as chimps. Who would go extinct then?

At the moment he didn't much care. He had felt real rage when the chimps—*his own kind!*—had turned against them, even when the raboons came within view. Why?

231

He worried at the issue, sure there was something here he had to understand. Sociohistory had to deal with such basic, fundamental impulses. The chimps' reaction had been uncomfortably close to myriad incidents in human history. *Hate the Stranger.*

He had to fathom that murky truth.

Chimps moved in small groups, disliking outsiders, breeding mostly within their modest circle of a few dozen. This meant that any genetic trait that emerged could pass swiftly into all the members, through inbreeding. If it helped the band survive, the rough rub of chance would select for that band's survival. Fair enough.

But the trait had to be undiluted. A troop of especially good rock throwers would get swallowed up if they joined a company of several hundred. Contact would make them breed outside the original small clan. Outbreeding: Their genetic heritage would get watered down.

Striking a balance between the accidents of genetics in small groups, and the stability of large groups—that was the trick. Some lucky troop might have fortunate genes, conferring traits that fit the next challenge handed out by the ever-altering world. They would do well. But if those genes never passed to many chimps, what did it matter?

With some small amount of outbreeding, that trait got spread into other bands. Down through the strainer of time, others picked up the trait. It spread.

This meant it was actually *helpful* to develop smoldering animosity to outsiders, an immediate sense of their wrongness. Don't breed with them.

So small bands held fast to their eccentric traits, and some prospered. Those lived on; most perished. Evolutionary jumps happened faster in small, semi-isolated bands which outbred slightly. They kept their genetic assets in one small basket, the troop. Only occasionally did they mate with another troop—often, through rape.

The price was steep: a strong preference for their own tiny lot.

They hated crowds, strangers, noise. Bands of less than ten were too vulnerable to disease or predators; a few losses and the group failed. Too many, and they lost the concentration of close breeding. They were intensely loyal to their group, easily identifying each other in the dark by smell, even at great distances. Because they had many common genes, altruistic actions were common.

They even honored heroism—for even if the hero died, his shared genes were passed on through his relatives.

Even if strangers could pass the tests of difference in appearances, manner, smell, grooming—even then, culture could amplify the effects. Newcomers with different language or habits and posture would seem repulsive. Anything that served to distinguish a band would help keep hatreds high.

Each small genetic ensemble would then be driven by natural selection to stress the non-inherited differences—even arbitrary ones, dimly connected to survival fitness . . . and so they could evolve culture. As humans had.

Diversity in their tribal intricacies avoided genetic watering down. They heeded the ancient call of aloof, wary tribalism.

Leon/Ipan shifted uneasily. Midway through his thinking, the word *they* had come in Leon's thinking to mean humans as well as chimps. The description fit both.

That was the key. Humans fit into civilization *despite* their innate tribalism, their chimplike heritage. It was a miracle!

But even miracles called out for explanation. How could civilization possibly have kept itself stable, using such crude creatures as humans?

Leon had never seen the issue before in such glaring, and humbling, light.

And he had no answer.

They moved on against the blunt, deep unease of their chimps.

Ipan smelled something that sent his eyes darting left and right. With the full tool kit of soothing thoughts and the subtle tricks he had learned, Leon kept him going.

Sheelah was having more trouble. The female chimp did not like laboring up the long, steep gullies that approached the ridgeline. Gnarled bushes blocked their way and it took time to work their way around. Fruit was harder to find at these altitudes.

Ipan's shoulders and arms ached constantly. Chimps walked on all fours because their immensely strong arms carried a punishing weight penalty. To navigate both trees and ground meant you could optimize neither. Sheelah and Ipan groaned and whined at the soreness that never left feet, legs, wrists, and arms. Chimps would never be far-ranging explorers.

Together they let their chimps pause often to crumble leaves and soak up water from tree holes, a routine, simple tool use. They kept sniffing the air, apprehensive.

The smell that disturbed both chimps got stronger, darker.

Sheelah went ahead and was the first over the ridgeline. Far below in the valley they could make out the rectangular rigidities of the Excursion Station. A flier lifted from the roof and whispered away down the valley, no danger to them.

He recalled a century ago sitting on the veranda there with drinks in hand and Kelly saying, *If you stayed in Helsinki you might be dead.* Also if you didn't stay in Helsinki . . .

They started down the steep slope. Their chimps' eyes jerked at every unexpected movement. A chilly breeze stirred the few low bushes and twisted trees. Some had a feathered look, burnt and shattered by lightning. Air masses driven up from the valleys fought along here, the brute clash of pressures. This rocky ridge was far from the comfortable province of chimps. They hurried.

Ahead, Sheelah stopped.

Without a sound, five raboons rose from concealment, forming a neat half-circle around them.

Leon could not tell if it was the same pack as before. If so, they were quite considerable pack hunters, able to hold memory and purpose over time. They had waited ahead, where there were no trees to climb.

The raboons were eerily quiet as they strode forward, their claws clicking softly.

He called to Sheelah and made some utterly fake ferocious noises as he moved, arms high in the air, fists shaking, showing a big profile. He let Ipan take over while he thought.

A raboon band could certainly take two isolated chimps. To survive this they had to surprise the raboons, frighten them.

He looked around. Throwing rocks wasn't going to do the trick here. With only a vague notion of what he was doing he shuffled left, toward a tree that had been splintered by lightning.

Sheelah saw his move and got there first, striding energetically. Ipan picked up two stones and flung them at the nearest raboon. One caught him on the flank but did no real harm.

The raboons began to trot, circling. They called to each other in wheezing grunts.

Sheelah leaped on a dried-out shard of the tree. It snapped. She snatched it up and Leon saw her point. It was as tall as she was and she cradled it.

The largest raboon grunted and they all looked at each other.

The raboons charged.

The nearest one came at Sheelah. She caught it on the shoulder with the blunt point and it squealed.

Leon grabbed a stalk of the shattered tree trunk. He could not wrench it free. Another squeal from behind him and Sheelah was gibbering in a high, frightened voice.

It was best to let the chimps release tension vocally, but he could feel the fear and desperation in the tones and knew it came from Kelly too.

He carefully selected a smaller shard of the tree. With both hands he twisted it free, using his weight and big shoulder muscles, cracking it so that it came away with a point.

Lances. That was the only way to stay away from the raboon claws. Chimps never used such advanced weapons. Evolution hadn't gotten around to that lesson yet.

The raboons were all around them now. He and Sheelah stood back-to-back. He barely got his feet placed when he had to take the rush of a big, swarthy raboon.

They had not gotten the idea of the lance yet. It slammed into the point, jerked back. A fearsome bellow. Ipan wet himself with fear but something in Leon kept him in control.

The raboon backed off, whimpering. It turned to run. In midstride it stopped. For a long, suspended moment the raboon hesitated—then turned back toward Leon.

It trotted forward with new confidence. The other raboons watched. It went to the same tree Leon had used and with a single heave broke off a long, slender spike of wood. Then it came toward Leon, stopped, and with one claw held the stick forward. With a toss of its big head it looked at him and half-turned, putting one foot forward.

With a shock Leon recognized the swordplay position. Ruben had used it. Ruben was riding this raboon.

It made perfect sense. This way the chimps' deaths would be quite natural. Ruben could say that he was developing raboon-riding as a new commercial application of the same hardware that worked for chimp-riding.

Ruben came forward a careful step at a time, holding the long lance between two claws now. He made the end move in a circle. Movement was jerky; claws were crude, compared with chimp hands. But the raboon was stronger.

It came at him with a quick feint, then a thrust. Leon barely managed to dodge sideways while he brushed the lance aside with his stick. Ruben recovered quickly and came from Leon's left. Jab, feint, jab, feint. Leon caught each with a swoop of his stick.

Their wooden swords smacked against each other and Leon hoped his didn't snap. Ruben had good control of his raboon. It did not try to flee as it had before.

Leon was kept busy slapping aside Ruben's thrusts. He had to have some other advantage or the superior strength of the raboon would eventually tell. Leon circled, drawing Ruben away from Sheelah. The other raboons were keeping her trapped, but not attacking. All attention riveted on the two figures as they poked and parried.

Leon drew Ruben toward an outcropping. The raboon was having trouble holding its lance straight and had to keep looking down at its claws to get them right. This meant it paid less attention to where its two hooves found their footing. Leon slapped and jabbed and kept moving, making the raboon step sideways. It put a big hoof down among some angular stones, teetered, then recovered.

Leon moved left. It stepped again and its hoof turned and it stumbled. Leon was on it in an instant. He thrust forward as the raboon looked down, feet scrambling for purchase. Leon caught the raboon full with his point.

He pushed hard. The other raboons let out a moaning.

Snorting in rage, the raboon tried to get off the point. Leon made Ipan step forward and thrust the tip into the raboon. The thing wailed hoarsely. Ipan plunged again. Blood spurted from it, spattering the dust. Its knees buckled and it sprawled.

Leon shot a glance over his shoulder. The others had surged into action. Sheelah was holding off three, screeching at them so loudly it unnerved even him. She had already wounded one. Blood dripped down its brown coat.

But the others did not charge. They circled and growled and stamped their feet, but came no closer. They were confused. Learning too. He could see the quick, bright eyes studying the situation, this fresh move in the perpetual war.

Sheelah stepped out and poked the nearest raboon. It launched itself at her in a snarling fit and she stuck it again, deeper. It yelped and turned—and ran.

That did it for the others. They all trotted off, leaving their fellow bleating on the ground. Its dazed eyes watched its blood trickle out. Its eyes flickered and Ruben was gone. The animal slumped.

With deliberation Leon picked up a rock and bashed in the skull. It was messy work and he sat back inside Ipan and let the dark, smoldering chimp anger come out.

He bent over and studied the raboon brain. A fine silvery webbing capped the rubbery, convoluted ball. Immersion circuitry.

He turned away from the sight and only then saw that Sheelah was hurt.

★ ★ ★ ★ ★

The station crowned a rugged hill. Steep gullies gave the hillside the look of a weary, lined face. Wiry bushes thronged the lower reaches.

Ipan puffed as he worked his way through the raw land cut by erosion. In chimp vision the night was eerie, a shimmering vista of pale greens and blue-tinged shadows. The hill was a nuance in the greater slope of a grand mountain, but chimp vision could not make out the distant features. Chimps lived in a close, immediate world.

Ahead he could see clearly the glowing blank wall ringing the Station. Massive, five meters tall. And, he remembered from his tourist tour of the place, rimmed with broken glass.

Behind him came gasps as Sheelah labored up the slope. The wound in her side made her gait stiff, face rigid. She refused to hide below. They were both near exhaustion and their chimps were balky, despite two stops for fruit and grubs and rest.

Through their feeble vocabulary, their facial grimacing and writing in the dust, they had "discussed" the possibilities. Two chimps were vulnerable out here. They could not expect to be as lucky as with the raboons, not tired out and in strange territory.

The best time to approach the Station was at night. And whoever had engineered this would not wait forever. They had hidden from fliers twice more this last day. Resting through the next day was an inviting option, but Leon felt a foreboding press him onward.

He angled up the hillside, watching for electronic trip wires. Of such technical matters he knew nothing. He would have to keep a lookout for the obvious and hope that the Station was not wired for thinking trespassers. Chimp vision was sharp and clear in dim light for nearby objects, but he could find nothing.

He chose a spot by the wall shadowed by trees. Sheelah panted in shallow gasps as she approached. Looking up, the wall seemed immense. Impossible . . .

Slowly he surveyed the land around them. No sign of any movement. The place smelled peculiar to Ipan, somehow wrong. Maybe animals stayed away from the alien compound. Good; that would make security inside less alert.

The wall was polished concrete. A thick lip jutted out at the top, making climbing it harder.

Sheelah gestured where trees grew near the wall. Stumps nearer showed that the builders had thought about animals leaping across from branches. But some were tall enough and had branches within a few meters of the top.

Could a chimp make the distance? Not likely, especially when tired. Sheelah pointed to him and back to her, then held hands and made a swinging motion. Could they *swing* across the distance?

He studied her face. The designer would not anticipate two chimps cooperating that way. He squinted up at the top. Too high to climb, even if Sheelah stood on his shoulders.

Yes, he signed.

A few moments later, her hands holding his feet, about to let go of his branch, he had second thoughts.

Ipan didn't mind this bit of calisthenics, and in fact was happy to be back in a tree. But Leon's human judgment still kept shouting that he could not possibly do it. Natural chimp talent conflicted with human caution.

Luckily, he did not have much time to indulge in self-doubt. Sheelah yanked him off the branch. He fell, held only through her hands.

She had wrapped her feet securely around a thick branch,

and now began to oscillate him like a weight on a string. She swung him back and forth, increasing the amplitude. Back, forth, up, down, centrifugal pressure in his head. To Ipan it was unremarkable. To Leon it was a wheeling world of heart-stopping whirls.

Small branches brushed him and he worried about noise and then forgot about that because his head was coming up level with the top of the wall.

The concrete lip was rounded off on the inside, so no hook could find a grip.

He swung back down, head plunging toward ground. Then up into the lower branches, twigs slapping his face.

On the next swing he was higher. All along the top of the wall thick glass glinted. Very professional.

He barely had time to realize all this when she let him go.

He arced up, hands stretched out—and barely caught the lip. If it had not protectively protruded out, he would have missed.

He let his body slam against the side. His feet scrabbled for purchase against the sheer face. A few toes got hold. He heaved up, muscles bunching—and over. Never before had he appreciated how much stronger a chimp could be. No man could have made it here.

He scrambled up, cutting his arm and haunch on glass. It was a delicate business, getting to his feet and finding a place to stand.

A surge of triumph. He waved to Sheelah, invisible in the tree.

From here on it was up to him. He realized suddenly that they could have fashioned some sort of rope, tying together vines. Then he could lift her up here. *Good idea, too late.*

No point in delaying. The compound was partly visible through the trees, a few lights burning. Utterly silent. They had waited until the night was about half over, he had nothing but Ipan's gut feelings to tell him when.

He looked down. Just beyond his toes razor wire gleamed, set into the concrete. Carefully he stepped between the shiny lines. There was room among the sharp glass teeth to stand. A tree blocked his vision and he could see little below him in the dim glow from the Station. At least that meant they couldn't see him, either.

Should he jump? Too high. The tree that hid him was close, but he could not see into it.

He stood and thought, but nothing came to him. Meanwhile Sheelah was behind him, alone, and he hated leaving her where dangers waited that he did not even know.

He was thinking like a man and forgetting that he had the capability of a chimp.

Go. He leaped. Twigs snapped and he plunged heavily in shadows. Branches stabbed his face. He saw a dark shape to his right and so curled his legs, rotated, hands out—and snagged a branch. His hands closed easily around it and he realized it was too thin, *too thin*—

It snapped. The *crack* came like a thunderbolt to his ears. He fell, letting go of the branch. His back hit something hard and he rolled, grappling for a hold. His fingers closed around a thick branch and he swung from it. Finally he let out a gasp.

Leaves rustled, branches swayed. Nothing more.

He was halfway up the tree. Aches sprouted in his joints, a galaxy of small pains.

Leon relaxed and let Ipan master the descent. He had made far too much noise falling in the tree but there was no sign of any movement across the broad lawns between him and the big, luminous Station.

He thought of Sheelah and wished there were some way he could let her know he was inside now. Thinking of her, he measured with his eye the distances from nearby trees, memorizing the pattern so that he could find the way back at a dead run if he had to.

Now what? He didn't have a plan. That, and suspicions.

Leon gently urged Ipan—who was nervous and tired, barely controllable—into a triangular pattern of bushes. Ipan's mind was like a stormy sky split by skittering lightning. Not thoughts precisely; more like knots of emotion, forming and flashing around crisp kernels of anxiety. Patiently Leon summoned up soothing images, getting Ipan's breathing slowed, and he almost missed the whispery sound.

Nails scrabbling on a stone walkway. Something running fast.

They came around the triangle peak of bushes. Bunched muscles, sleek skin, stubby legs eating up the remaining distance. They were well trained to seek and kill soundlessly, without warning.

To Ipan the monsters were alien, terrifying. Ipan stepped back in panic before the two onrushing bullets of muscle and bone. Black gums peeled back from white teeth, bared beneath mad eyes.

Then Leon felt something shift in Ipan. Primeval, instinctive responses stopped his retreat, tensed the body. No time to flee, so *fight*.

Ipan set himself, balanced. The two might go for his arms so he drew them back, crouching to bring his face down.

Ipan had dealt with four-legged pack hunters before, somewhere far back in ancestral memory, and knew innately that they lined up on a victim's outstretched limb, would go for the throat. The canines wanted to bowl him over, slash open the jugular, rip and shred in the vital seconds of surprise.

They gathered themselves, bundles of swift sinew, running nearly shoulder-to-shoulder, big heads up—and leaped.

In air, they were committed, Ipan knew. And open.

Ipan brought both hands up to grasp the canines' forelegs.

He threw himself backward, holding the legs tight, his hands barely beneath the jaws. The wirehounds' own momentum carried them over his head as he rolled backward.

Ipan rolled onto his back, yanking hard. The sudden snap slammed the canines forward. They could not get their heads turned around and down to close on his hand.

The leap, the catch, the quick pivot and swing, the heave—all combined in a centrifugal whirl that slung the wirehounds over Ipan as he himself went down, rolling. He felt the canines' legs snap and let go. They sailed over him with pained yelps.

Ipan rolled over completely, head tucked in, and came off his shoulders with a bound. He heard a solid thud, clacks as jaws snapped shut. A thump as the canines hit the grass, broken legs unable to cushion them.

He scrambled after them, his breath whistling. They were trying to get up, turning on snapped legs to confront their quarry. Still no barks, only faint whimpers of pain, sullen growls. One swore vehemently and quite obscenely. The other chanted, "Baaas'ard . . . baaas'ard . . ."

Animals turning in their vast, sorrowful night.

He jumped high and came down on both. His feet drove their necks into the ground and he felt bone give way. Before he stepped back to look he knew they were gone.

Ipan's blood surged with joy. Leon had never felt this tingling thrill, not even in the first immersion, when Ipan had killed a Stranger. Victory over these alien things with teeth and claws that come at you out of the night was a profound, inflaming pleasure.

Leon had done nothing. The victory was wholly Ipan's.

For a long moment Leon basked in it in the cool night air, felt the tremors of ecstasy.

Slowly, reason returned. There were other wirehounds. Ipan had caught these just right. Such luck did not strike twice.

The wirehounds were easy to see on the lawn. Would attract attention.

Ipan did not like touching them. Their bowels had emptied and the smell cut the air. They left a smear on the grass as he dragged them into the bushes.

Time, time. Someone would miss the canines, come to see.

Ipan was still pumped up from his victory. Leon used that to get him trotting across the broad lawn, taking advantage of shadows. Energy popped in Ipan' s veins. Leon knew it was a mere momentary glandular joy, overlaying a deep fatigue. When it faded, Ipan would become dazed, hard to govern.

Every time he stopped he looked back and memorized landmarks. He might have to return this way on the run.

It was late and most of the Station was dark. In the technical area, though, a cluster of windows blossomed with what Ipan saw as impossibly rich, strange, superheated light.

He loped over to them and flattened himself against the wall. It helped that Ipan was fascinated by this strange citadel of the godlike humans. Out of his own curiosity he peeked in a window. Under enamel light a big assembly room sprawled, one that Leon recognized. There, centuries ago, he had formed up with the other brightly dressed tourists to go out on a trek.

Leon let the chimp's curiosity propel him around to the side, where he knew a door led into a long corridor. The door opened freely, to Leon's surprise. Ipan strolled down the slick tiles of the hallway, quizzically studying the phosphor-paint designs on the ceiling and walls, which emitted a soothing ivory glow.

An office doorway was open. Leon made Ipan squat and bob his head around the edge. Nobody there. It was a sumptuous den with shelves soaring into a vaulted ceiling. Leon remembered sitting there discussing the immersion process. That meant the immersion vessels were just a few doors away down—

The squeak of shoes on tiles made him turn.

ExSpec Ruben was behind him, leveling a weapon. In the cool light the man's face looked odd to Ipan's eyes, mysteriously bony.

Leon felt the rush of reverence in Ipan and let it carry the chimp forward, chippering softly. Ipan felt awe, not fear.

Leon wondered why Ruben said nothing and then realized that of course he could not reply.

Ruben tensed up, waving the snout of his ugly weapon. A metallic click. Ipan brought his hands up in a ritual chimp greeting and Ruben shot him.

The impact spun Ipan around. He went down, sprawling.

Ruben's mouth curled in derision. "Smart professor, huh? Didn't figure the alarm on the door, huh?"

The pain from Ipan's side was sharp, startling. Leon rode the hurt and gathering anger in Ipan, helping it build. Ipan felt his side and his hand came away sticky, smelling like warm iron in the chimp's nostrils.

Ruben circled around, weapon weaving. "You *killed* me, you weak little dope. Ruined a good experimental animal too. Now I got to figure what to do with you."

Leon threw his own anger atop Ipan's seethe. He felt the big muscles in the shoulders bunch. The pain in the side jabbed suddenly. Ipan groaned and rolled on the floor, pressing one hand to the wound.

Leon kept the head down so that Ipan could not see the blood that was running down now across the legs. Energy was running out of the chimp body. A seeping weakness came up the legs.

He pricked his ears to the shuffle of Ruben's feet. Another agonized roll, this time bringing the legs up in a curl.

"Guess there's really only one solution—"

Leon heard the metallic click.

Now, yes. He let his anger spill.

Ipan pressed up with his forearms and got his feet under him. No time to get all the way up. Ipan sprang at Ruben, keeping low.

A tinny shot whisked by his head. Then he hit Ruben in the hip and slammed the man against the wall. The man's scent was sour, salty.

Leon lost all control. Ipan bounced Ruben off the wall and instantly slammed arms into the man with full force.

Ruben tried to deflect the impact. Ipan pushed the puny human arms aside. Ruben's pathetic attempts at defense were like spider webs brushed away.

He butted Ruben and pounded massive shoulders into the man's chest. The weapon clattered on the tiles.

Ipan slammed himself into the man's body again and again.

Strength, power, joy.

Bones snapped. Ruben's head snapped back, smacked the wall, and he went limp.

Ipan stepped back and Ruben sagged to the tiles. *Joy.*

Blue-white flies buzzed at the rim of his vision.

Must move. That was all Leon could get through the curtain of emotions that shrouded the chimp mind.

The corridor lurched. Leon got Ipan to walk in a sidewise teeter.

Down the corridor, painful steps. Two doors, three. Here? Locked. Next door. World moving slower somehow.

The door snicked open. An antechamber that he recognized. Ipan blundered into a chair and almost fell. Leon made the lungs work hard. The gasping cleared his vision of the dark edges that had crept in but the blue-white flies were there, fluttering impatiently, and thicker.

He tried the far door. Locked. Leon summoned what he could from Ipan. *Strength, power, joy.* Ipan slammed his shoulder into the solid door. It held. Again. And again, sharp pain—and it popped open.

Right, this was it. The immersion bay. Ipan staggered into the array of vessels. The walk down the line, between banks of control panels, took an eternity. Leon concentrated on each step, placing each foot. Ipan's field of view bobbed as the head seemed to slip around on the liquid shoulders.

Here. His own vessel.

He fumbled with the latches. Popped it open.

There lay Leon Mattick, peaceful, eyes closed.

Emergency controls, yes. He knew them from the briefing.

He searched the polished steel surface and found the panel on the side. Ipan stared woozily at the meaningless lettering and Leon himself had trouble reading. The letters jumped and fused together.

He found several buttons and servo controls. Ipan's hands were stubby, wrong. It took three tries to get the reviving program activated. Lights cycled from green to amber.

Ipan abruptly sat down on the cool floor. The blue-white flies were buzzing all around his head now and they wanted to bite him. He sucked in the cool dry air but there was no substance in it, no help . . .

Then, without any transition, he was looking at the ceiling. On his back. The lamps up there were getting dark, fading. Then they went out.

Leon's eyes snapped open.

The recovery program was still sending electrostims through his muscles. He let them jump and tingle and ache while he thought. He felt fine. Not even hungry, as he usually did after an immersion. How long had he been in the wilderness? At least five days.

He sat up. There was no one in the vessel room. Evidently Ruben had gotten some silent alarm, but had not alerted anyone else. That pointed, again, to a tight little conspiracy.

He got out shakily. To get free he had to detach some feeders and probes but they seemed simple enough.

Ipan. The big body filled the walkway. He knelt and felt for a pulse. Rickety.

But first, Kelly. Her vessel was next to his and he started the revival. She looked well.

Ruben must have put some transmission block on the system, so that none of the staff could tell by looking at the panel that anything was wrong. A simple cover story, a couple who wanted a really long immersion. Ruben had warned them, but no, they wanted it so . . . A perfectly plausible story.

Kelly's eyes fluttered. He kissed her. She gasped.

He made a chimp sign, *quiet,* and went back to Ipan.

Blood came steadily. Leon was surprised to find that he could not pick up the rich, pungent elements in the blood from smell alone. A human missed so much!

He took off his shirt and made a crude tourniquet. At least Ipan's breathing was regular. Kelly was ready to get out by then and he helped her disconnect.

"I was hiding in a tree and then—poof!" she said. "What a relief. How did you—"

"Let's get moving," he said.

As they left the room she said, "Who can we trust? Whoever did this—" She stopped when she saw Ruben. "Oh."

Somehow her expression made him laugh. She was very rarely surprised.

"*You* did this?"

"Ipan."

"I never would have believed a chimp could, could . . ."

"I doubt anyone's been immersed this long. Not under such stress, anyway. It all just, well, it came out."

He picked up Ruben's weapon and studied the mechanism. A standard pistol, silenced. Ruben had not wanted to awaken the rest of the Station. That was promising. There should be people here who would spring to their aid. He started toward the building where the Station personnel lived.

"Wait, what about Ruben?"

"I'm going to wake up a doctor."

They did—but Leon took him into the vessel room first, to work on Ipan. Some patchwork and injections and the doctor said Ipan would be all right. Only then did he show the man Ruben's body.

The doctor got angry about that, but Leon had a gun. All he had to do was point it. He didn't say anything, just gestured with the gun. He did not feel like talking and wondered if he ever would again. When you couldn't talk you concentrated more, entered into things. Immersed.

And in any case, Ruben had been dead for some time.

Ipan had done a good job. The doctor shook his head at the severe damage.

Kelly looked at him oddly throughout the whole time. He

did not understand why, until he realized that he had not even thought about helping Ruben first. Ipan was *himself,* in a sense he could not explain.

But he understood immediately when Kelly wanted to go to the Station wall and call to Sheelah. They brought her, too, in from the wild darkness.

A year later, when the industrial conspiracy had been uncovered and dozens brought to trial, they returned to the Excursion Station.

Leon longed to lounge in the sun, after a year of facing news cameras and attorneys. Kelly was equally exhausted with the rub of events.

But they both immediately booked time in the immersion chambers and spent long hours there. Ipan and Sheelah seemed to greet their return with something approximating joy.

Each year they would return and live inside the minds. Each year they would come away calmer, somehow fuller.

Leon's analysis of sociohistory appeared in a groundbreaking series of papers, modeling all of civilization as a "complex adaptive system." Fundamental to the intricately structured equations were terms allowing for primordial motivations, for group behavior in tension with individual longings, for deep motivations kindled in the veldt, over a thousand millennia ago. This was exact, complex, and original; his papers resounded through the social sciences, which had finally been made quantitative.

Fifteen years later the work received a Nobel Prize, then worth 2.3 million New Dollars. Leon and Kelly spent a lot of it on travel, particularly to Africa.

When questioned in interviews, he never spoke of the long trek he and Kelly had undergone. Still, in his technical papers and public forums, he did give chimpanzees as examples of complex, adaptive behavior. As he spoke, he gave a long, slow smile, eyes glittering enigmatically, but would discuss the subject no further.